THREE
STRONG
WOMEN

THREE STRONG WOMEN

a novel by

MARIE NDIAYE

translated by John Fletcher

ALFRED A. KNOPF · NEW YORK · 2012

THIS IS A BORZOI BOOK
PUBLISHED BY ALFRED A. KNOPF

www.aaknopf.com

Originally published in France as *Trois femmes puissantes* by Gallimard,
Paris, in 2009. Copyright © Editions Gallimard, Paris, 2009.

Library of Congress Cataloging-in-Publication Data
NDiaye, Marie.
[Trois femmes puissantes. English]
Three strong women : a novel / by Marie NDiaye ; translated by
John Fletcher.—1st ed.
p. cm.
"This is a Borzoi book."
ISBN 978-0-307-59469-3
1. Women—Senegal—Fiction.   2. Women—France—Fiction.
3. West Africans—France—Fiction.   4. Self-realization in women—
Fiction.   I. Fletcher, John.   II. Title.
PQ2674.D53T7613 2012
813'.914—dc23   2012003533

Jacket photograph by Ocean Photography/Veer
Jacket design by Gabriele Wilson

Manufactured in the United States of America
First American Edition

PART

I

*A*ND THE MAN waiting for her at the entrance to the big concrete house—or who happened to be standing in the doorway—was bathed in a light so suddenly intense that it seemed to radiate from his whole body and his pale clothing: yet this short, thickset man before her, who'd just emerged from his enormous house and was glowing bright as a neon tube, no longer possessed, Norah straightaway realized, the stature, arrogance, and youthfulness once so mysteriously his own as to seem everlasting.

He held his hands crossed over his belly and his head tilted sideways; his hair was gray, and under his white shirt the belly sagged limply over the waistband of his cream trousers.

There he stood, bathed in cold light, looking as if he might have dropped to the threshold of his pretentious house from the branch of one of the poincianas with which the garden was filled, for—it had occurred to Norah—as she approached the house staring through the railings at the front door, she hadn't seen it open to let her father out: and yet there he stood in the sunset, this glowing, shrunken man who at some point must have been dealt an enor-

mous blow to the head that further reduced the harmonious pro-
portions Norah remembered to those of a fat man, neckless with
short, thick legs.

He stood there watching her as she approached; nothing in his
rather lost, rather hesitant look indicated that he was expecting
her, indeed that he'd asked, even begged, her to come and see him
(insofar as a man like that, she thought, was capable of requesting
help of any kind).

He was simply there, perhaps indeed having flitted down from
the thick branch of a poinciana in whose yellow shade the house
stood, to land heavily on the cracked concrete of the doorstep; and
it was as if Norah had approached the railings at that instant by
pure chance.

This man who could transform every entreaty on his part into
an appeal made to him by someone else watched her opening the
gate and entering the garden. He had the look of a host who was
rather put out but trying to hide the fact; he was shading his eyes
despite the fading of the light that had left the doorway in shadows
but for his strange, shining, electric person.

"Well, well," he said, "it's you." His speech was muffled and
weak; despite his mastery of the language he was tentative in
French, as if the unease he'd always felt over certain mistakes that
were difficult to avoid now caused his voice to tremble.

Norah said nothing.

She gave him a quick hug but did not hold him tight: from the
almost imperceptible way the flabby skin on her father's arms
shrank under her grasp she remembered how much he detested
physical contact.

She thought she noticed a musty smell.

A smell emanating from the lush, wilting vegetation of the poinciana whose branches overhung the flat roof of the house and among whose leaves there perhaps nested this withdrawn and self-assured man ever on the alert—it pained Norah to imagine—for the slightest sound of footsteps approaching the gate at which he would take flight to land clumsily on the doorstep of his vast house with its rough concrete walls; or was it emanating—this smell—from her father's body or his clothes or his old, wrinkled, ashen skin: she couldn't say what it was, she'd no idea where it might be coming from.

At most she could say that this day he was wearing, and probably always wore now, a rumpled, sweat-stained shirt and trousers that were pale and shiny and hideously baggy at the knees, either the effect of his being too heavy a bird, one that fell over each time he landed, or—Norah reflected with rather weary compassion—of his having become after all another slovenly old man, indifferent or blind to lapses of hygiene while still clinging to the forms of conventional elegance, dressing as he'd always done in white and cream and never appearing on the threshold of his unfinished house without tightening the knot of his tie, whatever dusty room he'd emerged from, whatever poinciana, exhausted by flowering, he'd flown down from.

On landing at the airport Norah had taken a taxi, then walked in the heat for a long while because she'd forgotten her father's exact address and only found her way after she'd recognized the house. She felt sticky, dirty, and spent.

She wore a sleeveless lime-green dress covered with little yellow flowers rather like those strewn over the doorstep under the poinciana, and flat sandals in the same soft green.

And she noticed with a start that her father wore plastic flip-flops, he who had always made a point, it seemed to her, of never appearing in anything other than polished shoes in off-white or beige.

Was it because this untidy man had lost the right to cast a stern or disapproving eye over her, or because, as a confident thirty-eight-year-old, she no longer worried above all else what people thought of her appearance? Whatever the case, fifteen years earlier—she knew—she would have felt mortified to have arrived tired and sweating before her father, whose own aspect and bearing never betrayed in those days the slightest sign of weakness or susceptibility during a heat wave, whereas now she couldn't care less about showing him an un-made-up, shiny face that she hadn't bothered to powder in the taxi. Telling herself, with a rather sour, rancorous cheer, He can think of me what he likes, she recalled the cruel casual insults of this superior male when as teenagers she and her sister came to see him: remarks that always turned on his daughters' lack of elegance or want of lipstick.

She would have liked to say to him now, "You realize, don't you, that you spoke to us as if we were women whose duty it was to make themselves attractive, whereas we were just kids, not to mention your own daughters."

She would have liked to say this to him in a flippant, mildly reproachful way, as if all that had been just a rather crude form of humor on his part, and she'd have liked her father to show a little contrition, and for them to have laughed about it together now.

But seeing him standing there in his plastic flip-flops on the concrete doorstep strewn with rotting flowers perhaps knocked loose as he flew down from the poinciana on his tired, heavy wings, she realized that he no more would have understood or grasped the most insistent allusion to the nasty comments he used to make than he now cared to scrutinize her appearance and formulate a judgment about it.

He had a rather fixed, vacant, distant look.

She wondered then if he actually remembered having written asking her to come.

"Shall we go in?" she said, slipping her bag from one shoulder to the other.

"Masseck!" he shouted, clapping his hands.

The icy, bluish light seemed to shine more intensely from his misshapen body.

A barefoot old man in Bermudas and a torn polo shirt hurried forward.

"Take the bag," Norah's father ordered.

Then, turning to her, he said, "It's Masseck, d'you recognize him?"

"I can carry my bag," she said, immediately regretting her words, which could only have offended the servant, who, despite his age, was used to bearing the most awkward burdens, and so she passed it to him so impetuously that, being taken unawares, he tottered, before recovering his balance and tossing the bag onto his back, returned into the house with it, stooped over.

"When I last came," she said, "it was Mansour. I don't know Masseck."

"What Mansour?" her father asked with a suddenly wild, almost dismayed look that she'd never seen before.

"I don't know his surname, but that Mansour, he lived here for years and years," said Norah, who felt herself slowly gripped by a nauseating, stifling feeling of discomfort.

"It was perhaps Masseck's father, then."

"Oh no," she murmured, "Masseck is far too old to be Mansour's son."

And since her father seemed increasingly bewildered and even close to wondering whether she wasn't deliberately trying to confuse him, she quickly added, "Oh, it really doesn't matter."

"You're mistaken, I've never employed anyone called Mansour," he said with a subtle, condescending smile that was the first manifestation of his former self: however irritating that tiny, scornful smile, it had always warmed Norah's heart; it was as if, to this conceited man, it mattered less to be right than to have the last word.

For she was certain that a diligent, patient, efficient Mansour had been at her father's side for years on end, and that even if she and her sister had come to this house scarcely three or four times since they were children, it was Mansour whom they'd seen here and not this Masseck, whose face she didn't recognize.

Once inside, Norah noticed how empty the house was.

Outside, it was now quite dark.

The big living room was dark too, and silent.

Her father switched a lamp on, the kind that uses forty-watt bulbs and lights poorly. Nevertheless it revealed the middle of the room and its long, glass-topped table.

On the rough-plastered walls Norah recognized the framed photographs of the holiday village her father had owned and run and which had made him rich.

He took much pride in his success, and always allowed a large number of people to live in his house. Norah had always thought that this wasn't so much because he was a generous man but because he was keen to show that he could provide his brothers, sisters, nephews, nieces, and sundry other relatives with free board and lodging. As a result, whatever time of day she happened to be there, Norah had never seen the living room empty.

There were always children on the sofas, sprawling belly up like well-fed cats, men drinking tea and watching television, and women moving to-and-fro between the kitchen and the bedrooms.

But that evening the room was empty, harshly exposing the crude materials used in its construction, the shiny floor tiles, the cement rendering on the walls, the narrow window frames.

"Isn't your wife here?" asked Norah.

He picked up two chairs from the big table, moved them closer to each other, then changed his mind and put them back again.

He switched on the television, and then turned it off before it had time to light up.

He moved about the room without lifting his feet, so that his flip-flops scraped the tiles.

His lips trembled slightly.

"She's away traveling at the moment," he mumbled finally.

Oh, Norah thought anxiously, he can't admit she's probably left him.

"And Sony? Where's Sony?"

"Likewise," he said, exhaling.

"Sony's off traveling too?"

The thought that her father, who'd had so many wives and children, that this not particularly handsome but brilliant, clever, quick-witted, and ruthless man who'd been born into poverty but made his fortune, and had since then always lived surrounded by a grateful and submissive crowd, that this spoiled individual now found himself alone and perhaps abandoned, fed a hazy old grudge that Norah harbored in spite of herself.

It seemed to her that her father was at last being taught a lesson he should have learned much earlier.

But what sort of lesson?

It made her feel petty and base, thinking that.

For even if her father had always kept an open house to spongers, even if he'd never had any true friends, honest wives (with the exception, Norah thought, of her own mother), or loving children, and if now, old, ravaged, and probably much diminished, he wandered alone around his gloomy house—how was that justice served? What kind of satisfaction could that be for Norah, except that of a jealous daughter avenged at last for never having been welcomed into her father's inner circle?

And feeling petty and cheap she now also felt ashamed of her hot, damp skin and her rumpled dress.

As if to atone for her spiteful thoughts, by confirming he wouldn't be left alone for too long, she asked, "Will Sony be back soon?"

"He'll tell you himself," her father murmured.

"How can he, if he's away?"

Her father clapped his hands and shouted, "Masseck!"

Small yellow poinciana flowers fluttered down from his neck and shoulders onto the tiled floor, and with a swift movement he crushed them under the toe of one of his flip-flops.

It gave Norah the intimation of his doing likewise to the flowers, rather similar, covering her dress.

Masseck came in pushing a cart laden with food, plates, and cutlery, and proceeded to lay the table.

"Sit down," her father said, "and let's eat."

"I'm going to wash my hands first."

She found herself adopting the tone of peremptory volubility that she never used with anyone but her father, the tone intended to forestall his attempt to have Masseck, and before Masseck Mansour, do what she insisted on doing herself, insisted out of an awareness that he so hated seeing his guests perform the slightest labor in his house, thereby casting doubt on the competence of his servants, that he was quite capable of saying to her, "Masseck will wash your hands for you," without for a moment imagining that she would fail to obey him as those around him, young and old, had always done.

But her father had hardly heard her.

He'd taken a seat and was staring vacantly at what Masseck was doing.

She found that his skin was now blackish, less dark than before, and dull looking.

He yawned, his mouth wide open, not making a sound, just like a dog.

She now felt certain that the sweet fetid smell that she'd noticed at the threshold came both from the poinciana and from her father's body; in fact his whole person seemed steeped in the slow putrefaction of the yellowy-orange flowers, this man who, she remembered, had worn none but the chicest of perfumes, this haughty and insecure man who'd never wished to give off an odor that was his own!

Poor soul, who'd have thought he'd wind up a plump old bird, clumsy flying and strong smelling?

She walked toward the kitchen along a concrete corridor lit imperfectly by a bulb covered in fly specks.

The kitchen was the least commodious room in this badly proportioned house, as Norah remembered, having added it to the inexhaustible list of the grievances against her father, though knowing full well that she would mention none of them, neither the serious ones nor the less serious, and that, face-to-face with this unfathomable man, she could never summon up the courage—which she possessed in abundance when far away from him—to express her disapproval; and as a result she was not at all pleased with herself but, rather, very disappointed, and all the angrier for bowing and daring to say nothing.

Her father couldn't have cared less about making his servants work in a tight, uncomfortable space, where neither he nor his visitors ever set foot.

Any such consideration would have been incomprehensible to him. Indeed, he would put it down to the sentimentality that characterized her sex, the world she inhabited, and a culture he didn't share.

"We don't live in the same country, societies are very different," he would more or less say, in a pedantic, condescending manner, and perhaps summon Masseck to ask him in front of her whether the kitchen suited him—to which Masseck would say yes—and her father, not even looking at her, since that would give the subject an importance it didn't merit, would, with an air of triumph, simply consider the matter closed.

There's no point, no sense in having a father you literally can't communicate with, whose feelings for you have always been in question, she thought, yet again, but this time calmly, not shaking with rage, impotence, and despondency as so often in the past when circumstance had brought up the fundamental differences of perception, outlook, and education between her and this cold, passionless man who'd spent only a few years in France, where she, a vulnerable person of strong feeling, had lived all her life.

And yet here she was, in her father's house. When he'd called her, she had come.

If she'd possessed less of this capacity for emotion which he so heartily despised (lumping together, with his own daughter, the entire limp-wristed, feminized Western world), she would have found any excuse to avoid making such a journey . . . "And you would do me a great honor and give me the distinct pleasure if you were able—if you felt strong enough—to leave your family for a time, even for quite a while, and come here, to your father, because I've important things to say to you . . ."

Oh, how she already regretted having weakened, how she longed to return home now and get on with her life.

At the tiny sink in the kitchen a slim young girl in a T-shirt and threadbare skirt was washing some cooking pots.

The table was covered with dishes about to be served, Norah realized, to her father and herself.

She noticed roast chicken, couscous, saffron rice, a dark meat in a peanut sauce, and other dishes she could just make out under their steamy glass covers. The profusion was staggering. It was beginning to make her feel queasy.

She slipped between the table and the sink and waited until the girl, who was laboriously rinsing out a large stew pot, had finished.

The sink was so narrow that the pot kept hitting the edges or the tap and, since there was no draining board, the girl had to crouch to set the vessel down on the floor, where she'd spread out a dish towel on which to dry it, a sight that once again exasperated Norah, who quickly washed her hands, all the while smiling and nodding to the girl.

And when she'd asked her name and the girl, after a brief silence—as if, Norah thought, to give her answer a dignified setting—had replied, "Khady Demba," her calm assurance, firm voice, and limpid gaze both surprised and soothed Norah, calming her jumpy weariness and feelings of irritation and resentment.

At the end of the corridor her father's voice rang out, calling her impatiently.

She made haste to rejoin him and found him in a state of some annoyance, anxious to tuck into the prawn and fruit tabbouleh Masseck had served in the two plates set opposite each other.

She'd hardly sat down when he started eating greedily, with his face almost in his plate, and this voraciousness, entirely devoid of polite pretense or small talk, was so much at odds with the old-fashioned manners of this rather affected man that Norah nearly asked him if he'd been depriving himself of food, thinking that he was quite capable—if his financial difficulties were such as she supposed them to be—of trying to impress her by loading this dinner with all the provisions of the three preceding days.

Masseck brought out one dish after another, at such a pace that she couldn't keep up.

She was relieved to see that her father was paying no attention to what she ate.

He only raised his head to scrutinize gluttonously and suspiciously what Masseck had just put on the table, and when at one point he looked furtively at Norah's plate, it was with such childlike apprehension that she realized he was simply making sure Masseck had not served her more generously than him.

That really upset her.

Her father—normally so loquacious, so full of fine words—remained silent. The only sounds to be heard in the desolate house were the clatter of plates, the slip-slap of Masseck's feet on the tiles, and perhaps the rustle of the poinciana's upper branches brushing against the tin roof. She wondered vaguely whether the lone tree was calling out in the night for her father to come.

He went on eating, moving from the grilled lamb to the chicken in sauce, hardly pausing for breath between mouthfuls, joylessly stuffing himself.

For dessert, Masseck put a mango cut in pieces before him.

He pushed one piece into his mouth, then another. Norah saw him chewing with difficulty, and trying to swallow. In vain.

He spat out the mango pulp onto his plate.

Tears were pouring down his cheeks.

Norah felt her own cheeks burning.

She got up, heard herself mumbling something, she couldn't tell what, went over and stood behind him, and then didn't know what to do with her hands, never before having found herself in a position either to comfort her father or to show him anything other than a stiff, forced respect tinged with resentment.

She turned around, looking for Masseck, but after clearing the table he'd left the room.

Her father was still weeping silently, expressionless.

She sat down next to him and leaned forward to bring her head as close as possible to his tear-streaked face.

She could smell, under the odor of the food and the spicy sauces, the sickly sweet scent of the rotting flowers of the big tree, and since her father kept his head lowered, she could see how grubby the shirt collar was around his neck.

She remembered a piece of news that two or three years earlier her brother Sony had passed on but that her father hadn't seen fit to divulge to her or her sister. She'd resented this, but before long she'd forgotten both the news and her bitterness at not having been told. The two things now went through her mind simultaneously and as a result her tone was rather acerbic even though she'd tried to make her voice sound comforting.

"Tell me, where are your children?" she asked.

She remembered that he'd fathered twins but couldn't recall what gender they were.

He looked at her, distraught.

"My children?"

"The last ones you had. Or so I understand. Has your wife taken them with her?"

"The little girls? Oh, they're here, yes," he murmured, and turned his head. It was as if he were disappointed, as if he'd hoped that she would talk about something he didn't know, whose implications he hadn't grasped, something that, in a strange, magical way, would save him.

She couldn't contain a slight shiver of vengeful spite.

So Sony was the only son of this man who didn't care much for girls, or have much time for them.

Overwhelmed, weighed down by useless, crucifying females who weren't even pretty, thought Norah calmly, thinking of herself and her sister; they'd always had, for their father, the irremediable defect of being too much like him, that is, quite unlike their mother, and attesting to the pointlessness of his marriage to a Frenchwoman, because what good had it done him? No almost-white children, no well-built sons . . .

And it had been a failure.

Upset, overwhelmed by a feeling of ironic compassion, she laid her hand lightly on his shoulder.

"I'd like to meet them," she said, adding at once, so as not to give him time to ask what she meant, "your two daughters, the little girls."

Her father shook her hand off his fat shoulder in an involuntary gesture signifying that nothing could justify such familiarity on her part.

He rose heavily and wiped his face on his sleeve.

He pushed open an ugly glazed door at the other end of the room, and switched on the solitary bulb that lit another long, gray concrete corridor, off which, she recalled, doors opened onto small square rooms like monastic cells that once were inhabited by her father's numerous kin.

From the way their footsteps and her father's loud irregular breathing echoed in the silence, she was sure that the rooms were now empty.

They seemed to have been walking already for several long minutes when the corridor swung first to the left, then to the right, getting almost dark, and so stuffy that Norah nearly turned back.

Her father stopped in front of a closed door.

He grasped the handle and stood still for a moment with his ear against the panel. Norah couldn't tell if he was trying to listen to something inside or was summoning up the will to open the door. But the attitude of this man, at once scarcely recognizable and illusory as ever—oh, what incorrigible naïveté to think, even not having seen him for years, that time might have altered him and brought them closer together—worried and annoyed her now more than it ever had in the past, when she could never be sure whether, in his brazen recklessness and arrogant flippancy, and utter lack of humor, he wasn't going to hurl some unforgettably cruel remark at her.

With a quick movement, as if to catch someone in flagrante, he opened the door.

With an air of fear and repugnance, he stood aside and let Norah in.

The tiny room was lit by a lamp with a pink shade. It stood on a small table placed between two beds, on the narrower of which sat the girl whom Norah had seen in the kitchen and who had told her she was called Khady Demba. The lobe of her right ear, Norah noticed, was slit in two.

Sitting cross-legged on the mattress, she was sewing a small green dress.

Looking up briefly, she smiled at Norah.

Two little girls were asleep on the other bed, lying face-to-face under a white sheet.

With a start Norah realized that the faces of the two children were the most beautiful she had ever seen.

Awakened perhaps by the stuffiness of the corridor flooding

into the air-conditioned room, or by an imperceptible change in the quiet atmosphere surrounding them, the two little girls opened their eyes at the same time.

They looked at their father gravely and without warmth or feeling. They showed no fear at seeing him, but no pleasure either. As for him, Norah noted with surprise, he seemed to melt under their gaze. His shaven head, his face, his neck in its grubby collar, all were suddenly dripping with sweat and reeking of that acrid odor of flowers crushed underfoot.

This man, who'd managed to maintain around himself a climate of dull fear and who'd never let anyone intimidate him, now seemed terrified.

What could such small girls be making him afraid of? Norah wondered. They—the miraculous offspring of his old age—were so marvelously pretty as to make him forget that they belonged to the lesser sex, and perhaps even forget the plainness of his first two daughters, Norah and her sister.

She went toward the bed and knelt down. Looking into the two small identical faces, round, dark, and delicate like the heads of seals resting on the sand, she smiled.

At that moment the first bars of "And here's to you, Mrs. Robinson . . ." rang out in the room.

Everyone jumped—even Norah, though it was the ringtone of her cell phone. She reached for the phone in the pocket of her dress. She was about to turn it off when she noticed that the call was coming from her own home. Awkwardly, she put the phone to her ear. The silence of the room seemed to have changed. Calm, ponderous, and lethargic just a moment ago, it had suddenly become alert and vaguely hostile, as if the chance of overhearing something clear and definitive might help them to decide between keeping her at a distance and welcoming her into their midst.

"It's me, Mummy!" Lucie's voice rang out.

"Hello, darling! You don't have to shout, I can hear you quite clearly," Norah said, red in the face. "Is everything okay?"

"Yes! At the moment we're making crepes with Grete. Then we're off to the movies. We're having a lovely time."

"Splendid," said Norah softly. "Lots of love! Speak to you soon."

She snapped the phone shut and slipped it into her pocket.

The two little girls pretended to be asleep. Their eyelids flickered and their lips were pressed together.

Disappointed, Norah stroked their cheeks, then got up and nodded to Khady before leaving the room with her father, who closed the door carefully behind him.

She thought, plaintively, of what seemed yet another failure on this man's part to establish a straightforward loving relationship with his children. A man who provoked such a pitiless gaze did not deserve the beautiful little girls born to him in his old age, and nothing, no one could change a man like that except by tearing out his heart.

But as she followed him back down the gloomy corridor, her cell phone knocking gently now against her thigh, she admitted grimly that her irritation with her father was amplified by the outsize excitement in Lucie's voice, and that the barbs she couldn't or wouldn't dare utter to Jakob, the man she'd been living with for a year, would be planted there, in her father's back, as he walked innocently before her, bowed and overweight, along the obscure passage.

For in her mind's eye she could see her beloved Paris apartment, the intimate, discreet emblem of her perseverance, of her modest success, into which, having lived there for a few years alone with Lucie, she'd introduced Jakob and his daughter, Grete, and with them, at a stroke, confusion and disorder, whereas the motivation behind the purchase of the three-room apartment in Montmartre (financed by a thirty-year loan) had precisely been her spiritual longing to put an end to the lifelong confusion of which her now elderly, threadbare father, his wings folded under his shirt, looming huge and incongruous in the gloomy corridor, had been the agonizing incarnation.

Oh, she'd quickly sensed in Lucie's tone—panting, urgent, and shrill—that the apartment was at that very moment the scene of another demonstration of fatherly ardor, a detestable display informed by Jakob's ostentatious refusal to lay down any limits or exercise the slightest authority over two seven-year-old girls, and by his habit of undertaking, with extravagant commentary, great energy, and much gusto, culinary preparations he usually lacked the ability, will, or patience to see through, so that pancake or cake batter was never set to cook, because in the meantime he'd suddenly suggested going out or doing something else, in the same panting, urgent, shrill tone that the girls adopted, and that got them so overexcited that they often ended up exhausted, fretful, and in tears, a situation made worse, Norah thought, by a vague feeling that, for all the screaming and laughter, the day had been pointless, awkward, and weird.

Yes, she'd been quick to sense all that in Lucie's voice. She was already worried about not being there. Or rather, the disquiet that she'd started to feel as the day of her departure approached and that she'd firmly suppressed, she now gave free rein to. Not that there was anything that could objectively be considered dangerous in leaving the girls in Jakob's care, but she was concerned that the discipline, thrift, and high moral values that, it seemed to her, she'd established in her little apartment and that were meant to affirm and adorn her own life and form the basis of Lucie's upbringing were being demolished in her absence with cold, methodical jubilation by a man. As for bringing the man into her home, nothing had obliged her to do that: only love, and hope.

Now she was unable to recognize that love any longer; it lay smothered by disappointment. She had lost all hope of an ordered, sober, harmonious family life.

She had opened her door and evil—smiling, gentle, and stubborn—had entered.

After years of mistrust, having left Lucie's father and bought the apartment, after years of austerely constructing an honorable existence, she had opened her door to its destruction.

Shame on her; she couldn't tell anyone about it. There seemed to be nothing expressible or understandable about the mistake she'd made: a mistake, a crime against her own efforts.

Neither her mother nor her sister nor her few friends could conceive how Jakob and his daughter, Grete—both of them gentle and considerate, well brought up and likable—were working subtly to undermine the delicate balance that had finally been achieved in the lives of Norah and Lucie, before Norah—as if blinded in the end by an excess of mistrust—had obligingly opened her door to the charming incarnation of evil.

How lonely she felt!

How trapped, how stupid!

Shame on her.

But what words could she find sufficiently precise to comprehend the anger and disquiet that she'd felt two or three days before, during one of those family arguments that epitomized for her Jakob's nasty underhandedness and her own feeblemindedness, she who had so aspired to simplicity and straightforwardness, she who had been so afraid of twisted thinking while she and Lucie lived alone together that she'd run a mile at the slightest hint of it, determined never to expose her child to eccentric or perverse behavior?

But she had been ignorant of the fact that evil can have a kindly face, that it could be accompanied by a delightful little girl, and that it could be prodigal in love—though, in fact, Jakob's vague, impersonal, and inexhaustible love cost him nothing; she knew that now.

As on every other morning, Norah had gotten up first, made Grete and Lucie's breakfast, and gotten them ready for school. Jakob, who normally only woke up after the three of them had left the house, emerged from the bedroom that morning just as Norah was finishing her hair in the bathroom.

The girls were putting on their shoes, and what should he do but start teasing them, undoing one girl's laces and stealing the other's shoe, running and hiding it under the sofa with howls of laughter like a mocking child, oblivious of the time and the distress of the girls, who, amused at first, ran around the apartment in pursuit, begging him to stop his tricks, on the verge of tears but trying to smile because it was all supposed to be comical and in good fun. Norah had to intervene and order him, like a dog, in that faux-gentle tone, pulsing with suppressed anger, that she used only with Jakob, to bring the shoe back at once, which he did with such good grace that Norah, and the girls too, suddenly looked like petty, sad women whom an impish teaser had only tried to cheer up.

Norah knew that she had to hurry now or be late for the first appointment of the day, so she refused tartly when Jakob offered to go with them. But the girls had encouraged him and backed him up, so Norah, weary and demoralized all of a sudden, gave in. Standing silently in the hallway with their coats, shoes, and scarves on, they had to wait for him to get dressed and join them. He had a way of being gay and lighthearted that seemed forced, almost threatening, to Norah. Their eyes had met as she glanced anxiously at her watch. All she saw in Jakob's look was cruel spite, bordering on hardness, under his stubbornly effervescent manner.

It made her head spin, wondering what kind of man she'd allowed into her home.

He'd then taken her in his arms and embraced her more tenderly than anyone had ever done. Feeling miserable, she chided herself: Who can enjoy a taste of tenderness and then willingly give it up?

They had then trudged through the muddy slush on the pavement and clambered into Norah's little car. It was cold and uncomfortable.

Jakob had gotten into the back with the girls (as was his annoying habit, Norah thought: as an adult, wasn't his place in the front, next to her?), and while she let the engine warm up, she'd heard him whisper to the girls that they needn't fasten their seat belts.

"Oh, why needn't we?" Lucie had asked in astonishment.

"Because we're not going far," he'd said in his silly, excited voice.

Norah had gripped the steering wheel, and her hands had begun to tremble.

She'd ordered the girls to fasten their seat belts at once, the fury she felt against Jakob hardening her tone. Her anger had seemed aimed at them, the unfairness of which Grete and Lucie had expressed to Jakob with a pained look.

"We're really not going far," he'd said. "Anyway, I'm not going to fasten my seat belt."

Norah pulled out.

She, who made a point of never being late, was certainly late now.

She was on the brink of tears.

She was a lost, pathetic creature.

After some hesitation, Grete and Lucie had given up fastening their seat belts and Norah said nothing, furious with Jakob for seeking always to cast her in the role of a killjoy or a villain, but also disgusted with herself for being, she felt, a coward, unworthy.

She'd felt like heaving the car against a bus, just to show him that fastening seat belts wasn't pointless, but he knew that, didn't he?

That wasn't the issue. What was *she* doing? What did she want from this man who was hanging on her back with his adorable child in tow? What did she want from this man with the soft, pale eyes, who'd sunk his painless little claws in her flanks so that no matter what she did she couldn't shake him off?

That's what she could not, dare not, explain to her mother or her sister or her few remaining friends: the sheer ordinariness of such incidents, the narrowness of her concerns, the emptiness of such a life beneath the appearance of fullness that—such was the terrible power of enchantment wielded by Jakob and his daughter—so easily deceived mother, sister, and friends.

Norah's father stopped in front of one of the cells that lined the corridor.

He opened the door carefully and immediately stood back.

"You'll be sleeping here," he said.

Gesturing toward the far end of the corridor, he added—as if Norah had shown a slight hesitation about this particular assignment—"There're no longer any beds in the other rooms."

Norah switched on the ceiling light.

The walls were covered with posters of basketball players.

"Sony's room?" she mumbled.

Her father nodded.

He was breathing more audibly, with his mouth wide open, his back against the wall.

"What are the girls called?" asked Norah.

He shrugged, pretending to think.

She laughed, slightly shocked.

"Don't you remember?" she asked.

"Their mother chose their names, rather strange names, I can never remember them," he replied, laughing too, but mirthlessly.

To her great surprise she sensed in him an air of desperation.

"What do they do during the day, when their mother isn't there?"

"They stay in their room," he said abruptly.

"All day?"

"They have all they need. They don't lack for anything. That girl takes good care of them."

Norah then wanted to ask why he'd summoned her.

But though she knew her father well enough to be aware that it couldn't have been for the simple pleasure of seeing her after so long and that he must be after something from her in particular, he seemed at that moment so old and vulnerable that she refrained from asking the question. When he's ready, he'll let me know, she said to herself, but she couldn't help telling him, "I can only stay a few days."

She thought of Jakob and the two overexcited girls, and her stomach tightened.

"Ah no," he said, agitated all of a sudden, "you must stay a lot longer, it's absolutely essential! Well, see you tomorrow."

Slipping into the corridor, he trotted away, his flip-flops clacking on the concrete, his fat hips wiggling under the thin fabric of his trousers.

With him went the bittersweet smell of rotting flowers, of flowers in full bloom crushed under an indifferent foot or bitterly trampled, and when she removed her dress to go to sleep she took particular care to spread it out on Sony's bed so that the yellow flowers embroidered on the green cotton cloth remained fresh and distinct to the eye and bore no resemblance to the poinciana's wilting flowers and the guilty, sad smell left in her father's wake.

She found her backpack at the foot of the bed.

She sat in her nightgown on her brother's bed. It was covered with a sheet bearing the insignias of American basketball teams. She cast a pained look at the small chest of drawers covered with dusty knickknacks, the child's desk with its low top, the basketballs piled up in a corner, most of them burst or deflated.

She recognized every object, every poster, every piece of furniture.

Her brother Sony was thirty-five and Norah hadn't seen him for many years, but they had always been close.

His room hadn't changed at all since his adolescence.

How was it possible to live like that?

She shivered in spite of the heat.

Outside the small square window everything was pitch black and totally silent.

No sound came from within the house nor from outside it, except perhaps—she couldn't be sure—from time to time that of the poinciana's branches rubbing against the corrugated-iron roof.

She picked up her cell phone and phoned home.

No reply.

Then she remembered that Lucie had mentioned going to the movies, which annoyed her because it was Monday and the girls had to be up early the next day for school, and she had to struggle against a sense of impending catastrophe, of terrifying disorder, that swept over her every time she wasn't there to see, simply see, what was going on, even if she couldn't always do much about it.

She considered such worries as failings on her part, not weaknesses.

Because it would be too arrogant to think that she alone knew how to organize Lucie and Grete's life properly, that she alone, through the power of her reason, of her anxious concern, could prevent disaster from crossing the threshold and entering her life.

Had she not already opened her door to evil in a kindly, smiling form?

The only way to mitigate the effects of this great blunder was to be constantly, anxiously, on the alert.

But when her father called she'd simply left.

Sitting on Sony's bed, she now regretted it.

What was her father—this selfish old man—to her, compared with her daughter?

What did her father's existence matter now, when her own hung by a thread?

Although she knew that, if Jakob was sitting in a movie theater at that moment, it was pointless, she still dialed his cell phone.

She left an exaggeratedly cheery message.

She could see his affable face, the calm, clear, sensible look in his eyes, the slight droop of his lips, and the general pleasantness of his finely wrought features. She was still able to acknowledge that such amiability had inspired her with confidence, to the extent that she had not dwelled on the puzzling aspects of the life of this man who'd come from Hamburg with his daughter, on the slightly differing versions he'd given of his reasons for coming to France, on the vagueness of his explanations for his less than assiduous attendance at law school, or the fact that Grete never saw, and never spoke about, her mother, who, he claimed, had stayed in Germany.

She knew now that Jakob would never become a lawyer, or anything else, for that matter, that he would never contribute meaningfully to the expenses of the household even if he did receive from time to time—from his parents, he said—a few hundred euros, which he spent immediately and ostentatiously on expensive meals and on clothes the children didn't need, and she knew too—finally admitting it to herself—that she had quite simply set up in her home a man and a little girl whom she had to feed and care for, whom she could not throw out, and who had her boxed in.

That was the way it was.

She dreamed sometimes that she would return home one evening to find Lucie all by herself, relaxed and happy as she used to be in the past, unaffected by the hollow excitement Jakob provoked, and that Lucie would tell her calmly that the others had left for good.

That was the way it was. Norah knew that she would never have the strength to throw them out.

Where would they go, how would they manage?

Only a miracle, she sometimes thought, could rid her of them, could free her and Lucie from life with this amiable but subtly evil pair.

Yes, that was the way it was, she was trapped.

She got up, took a toiletries bag out of her backpack, and went into the corridor.

So deep was the silence that she seemed to hear it vibrating.

She opened a door that she remembered concluding was the bathroom.

But it was her father's room. It was empty, and the double bed had not been slept in. Something about the stillness of the air and of everything else made her think that the room was no longer used.

She followed the corridor to the living room and groped her way through it.

The front door was not locked.

Hugging her toiletries bag to her chest and feeling her night-gown rubbing against the back of her knees, she went outside. With her bare feet on the warm cement she felt herself trampling on the invisible flowers that had fallen from the poinciana. She dared at last to look up at the tree, in the vain hope of seeing nothing there, of not discerning in the crisscross of branches the pale shape, the cold luminescence of her father's hunched body. She thought she could hear, coming from the shadows, loud, painful breathing, desolate panting, and even stifled sobs and little groans of distress.

Overcome with emotion, she wanted to call out to him.

But what word could she use to address him?

She'd never been comfortable saying "Daddy," and couldn't imagine using his first name, which she barely knew.

Her urge to call out to him remained stuck in her throat.

For a long while she watched him rocking very slightly above her head. She couldn't see his face, but she recognized, gripping the biggest branch, his old plastic flip-flops.

The body of her father, this broken man, shone palely.

What a bad omen!

She wanted to run away from this funereal house as quickly as possible, but she felt that, having agreed to return to it and having managed to locate the tree her father was perching in, she was now too deeply committed to be able to abandon him and go back home.

She returned to Sony's room, having given up on the idea of trying to find the bathroom, so fearful was she now of opening a door on a scene or situation that would cause her to feel more guilty.

Sitting on Sony's bed again, she toyed with her cell phone, deep in thought.

Should she try again to call home, at the risk of waking the children if they'd gotten back from the movies?

Or go to sleep with the guilty feeling of having done nothing to avert a potential catastrophe?

She'd have liked to hear Lucie's voice again.

A hideous thought went through her mind, so fleeting that she forgot the exact form it took, but long enough for her to feel the full horror of it: Might she never hear her daughter's voice again?

And what if, in hastening to her father's side, she'd unwittingly chosen between two camps, two possible ways of life, the one inevitably excluding the other, and between two forms of commitment fiercely jealous of each other?

Without further ado she dialed the number of the apartment, and then, since no one picked up, the number of Jakob's cell phone, also in vain.

Having slept little and badly, she got up at dawn, slipped on her green dress and sandals, and went in search of the bathroom, which was, in fact, next door to Sony's room.

She went back to the little girls' room.

She gently opened the door.

The young woman was still asleep. The two little girls were awake and sitting up in bed. Their perfectly identical pairs of eyes were wide open, gazing sternly at Norah.

She smiled at them, murmuring from a distance the tender things she habitually said to Lucie.

The little girls frowned.

One of them spat at her. The thin spittle dribbled onto the sheet.

The other began to imitate her, puffing out her cheeks.

Norah shut the door, not offended, but unsettled.

She wondered if she should be doing something for these little waifs, and in what capacity—as a half sister, a kind of mother, an adult morally responsible for every child one came across?

She once again felt her heart bursting with impotent rage at that thoughtless man who after so many failures couldn't wait to marry again and produce more children who meant nothing to him, a man whose capacity for love and for showing consideration to others was so small, seemingly used up in his youth in his relationship with his old mother, long dead, whom Norah had never known.

It's true he'd shown some affection toward Sony, his only son.

But what need had he for a new family, this unfeeling man, incomplete, detached?

He was already eating when she reentered the living room. He was sitting at the table as on the previous evening, dressed in the same pale shabby clothes, his face bent over his plate, stuffing himself with porridge, so that she had to wait until he'd finished and had hurled himself backward, as if after enormous physical exertion, panting and sighing. Only then could she ask, looking him straight in the eye, "Now, what's this all about?"

That morning her father had a look that was even more evasive than usual.

Was it because he knew that she'd seen him in the poinciana?

But how could that embarrass him, this cynical man who had never batted an eyelid over much more degrading situations?

"Masseck!" he shouted hoarsely.

He then asked Norah, "What'll you have? Tea? Coffee?"

She tapped on the table lightly with her fist, thinking, with a vacant, worried air, that it was time for Lucie and Grete to get up and go to school, and that Jakob would perhaps have forgotten to set his alarm clock, which would mean that the whole day would bear the mark of failure and neglect. But wasn't she herself much too virtuous, punctual, and scrupulous? Wasn't she in reality that tiresome woman whom she reproached Jakob for painting her as?

"Coffee?" asked Masseck, offering her a full cup.

"Will you please tell me why I've come?" she said calmly, looking her father in the eye.

Masseck scurried away.

Her father then started breathing so violently and with such difficulty that Norah leaped from her chair and went up to him.

She stood there, awkwardly, and would have put her question to him again if she'd been able.

"You must go and see Sony," he murmured painfully.

"Where's Sony?"

"In Reubeuss."

"What on earth's Reubeuss?"

No answer.

He breathed less painfully, slumped in his chair, his belly sticking out, surrounded by the syrupy odor of poinciana flowers in full bloom.

Then she was deeply moved to see tears running down his gray cheeks.

"It's the prison," he said.

She took a step, almost a leap, backward.

"What've you done with Sony?" she cried out. "You were supposed to be looking after him!"

"He was the one who committed the offense, not me," he whispered, almost inaudibly.

"What offense? What's he done? Oh God, you were supposed to be taking care of him and bringing him up properly!"

She stepped back and sank onto her chair.

She gulped down the coffee, which was acrid, lukewarm, and tasteless.

Her hands trembled so much that she dropped the cup onto the glass-topped table.

"That's another broken cup!" her father said. "I spend all my time buying crockery in this house."

"What did Sony do?"

He got up, shaking his head, his old wizened face ravaged by the impossibility of talking.

"Masseck will drive you to Reubeuss," he croaked.

He walked backward toward the door to the corridor, slowly, as if trying to escape without her noticing.

His toenails were long and yellow.

"So," she asked calmly, "is that why there's no one here anymore? Is that why everyone has left?"

Her father's back met the door; he groped behind him, opened it, and scurried away down the corridor.

Once, in a meadow in Normandy, she'd seen an old abandoned donkey whose hooves had grown so much he could hardly walk.

Her father was quite capable of trotting along when it suited him!

Her immense feeling of resentment lit up her mind and sharpened her thoughts.

No one, nothing, could ever excuse their father for his failure to keep Sony on the straight and narrow.

Because when, thirty years earlier, wishing to abandon their mother and France and his dead-end office job, he'd suddenly left, taking Sony, then age five, with him—abducting Sony, in truth, because he knew the mother would never agree to let him take her little boy—when he'd thereby plunged Norah, her sister, and their mother in a despair the mother would never really get over, when he'd promised in a letter left on the kitchen table to take better care of the child than of himself, his business affairs, and his personal ambitions, their mother, in her grief, had clung to that promise, convincing herself that Sony would have a brilliant career and great opportunities that she, a simple hairdresser, couldn't perhaps have managed to give him.

Norah couldn't recall without gasping for breath the day she came home from school to find her father's letter.

She was eight, her sister nine, and from the bedroom the three children shared Sony's things were gone: his clothes in the chest of drawers, his bag of Legos, his teddy bear.

Her first thought was to hide the letter and, by some miracle, the reality of Sony and their father's departure, so that her mother wouldn't notice.

Then, grasping how powerless she was, she'd wandered around

the small, dark apartment, dizzy with worry and pain, staggered by the realization of what had happened, of the huge suffering already inflicted and certain to go on being inflicted, and of the fact that nothing could undo the terrible thing that had occurred.

She'd then taken the metro to the salon where her mother worked.

Even now, thirty years later, she couldn't summon the strength to recall precisely the moment when she told her mother what had happened and what suffering still lay in wait.

It was all she could do to remember, little by little, her mother's wild stare as she sat on Sony's bed, frantically smoothing the pale blue chenille coverlet and repeating shrilly, monotonously, "He's too young to live without me. Five years old, that's much too small!"

Their father had phoned the day after his arrival. He was triumphant, full of gusto, and their mother had made an effort to be conciliatory, to sound almost calm, fearing above all that this man who hated open conflict would break off all relations if he thought she was making a big fuss.

He'd let Sony talk on the phone but had grabbed the receiver back when the child, hearing his mother's voice, had started to cry.

Time had passed, and the bitter, heartrending, unacceptable situation had become diluted in the routine of everyday life, had melted in the normality of an existence only disrupted at regular intervals by the arrival of a clumsy, stilted letter from Sony, which Norah and her sister had to answer in a similarly formal way so that—their mother calculated—it would appear to their father that there was no risk in allowing greater contact.

How accommodating and sadly devious this gentle, benumbed

woman had shown herself to be in her distress! She'd gone on buying clothes for Sony, folding them carefully, and putting them away in the little boy's chest of drawers.

"For when he gets back," she'd say.

But from the outset Norah and her sister had been fully aware that Sony would never come back, knowing as they did their father's lack of feeling, his indifference to the feelings of others, and his penchant for imposing his iron will on those around him.

Once he'd decided that Sony was his by right he would ignore everything that could restrain his desire to have his only son at his side.

He considered of little importance the unhappiness that Sony felt about his exile, just as he viewed the suffering of his wife as unavoidable and purely temporary. For he was like that: implacable and terrifying.

Throughout the time their mother still expected Sony to return, Norah and her sister knew that she hadn't gotten the full measure of her husband's intransigence. He would stubbornly refuse, for instance, to send the boy back to France for the holidays.

For he was like that: an implacable, terrifying man.

The years passed and the painful subservience of their mother was rewarded only by an invitation to Norah and her sister to visit their brother.

"Why won't you let Sony come and see us?" their mother shouted into the phone, her face contorted in grief.

"Because I know that you wouldn't let him go again," their father, calm and self-assured, probably answered, slightly annoyed perhaps because he loathed weeping and shouting.

"Of course I would, I swear to you!"

But he knew she was lying, and she knew it too. Choking and gasping, she couldn't go on.

That their father would never want to be burdened with his two daughters, that he'd do nothing to keep them, was so blindingly obvious that their mother let them go to see him, sending Norah and her sister as emissaries and witnesses to her immense affliction, to her somewhat disembodied love for a boy whose photograph his father from time to time sent to her, a badly taken picture, always blurred, which invariably showed Sony smiling broadly, in excellent health, amazingly handsome, and expensively dressed.

Their father had acquired a holiday village while it was still under construction. He'd given it a complete, luxurious makeover, and it was now making him a wealthy man.

Meanwhile, in Paris, in a symmetrical but contrary manner, as if she felt she had to atone for her misfortune by letting things slide, their mother was experiencing money troubles. She kept getting into debt and having to negotiate endlessly with credit card companies.

Their father sent a little money at irregular intervals, different amounts each time, doubtless because he wished to convey the impression that he was doing all he could.

He was like that, implacable and terrifying.

He was incapable of compassion and remorse, and because as a child he'd been tormented by hunger on a daily basis, he was determined now to gorge himself and apply his quick intelligence to no aim but ensuring his comfort and establishing his power. He had no need to tell himself, "I deserve all this," because he never doubted for a second that his privileges and the wealth amassed so quickly were his by right.

Meanwhile their conscientious, desperate, insecure mother was getting into a mess with her accounts. Eventually, that meant she had to move. In the rue des Pyrénées they took a two-bedroom apartment that looked onto an inner courtyard. Sony's drawer was stocked with fewer and fewer new clothes.

So when the two girls, aged twelve and thirteen, arrived for the first time in their father's enormous house, stricken with emotion and exhausted by the heat, they brought with them the decorous, austere, repressed sadness in which they lived, a sentiment betrayed by their short, simple haircuts, their denim dresses bought too big so as to last longer, and their graceless missionary sandals. It all aroused an overwhelming feeling of disgust in their father, made only worse by the fact that they were neither of them very pretty, as well as suffering from acne and being overweight. As they grew older they shed the extra pounds, but they would always, in a way, look fat to their father, because he was like that: a man deeply shocked and repelled by ugliness.

That's why, Norah thought, he'd loved Sony as much as he could love anyone.

Their younger brother appeared on the threshold of the house. He hadn't dropped from the poinciana, then still a small and delicate shrub, but had just dismounted from a pony on which he'd been slowly trotting around the garden.

Dressed in a cream-colored riding outfit and wearing real riding boots, he stood with one foot forward, his riding hat tucked under his arm.

No smell of rotting flowers clung to his lithe, elegant frame. The nine-year-old boy's narrow chest was not lit from within by any unusual glow.

He was simply there, smiling, happy, and magnificent, stretching his arms out to his sisters, as dazzling and carefree as they were dull and serious.

And Sony treated them with extreme unpretentious kindness throughout their stay, during which, though scared and reproachful, they tasted a life of luxury beyond their wildest imaginings.

He greeted every remark they made, every question they asked, with a gentle smile and a few noncommittal words, making a joke of it, so they failed to notice that they never got a straight response to anything.

He remained silent whenever they mentioned their mother.

He gazed into space and his lower lip quivered slightly.

But it didn't last; he quickly became once again the happy, calm, unpretentious, smooth-skinned, almost too gentle boy whom their father would gaze at proudly, obviously comparing him with his two lumpish anxious-looking daughters and telling himself—Norah supposed—that he'd done right in not leaving Sony behind, in removing him from his mother's baleful influence, which had transformed two amiable little girls into a pair of tubby nuns, particularly since the beautiful woman with the scornful expression and slightly bulging eyes whom he'd married two or three years earlier and who wandered the property silently with a weary, irritated, melancholy, and intimidating air, had yet to give him a child and never would.

When at the end of three weeks Norah and her sister returned home they were actually relieved to escape a way of life that their loyalty to their mother made them feel duty bound to condemn ("Mummy has money troubles," they'd found the courage to tell their father on learning that Sony was being sent to a prestigious

private school, to which he'd responded with a sigh, "My poor
dear girls, who doesn't have money troubles!"). They were also
deeply saddened to be leaving Sony behind.

Standing on the threshold with one foot in front of the other,
dressed this time in his basketball uniform, his ball under his arm,
and making every effort to smile, Sony had said good-bye, his
lower lip trembling slightly, but otherwise maintaining the kind,
inscrutably smooth, and submissive air he'd shown throughout.

Their father was there too, standing up straight beneath the
scanty foliage of the young poinciana, looking elegant, his narrow
hips turned slightly away.

He'd laid a hand on Sony's shoulder, at which the boy had
seemed to cringe, almost as if doubling over, greatly surprising
Norah, who had thought, He's afraid of him, but then, before getting into the car to be driven away by Mansour, rejecting the idea,
since it bore no relation to anything she'd seen during their stay.

Because their father, that terrifying, unbending man, had always
treated Sony with great kindness.

He had even shown him some tenderness.

But then Norah had tried to imagine how distraught her
five-year-old brother must have been to have found himself in this
unknown country, alone in a hotel with his father, then in this hastily rented house soon invaded by numerous unfamiliar relatives,
and how it must have slowly dawned on him that he was embarking on a new existence and that there was no longer any question
of his ever returning to live with his mother and sisters in the little
apartment in the twelfth arrondissement that up till then had constituted his whole universe.

She felt very sorry for Sony and no longer envied him his father's love or the pony in the garden.

And the life those three lived, grim and solemn, thrifty and deserving, suddenly struck her as free and easy compared with that of Sony, the pampered little prisoner.

Their mother, hungry for news, listened dejectedly and in silence to the two sisters' cautious account of what they'd seen and heard.

Then she burst into tears and kept repeating, "So he's lost to me, lost!" as if the education and affluence Sony enjoyed was erecting an impenetrable barrier between herself and the boy, were she even able to see him again.

It was at this time that their mother's behavior changed.

She left the hairdresser's where she'd been slaving away for twenty years or more and began going out in the evening. Although Norah and her sister never suspected it at the time, they would gather years later that their mother must have worked as a prostitute and that this activity, which her outward cheerfulness belied, was the particular form her grief took.

Norah and her sister would return to their father's on holiday once or twice.

But no longer did their mother ever want to be told anything about what they'd seen there.

She'd assumed a hard, determined look; her face was smooth under her makeup; and whatever the context, with a sarcastic curl of the lip and an angry sweep of the hand, she was given to saying, "Oh, what do I care?"

This new demeanor and this gritty bitterness enabled her to

meet exactly the kind of man she was looking for. She married a bank manager, who like her was divorced and remained her husband to this day. He was an uncomplicated, likable, and well-paid man, very kind to Norah and her sister, even to the point of—at their father's invitation—taking them with their mother to see Sony all together for the first time.

Their mother hadn't seen the boy since he'd left.

Sony was now sixteen.

On learning that their mother had remarried, their father wasted no time inviting them, and reserving several nights' accommodation for them in the town's best hotel. It was as if—Norah thought—he'd been waiting for their mother to make a new life for herself before he could stop worrying that she'd try to abduct Sony.

And that's how they all found themselves, like a big, happy, reconstituted family, Norah and her sister, their mother and her husband, Sony and their father, seated in the hotel dining room eating local delicacies, their father and the new husband discussing calmly, with only a hint of awkwardness, the international situation, while the boy and his mother, sitting close together, shot furtive, uneasy glances at each other.

Sony was as usual superbly turned out: he wore a dark linen suit; his skin was soft and smooth, and he had a short Afro haircut.

Their mother's face wore its new fixed expression. Her mouth was slightly twisted, her heavily lacquered hair was dyed pale blond, and Norah noticed as her mother asked Sony about school and his favorite subjects that she took care with her grammar and syntax, knowing that Sony was now much better educated and

more refined than herself, a mortifying and uncomfortable awareness.

Their father looked at them with a happy air of relief, as if at
long last he'd managed to reconcile old enemies.

Is that what he really thinks now? Norah wondered, cross and
astonished. Has he managed to convince himself that it was Sony
and our mother all these years who were unwilling to meet?

Long before, when, wild with grief, their mother had told him
on the telephone that if he refused to send Sony to spend the holidays with her she would borrow the airfare to visit her son in his
house, their father had said, "If I see you getting off that plane, I'll
slit his throat and mine right before your eyes!"

But was he really man enough to cut his own throat?

There he was now, seated at the head of the table, handsome,
charming, exquisitely polite, his cold dark eyes shining with love
and pride whenever he gazed at Sony's adorable face.

Norah noticed that her brother never looked anyone straight
in the eye. His affable, impersonal gaze flitted from one person to
another without dwelling on any face in particular, and when spoken to he stared fixedly at an invisible point in the distance, without
ceasing to smile or to adopt an expression of serious interest in
whatever was being said to him.

He was particularly careful, Norah thought, not to be caught
unawares by their father's gaze. Even then, even when their father
looked at him and Sony glanced elsewhere, he seemed to withdraw, to curl up in the depths of his being, where he was safe from
every judgment, every feeling that involved him.

He exchanged a few words with his mother's husband, and then with her, haltingly, because she had reached the limit of what she dared ask him.

After the meal they went their separate ways, and although it was a few days before their departure, Sony and their mother never saw each other again and never again would their mother mention him.

Their father had organized a lavish program of tourism, had hired a guide and a chauffeur for them, even paying for a few extra nights at one of the chalets in his holiday village in Dara Salam.

All that, however, their mother refused, dismissing the guide and the chauffeur, and bringing forward their departure date.

She no longer left the hotel. She just went back and forth between her room and the pool, smiling in the same mechanical, distant, very calm way that Sony did, leaving Norah and her sister to entertain the husband, who took pleasure in everything and found nothing to complain about, until the last evening, when, at a loss where to go, they took him to dinner at their father's, and the two men chatted until two in the morning, parting with reluctance and promising to see each other again.

That had really annoyed Norah. "He was making fun of you the whole time," she said to the husband, with a snicker, as they went back to the hotel.

"What? Not at all. He's a very nice man, your dad!"

And Norah immediately felt guilty for her spiteful remark, allowing that it was indeed perfectly possible that their father had genuinely enjoyed the company and that she was simply angry with the two of them for appearing to trivialize her mother's immense unhappiness, and also that it was her mother, after all, who had accepted the unseemly idea to bring her husband to their father's house in the obscure hope, no doubt, of provoking an almighty row, at the end of which she and Sony would be avenged and their father confounded, his cruelty having been exposed and acknowledged, but ought she not to have understood that this ideal husband was not the sort of person to make a scene?

Their mother never saw Sony again, never once wrote to him or telephoned him, and never even mentioned his name.

She and her husband had moved to a house in the outer suburbs. From time to time Norah brought Lucie to see her. She had the impression that since their return her mother had never stopped smiling, a faint smirk that seemed disconnected from her face floating lightly in front of her, as if she'd snatched it from Sony to mask her pain.

Norah continued passing on to her the odd bits of news she got from Sony or their father—about Sony's studies in London, or his return to their father a few years later—but it often seemed that their mother, through her smiles and nods, was trying not to listen.

Norah spoke about Sony to her less and less, then stopped altogether on learning that, after getting a very good degree, he had ended up in his father's house, and was leading a strangely passive, idle, lonely existence.

Her heart of course often missed a beat when she thought of him.

Should she not have gone to see him more often, or made him come and see her?

Wasn't he, despite his money and opportunities, just a hapless boy?

As for Norah, she'd managed to train to become a lawyer. She'd not found life easy, but she'd kept at it.

No one had helped her, and neither her mother nor her father had ever told her that they were proud of her.

And yet she bore no grudge and even felt guilty about not going to help Sony in some way.

But what could she have done?

A devil had possessed the five-year-old boy and had never let go of him.

What could she have done?

That's what she kept asking herself as she sat on the backseat of the black Mercedes driven by Masseck. As the car moved slowly down the deserted street she gazed in the rearview mirror at her father standing motionless by the gate, waiting perhaps to be alone before lofting himself heavily up again into the deep shade of the poinciana and sitting on the branch stripped and polished by his flip-flops—that was what she kept wondering as she fanned through the official documents stamped everywhere, which her father had given her: had she not, in her carelessness, really let Sony down?

The Mercedes was dirty and dusty, the seats covered in crumbs.

In the past her father would never have put up with such slovenliness.

She leaned toward Masseck and asked him why Sony was in prison.

He clicked his tongue and snickered. Norah realized that he'd been badly put out by her question and wouldn't answer it.

Deeply embarrassed, she forced herself to laugh too.

How could she have done that?

Obviously it wasn't his place to tell her.

She'd been thrown. She felt ashamed.

Just before getting into the car she'd tried to contact Jakob. In vain: the phone in the apartment rang, but no one answered.

It seemed to her unlikely that the children had already left for school, and just as unlikely that all three were sleeping so soundly as to not be aroused by the phone's insistent ringing.

So what was going on?

Her legs were shaking nervously.

She would have been grateful, at that moment, to take refuge herself in the fragrant golden semidarkness of that big tree!

She smoothed her hair back, retied her bun, and, as she stretched forward to see her reflection in the rearview mirror, thought that Sony would perhaps have difficulty recognizing her because, when they'd last met, eight or nine years earlier, she didn't have those two furrows on either side of her mouth or the rather thick, pudgy chin, against which she remembered having struggled ferociously when younger, guiltily aware that her father found rolls of fat disgusting, before, later, without remorse, and even with a certain provocative satisfaction, she'd allowed it to bloom, knowing full well that such a chin would offend that slender man who admired women, and it was from that moment she'd resolved to be free, to cast aside all concerns about pleasing a father who did not love her.

As for him, well, he'd gotten completely fat.

She shook her head, afraid and lost in thought.

The car was crossing the town center, and Masseck was driving slowly in front of the big hotels, calling out their names in a rather grand tone of voice.

Norah recognized the one where their mother and her husband had briefly stayed, back in the days when Sony, a first-rate student in high school, seemed destined for great things.

She'd never bothered to consider why Sony should have returned to live with his father after studying political science in London, and above all why he seemed to have made nothing of his life or his gifts.

That was because she considered him at the time to be much luckier than she was. She'd had to work her way through college in a fast-food restaurant, so she didn't think herself under any obligation to worry about her spoiled younger brother's mental state.

He'd fallen into a devil's clutches and had never been able to break loose.

Sony must have suffered greatly from clinical depression. Poor, poor boy, she thought.

It was at that moment that she saw before her eyes Jakob, Grete, and Lucie sitting at the hotel terrace where they'd all had lunch before.

Her blood ran cold. She closed her eyes.

When she opened them again, Masseck had turned into another street.

They were running along the coast road, and the car was filled with the smell of the sea.

Masseck had fallen silent, and his face, which Norah could see in profile, had taken on a sullen, stubborn, hurt look, as if being made to drive to Reubeuss were some personal slight.

He parked opposite the high gray walls of the prison.

Standing in the hot, dry wind, she got in line behind a large number of women. Noticing that they'd all put down on the pavement the baskets and parcels they'd brought with them, she did the same with the plastic bag Masseck had handed to her, telling her grudgingly, with a scornful air, that it contained coffee and food for Sony.

Then, as he had to wait for her with his door wide open so it didn't get too hot in the car, he settled down in his seat and turned his face away from her.

"There's nothing to be ashamed of," she'd nearly told him.

But she'd stopped herself, wondering whether it was in fact true.

Her stomach was churning. Who, in reality, were the three people she'd seen on the hotel terrace? Herself and her sister, when they were small, accompanied by some stranger?

Oh no, she was sure it was her daughter and Grete with Jakob. The children were wearing little striped dresses with matching sun hats that she'd bought them the previous summer. She'd felt a spasm of guilt as she left the shop, she remembered, because the outfits were perhaps too elegant for little girls, not at all the sort she and her sister would have ever worn.

What devil had gotten her sister into his clutches?

After a long wait outside the prison she was called into an office where she handed over her passport together with the documents her father had given her which certified that she had the right to visit her brother.

She also handed over the bag of food.

"Are you the lawyer?" asked a guard. He wore a tattered uniform. He had red, shining eyes, and his eyelids twitched nervously.

"No, no," she said, "I'm his sister."

"It says here you're the lawyer."

Circumspectly she replied, "I am a lawyer, but today I'm just here to see my brother."

He hesitated and gazed fixedly at the little yellow flowers on Norah's green dress.

Then she was shown into a big room with pale blue walls, divided down the middle by metal grating. The women who had been waiting with her on the pavement outside were already there.

She went up to the grating and saw her brother Sony entering at the other end of the room.

The men who came in with him rushed toward the grating, making such a din that she couldn't hear Sony's greeting.

"Sony, Sony!" she shouted.

She felt giddy and clung to the grating.

She got as close as she could to the dirty, dusty metal framework, trying to see as clearly as she could this thirty-year-old man who was her younger brother. Under the blemished skin, behind the eczema scars, she recognized his long handsome face and gentle, rather vague expression. When he smiled, it was the same distant, radiant smile that she'd always known him to wear and that had perpetually tugged at her heartstrings, because she'd always sensed, as she now knew, that it served merely to conceal and contain an inexpressible sadness.

His cheeks were covered in stubble, and his hair, some strands of which were long and some were short, stood up on his head except where it was flattened, on the side he slept on, no doubt.

He was talking to her, smiling—smiling all the time—but she couldn't hear a word because of the din.

"Sony!" she shouted, "what did you say? Speak up!"

He was scratching his forehead savagely. It was pale with eczema.

"You need a cream for that?" she yelled. "Is that what you're saying?"

He seemed to hesitate for a moment, then nodded, as if it didn't matter much whether she'd misunderstood, as if "cream" were as good a reply as any.

He shouted something, a single word.

This time Norah clearly heard the name of their sister.

A fleeting sensation of panic drove every thought out of her mind.

Now a devil had grabbed hold of her, too.

Now it seemed impossible to explain to Sony, to shriek at him that their sister had become an alcoholic and was so far gone—as she herself acknowledged—that she could find no refuge except in a mystical sect, from which she occasionally wrote Norah wild, fanatical, sloppy letters enclosing the odd photo showing her with long gray hair, thin as a rail, meditating on a dirty rubber mat and sucking on her lower lip.

Norah couldn't very well bellow at Sony, "And all that because our father took you from us when you were five!"

No, she couldn't, she could say nothing to this haggard face, those hollow, dead eyes, and those dry lips that seemed detached from the smile that played on them.

The visit was over.

The jailers were leading the prisoners out.

Norah glanced at her watch. Only a few minutes had elapsed since she'd entered the room.

She waved to Sony and shouted, "I'll be back again!" as he moved away, dragging his feet, a tall and gaunt figure in a grubby T-shirt and an old pair of trousers cut off at the knee.

He turned and made the gesture of putting a cup to his lips.

"Yes, yes," she shouted, "there's coffee there, and something for you to eat!"

The room was stiflingly hot.

Norah clung to the grating, afraid she'd pass out if she let go.

She was then dismayed to discover she'd lost control of her bladder, as she felt a warm liquid running down her thighs and calves and onto her sandals. But she could do nothing about it and even the sensation of passing urine seemed to elude her.

She stepped away from the puddle in horror.

But in the rush for the exit no one appeared to have noticed.

She was shaking so violently with fury against her father that her teeth were chattering.

What had he done to Sony?

What had he done to them all?

He was ubiquitous, inhabiting each one of them with impunity, and even in death he would go on hurting and tormenting them.

She asked Masseck to drop her at the hotel.

"You can go home," she said. "I'll manage, I'll take a taxi."

To her intense embarrassment the smell of urine soon filled the Mercedes.

Without saying a word Masseck lowered the windows in front.

She was relieved to find the hotel terrace empty.

But the vision of Jakob and the girls continued to haunt her. The subtle but clearly perceptible shadow of their cheerful, conspiratorial presence hung over her, so that when she felt a puff of wind she looked up. But all she could see above her head was a large bird with pale feathers outlined against the sky. It flapped its wings heavily and clumsily, casting over the terrace a huge, cold, unnatural shadow.

Once again she felt a spasm of anger, but it passed as soon as the bird did.

She went into the hotel and looked for the bar.

"I'm looking for Monsieur Jakob Ganzer," she said to the man at the reception desk.

He nodded, and Norah made her way to the bar in her wet sandals. The green carpet with its golden leafy pattern was the same as it had been twenty years earlier.

She ordered tea and went to the toilet to wash her legs and feet.

She took her panties off, rinsed them in the basin, squeezed the water out of them, and held them for a long time under the hand dryer.

She was afraid of what awaited her in the bar, where she'd noticed that there was a computer connected to the Internet that customers could use.

Sipping her tea slowly, so as to postpone as long as possible the moment when she'd have to start her Internet search, she eyed the barman as he watched a soccer match on the big screen above the bar, and she kept thinking that for the children of a dangerous man like her father there was no worse fate than to be loved by him.

Because Sony was certainly the one who'd paid most dearly for being the child of such a man.

As for herself, well, it was true that nothing irreparable had happened yet, just as it was possible she hadn't yet understood what was in store for her and Lucie, or even realized that the devil gripping her was crouching there and biding his time.

She paid for thirty minutes of connection time and soon found, in the archives of the paper *Le Soleil,* a long article about Sony.

She read and reread it with increasing horror, going over the same words again and again.

Holding her head in her hands she stammered, "Oh my God, Sony, oh my God, Sony," unable at first to imagine her brother connected to such an appalling crime, then, almost despite herself, lingering on the precise details, such as his date of birth and physical description, which banished all hope that it could have been a case of mistaken identity.

And who else could have been the son of the father mentioned in the article? Who else could have shown, in the midst of such horror, the immense kindness that the writer of the article singled out as being particularly despicable?

She started to moan, "My poor, dear Sony," but immediately swallowed the words like a mouthful of spit, realizing that a woman was dead and remembering that she herself was a defender of women who'd died in such circumstances, one who felt no pity for their tormenters even if they were gentle, smiling, unhappy men who'd been in the grip of a devil since the age of five.

She carefully logged off from the newspaper's Web site and walked away from the computer, eager now to get back as soon as possible to her father's house to ply him with questions, almost afraid that if she lingered he might fly off for good.

She was crossing the terrace when she saw them—Jakob, Grete, and Lucie—sitting where they'd been before. They were being served bissap juice.

They hadn't seen her yet.

The two little girls, wearing sun hats that matched the

red-and-white-striped dresses with short puff sleeves and smock tops that she'd later regretted buying (though at the time having imagined her father would have approved of the choice, of the vague longing to transform the girls into expensive dolls), were chatting gaily, addressing the occasional remark to Jakob, which he answered in the same cheerful, level tone.

And that was what Norah noticed straightaway: their calm, ready banter. She was filled with a strange melancholy.

Could it be that the unhealthy excitement that she suspected Jakob of provoking and feeding was triggered by her presence, and that in the end everything went well when she was not there?

It seemed to her that she'd never been able to create for the children the serene atmosphere that she now observed bathing the little group.

The pink shade of the umbrella cast a fresh, innocent blush on their skin.

Oh, she thought, that unhealthy feverishness, was she perhaps not the source of it?

She went up to their table, pulled up a chair, and sat down between Grete and Lucie.

"Hello, Mum," Lucie said, getting up to kiss her on the cheek.

And Grete said, "Hello, Norah."

They went on with their conversation, about a character in a cartoon they'd been watching that morning in their room.

"Have a taste of this, it's delicious," said Jakob, pushing his bissap juice toward her.

She found that he'd already gotten a tan, and that the long fair hair that hung over his forehead and down the back of his neck seemed even more bleached by the sun.

"Go up and get your things," he told the girls.

They left the table and went into the hotel with their arms around each other. One girl was fair and the other dark. Their closeness had never seemed entirely credible to Norah, because, while they got on very well, they were always silently jockeying for the first place in Norah and Jakob's affections.

"You know my brother, Sony," Norah hastened to say.

"Yes?"

She took a deep breath but couldn't help bursting into tears, into a flood of tears that her hands were powerless to wipe away.

Jakob picked up a tissue, dried her cheeks, took her in his arms, and patted her back.

She suddenly wondered why she'd always had the vague feeling, whenever they made love, that it was work for him, that he was paying for his and Grete's keep, because, at that moment, she felt great tenderness in him. She held him tight.

"Sony's in prison," she said quickly, her voice breaking.

Glancing around to make sure the children were not back, she told Jakob that four months earlier Sony had strangled his stepmother, the woman his father had married a few years before but whom Norah had never met.

Sony had informed her at the time that their father had remarried and that his new wife had given birth to twin girls, something the old man had not seen fit to tell her himself.

But Sony hadn't revealed that he'd embarked on a relationship with his stepmother, nor that, as the article in *Le Soleil* put it, they'd planned to run away together. He'd never mentioned having fallen head over heels in love with the woman, who was about his own age, much less that she changed her mind, broke off the affair, and asked him to move out of the house.

He'd lain in wait for her in her bedroom, where she slept alone.

"I know why my father wasn't there," Norah said. "I know where he goes at night."

Standing by the door he'd waited in the shadows while she put her children to bed in another room.

When she entered he grabbed her from behind and strangled her with a length of plastic-coated clothesline.

He'd then carefully set the woman's body onto the bed and gone back to his own room, where he'd slept until morning.

All that he had himself described, without prompting and with dazzling affability, as the newspaper article, very reproachfully, stressed.

Jakob listened closely, gently shaking the ice cubes at the bottom of his glass.

He was wearing jeans and a newly laundered blue shirt that smelled nice and fresh.

Norah said nothing, afraid she might be about to pee again without realizing it.

It came back to her, the burning, suffocating, scandalized incomprehension she'd felt on reading the article, but her indignation stubbornly refused to remain focused on Sony. Their father alone was to blame. He'd gotten into the habit of replacing one wife with another, of expecting a woman too young for him, a woman he'd bought in one way or another, to live with his aging body and damaged spirit.

What right had he to snatch from the ranks of men in their thirties a love that was their due, to help himself so freely to that store of burning passion, this man who'd been perching for so long on the big branch of the poinciana that his flip-flops had made it shine?

Grete and Lucie came out of the hotel with their backpacks on and stood beside the table, ready to leave.

Norah gazed intently, sorrowfully, at Lucie's face. It suddenly seemed to her that this beloved face meant nothing to her anymore.

It was the same face, with its delicate features, smooth skin, tiny nose, and curly forehead, but she didn't recognize it.

She felt alive but, as a mother, distant, distracted.

She'd always loved her daughter passionately, so what was this?

Was it simply the humiliation of feeling that behind her back Jakob and the children had taken advantage of her absence to become closer?

"Right," said Jakob, "let's go, I've already paid the bill."

"Go where?" asked Norah.

"We can't stay in the hotel, it's too expensive."

"True."

"We can go to your father's, can't we?"

"Yes," said Norah airily.

He asked the girls if they'd been sure to sort their things carefully into their two backpacks and to leave nothing behind. Norah couldn't help noticing that he was now able to talk to them with just that gentle firmness she'd always wanted to see him adopt.

"And school?" she asked casually.

"The Easter holidays have begun," Jakob said, somewhat surprised.

"I'd forgotten that."

She was upset and started trembling.

Things like that had always been her responsibility.

Was Jakob lying to her?

"My father never liked girls much. Now there are suddenly going to be two more!"

Faced with their serious expression she giggled nervously, ashamed to admit having such a father and also for making fun of him.

Yes, nothing ever emerged from that house but heartbreak and dishonor.

In the taxi she had some difficulty indicating precisely where her father lived.

She had only a rough idea of the address, just the name of the district, "Point E," and so many homes had been built in the last twenty years that she was soon quite lost. She once again misdirected the driver and for a moment worried that Jakob and the children would think she'd made it all up, the existence of the house and of its owner.

She'd taken Lucie's hand and was alternately squeezing it and stroking it.

In her distress she thought that genuine motherly love was melting away: she no longer felt it, she was cold, jittery, in total disarray.

When they stopped at last in front of the house she jumped out and ran to the door, where her father appeared, still in the same rumpled clothes, his long yellow toenails sticking out from the same brown flip-flops.

He gazed suspiciously past Norah at Jakob and the girls taking their bags out of the trunk.

She asked him nervously if they could stay in the house.

"The redhead is my daughter," she said.

"So you have a daughter?"

"Yes, I wrote to you when she was born."

"And him, he's your husband?"

"Yes."

"You're really married?"

"Yes."

It annoyed her to lie, but she did, knowing how much the pro-prieties mattered to her father.

He smiled with relief and shook hands affably with Jakob and then with Grete and Lucie, complimenting them on their nice dresses, speaking with the same urbane, winning drawl that he used when showing VIPs around his holiday village.

After lunch—another bout of tortured gluttony, during which he leaned back heavily in his chair to get his breath back every so often, his mouth wide open and his eyes closed—she led him off to Sony's room.

He showed great reluctance to go in, but being bloated he could not do otherwise than flop down on the bed.

He was gasping like a dying animal.

Norah stood leaning against the door.

He pointed toward a drawer, and Norah opened it. She found on top of Sony's T-shirts the framed photo of a very young woman with round cheeks and laughing eyes who was making her thin white dress swirl around her slender, beautiful legs.

Norah felt bitter, full of pity for this woman, and shrieked at her father: "Why did you marry again? What more did you want?"

He made a limp, slow gesture with his hand and muttered that he wasn't interested in being lectured to.

Then, slowly catching his breath, he said, "I asked you to come because I want you to take on Sony's defense. He hasn't got a lawyer. I can't afford a lawyer."

"He hasn't got a lawyer yet?"

"No, I tell you. I can't afford a good lawyer."

"Can't afford it? What about Dara Salam?"

She didn't like the sound of her voice, its spiteful, nagging tone. She didn't like being drawn into a fight with this baneful man, her father, when she'd tried so hard to keep their relationship bland and innocuous.

"I know where you spend your nights," she said, more calmly.

He glanced at her askance. There was hostility and menace in his hard, round eyes.

"Dara Salam went bankrupt," he said. "So there's nothing there. You'll have to take on Sony's case."

"But that's not possible, I'm his sister. What makes you think I can be his defense lawyer?"

"It's not forbidden, is it?"

"No, but it's not done."

"So what? Sony needs a lawyer, that's all that matters."

"You still love Sony?" she cried out, trying to understand.

He turned over on the bed and put his head in his hands.

"That boy is all I have to live for," he whispered.

He lay there, curled up in a fetal position, old and enormously fat, and Norah suddenly realized that one day he would be dead. Up till then she'd always thought, with some annoyance, that nothing human could ever happen to him.

He stirred, and sat up on the edge of the bed. He then had difficulty getting up.

He turned his eyes from the pile of balls in the corner to the photo Norah still held in her hand.

"She was evil, that woman, it was she who ensnared him. He would never have dared look at his dad's wife."

"That may be so," Norah hissed, "but she's the one who's dead."

"How long will Sony get? What do you think?" he asked in a tone of utter helplessness. "Surely he won't spend the next ten years in jail. Will he?"

"She's dead, he strangled her, she must have suffered a great deal," Norah murmured. "The little girls, the twins, what did you tell them?"

"I didn't tell them anything, I never speak to them. They're no longer here."

He looked stubborn and annoyed.

"What do you mean, no longer here?"

"I sent them north this morning, to her family," he said, jutting his chin at the photo of his wife.

Suddenly Norah couldn't bear looking at him any longer. She felt trapped. He'd gotten her in his grip. In truth he had them all in his grip, ever since he first abducted Sony and put the stamp of his ferocity on their very existence.

By sheer strength of will she'd gotten herself an education that had led to a partnership in a law firm. She'd given birth to Lucie and bought an apartment. But she would have given it all up if only she could turn back the clock and prevent Sony from being snatched from them.

"You said once, if I remember rightly, that you would never let go of Sony," her father exclaimed.

A few yellow flowers had stained the sheet. They'd fallen from his shoulders and been crushed beneath his bulk.

How heavy the devil must now be who held Sony in his grasp, Norah thought.

It was at dinner that night, when Jakob and her father were chatting amiably, that Norah heard him say, "When my daughter Norah lived here . . ."

"What're you talking about? I've never lived in this house!" she exclaimed.

He was holding a leg of roast chicken. He bit off a chunk, took his time chewing it, then said calmly, "No, I know. I meant when you were living in this town, in Grand Yoff."

He then looked as if a wad of cotton wool had gotten stuck in his throat. His ears started throbbing gently.

The voices of Jakob and her father, and of the girls conversing in an unduly measured way, seemed to be fading, becoming muffled and almost inaudible.

"Look here," she muttered angrily, "I've never lived in Grand Yoff, nor anywhere else in this country."

But she wasn't sure of having spoken, or if she had, of being listened to.

She cleared her throat and repeated more loudly, "I've never lived in Grand Yoff."

Her father raised his eyebrows in amused astonishment.

Jakob looked hesitantly first at Norah, then at her father, and the girls had stopped eating, so Norah, dismayed at appearing to beg just so they'd believe her, felt obliged to say, yet again, "I've never lived anywhere but France, you ought to know that."

"Masseck!" his father shouted. He said a few words to Masseck, who went to fetch a shoebox, which he put on the table. Norah's father started rummaging in it impatiently.

He pulled out a small square photo, which he held out to Norah.

Like all the photos he'd ever taken, this one was, intentionally or not, somewhat blurred. He manages to make them fuzzy so he'll be able to say what he likes about them, Norah thought.

The plump young woman was standing in front of a little house with pink walls and a blue corrugated-iron roof. She was wearing a lime-green dress with yellow flowers.

"That's not me," Norah said with relief. "That's my sister. You've always mixed us up, even though she's older than I am."

Without answering her he showed the photo to Jakob, then to Grete and Lucie. Embarrassed, the girls gave it a cursory glance.

"I'd have thought it was you, too," said Jakob with a nervous laugh. "You look very alike."

"Not really," Norah murmured. "It's a bad photo, that's all."

Her father waved it in front of Lucie, who'd lowered her eyes and was blushing slightly.

"Come on, Lucie, it's your mum in the photo, isn't it?"

Lucie nodded vigorously.

"You see," he said, "your own daughter recognizes you."

Furtively, but harsh as always, he glanced sideways at her.

"Didn't you know your sister once lived in Grand Yoff?" Jakob asked, obviously trying to be helpful. But Norah thought, I don't need anyone's help with this.

How absurd it all was!

She suddenly felt very tired. "No, I didn't know. When she's away proselytizing for her weird sect my sister hardly ever tells me what she's up to or where she's going." Without looking him in the eye, Norah asked her father, "What was she doing here?"

"It was you who were here, not your sister. You must know why you came."

In the night, as Jakob slept, she left the house and its oppressive atmosphere and went outside, knowing full well that she would find no peace there either, with her father standing watch up in the branches of the poinciana.

And although in the pitch-black darkness she couldn't see him, she could hear, hear the noises he made in his throat, the tiny movements of his flip-flops on the branch. All those sounds were amplified in her skull, to the point almost of deafening her.

She stood there, motionless, with her bare feet on the rough warm concrete of the threshold, aware that her arms, legs, and face were paler than the night and would probably be shining with an almost milky brightness, and that doubtless he could see her as she could now see him, his face in shadow, crouching in his white clothes.

She was torn between satisfaction at having found him out and horror at sharing a secret with this man.

She now felt that he would always resent her being party to this mystery, even though she had never sought to know anything about it.

Was that the reason why he'd tried to sow confusion with that story about a photo taken in Grand Yoff?

She couldn't remember ever having set foot there.

The only troubling detail—as she freely acknowledged—was that her sister was wearing a frock very similar to hers, because her mother had made the lime-green, yellow-flowered dress thanks to a Bouchara fabric voucher that Norah had found.

Her mother couldn't have made two dresses out of that one piece of cotton cloth.

Norah went back inside and walked along the corridor to the twins' room, where Masseck had put up Grete and Lucie.

She pushed the door open gently and, on sniffing the warm smell of the children's hair, suddenly felt overwhelmed by the love that had earlier deserted her.

But then it faded away, vanished, and once again she felt hard, distracted, remote, as if possessed by something that had quietly and without cause entered her being, refusing now to yield to anyone or anything.

"Lucie, my poppet, my little ginger-haired darling," she murmured. Her disembodied voice made her think of Sony's smile, or of their mother's, because it seemed not to issue from her lips but merely to float in the air before them, a product entirely of the atmosphere; and it seemed that feeling no longer dwelled in those words she had so often uttered.

Once more she found herself in front of Sony, separated from him by the grating against which they had to press their lips in order to have any hope of hearing each other.

She told him that she'd brought him some ointment for his eczema, which would be given to him in the prison infirmary once it had been checked. Sony burst out laughing, and in the affable tone he used whatever the subject, he said that he'd never see it.

Despite his gauntness, the scabs on his skin, and his unkempt beard, she could now at least recognize her brother's kind, saintly face, and tried to discern in it any signs of distress, suffering, or remorse.

There were none.

"I can't believe it, Sony," she said.

She thought, with pain and bitterness, of the many occasions when she'd heard the same vain words uttered pitifully by a criminal's family.

But Sony had been, really, a sort of mystic.

Scratching his face, he shook his head.

"I'm going to defend you. I'm going to be your lawyer. I'll have the right to visit you more frequently."

Still scratching his cheeks and forehead furiously, he kept shaking his head.

"It wasn't me, you know," he said calmly. "I wouldn't do anything to hurt her."

"What? What's that you're saying?"

"It wasn't me."

"It wasn't you who killed her? Oh my God, Sony!"

Her teeth hit the grating. Her lips tasted of rust.

"So who killed her, Sony?"

He shrugged his painfully thin shoulders.

He'd already told her that he was hungry the whole time because among the hundred or so prisoners with whom he shared his vast cell there were some who stole part of his rations every day.

Now all he ever dreamed about at night—he told her with a smile—was food.

"It was him," Sony said.

"Our father?"

He nodded, moistening his dry lips with his tongue over and over again.

Then, realizing that the visit was nearly over, he started speaking very quickly: "You remember, Norah, when I was little and we were still living together, there was this game we played: you'd pick me up, swing me up and down, and shout, 'With a one, with a two,' and on 'with a three!' you'd throw me onto the bed, saying that it was the ocean and I had to swim back to the shore, do you remember?"

Throwing his head back, he chuckled with delight, and Norah recognized at once, with a shock, the little boy with the wide-open mouth whom she used to throw on the blue chenille counterpane that covered his bed.

"How are the twins?" he asked.

"He's sent them to their mother's family, I believe." She spoke with difficulty. Her teeth were clenched and her tongue was thick.

As he moved away from the grating, following the other prisoners, he turned around and said gravely, "The little girls, the twins, they're my daughters, not his. He knew that, you understand."

For a long while she walked up and down the pavement in front of the prison, in the scorching midday sun, trying to summon up the strength to rejoin Masseck in the car.

So everything is falling into place at last, she thought, with icy exultation.

It seemed to her that she was staring into the eyes of the devil holding her brother in his clutches, thinking, I'll make him let go, but what is it all about, and who can ever restore all that's been taken away over years?

What, indeed, was it all about?

Masseck returned by a different route from the usual one, she noticed, but she didn't pay it much mind until he stopped in front of a little house with pink walls and a blue corrugated-iron roof, turned the engine off, and put his hands on his knees. She was determined not to ask any questions, to avoid taking a single step toward a possible trap.

For Sony's sake, and her own, she had to be a strong, skilled operator. The unsuspected won't trip me up again, she resolved.

"He told me to show you this house," Masseck said, "because that's where you lived."

"He's wrong, my sister did."

Why was she so reluctant to look closely at the house?

Feeling disconcerted, she cast an eye over the faded pink walls, the narrow balustrade in front, and the humbler houses nearby where children were playing.

Since she'd seen the photo, she thought she could not help remembering the place.

But didn't the memory come from further back?

Were there not, behind the pink walls, two small rooms with

dark blue tiles, and at the back, a tiny kitchen that smelled of curry?

During dinner she noticed that Jakob and her father were chatting contentedly and even that the latter, who could scarcely pretend to be interested in children, nonetheless managed to make an occasional face at Lucie and Grete, accompanied by funny noises intended to make them laugh.

He was relaxed, almost merry, as if—Norah thought—she'd lifted the terrible weight of Sony's incarceration off his shoulders, as if all he had to do now was wait until she sorted things out, as if she'd taken upon herself the moral burden, relieving him of it forever.

Even in her father's way with the girls she sensed an element of his courting her favor.

"Masseck showed you the house?" he suddenly asked.

"Yes, he showed me where my sister must have lived."

He gave a knowing, offhand laugh.

"I know," he said, "why you came to Grand Yoff, I've given it some thought, and now I remember."

She was dizzy all of a sudden and felt like jumping up from her chair and rushing into the garden, but she thought of Sony and suppressed every fear and doubt, every discomfort and disappointment.

It didn't matter what he might say to her, because she'd get him to cough up the truth.

"You came in order to get closer to me, yes. You must have been, I'm not sure exactly, twenty-eight or twenty-nine."

He spoke in a very neutral tone, as if he wanted to dispel any hint of conflict between them.

Jakob and the children were listening carefully. Norah felt that her father's affable manner, together with the air of authority conferred on him by his years and by the vestiges of wealth, ensured that those three gave him the benefit of the doubt where she never could: indeed, they were now inclined to believe him and not her.

And didn't they have a point?

Weren't all her child-rearing principles being called into question, their rigor, their fierceness, their luster?

For if Jakob, Grete, and Lucie came to think that she'd lied, dissembled, or somehow weirdly managed to forget, would she not seem all the more culpable for having, in their home life, preached and insisted on such rectitude?

A warm dampness slid along her thighs and insinuated itself between her buttocks and the chair.

She felt her dress anxiously.

In despair she wiped her wet fingers on her napkin.

"You were keen to know what it was like to live near Sony and me," her father went on in his kindly voice, "so you rented that house in Grand Yoff. I suppose you wanted to be independent, because of course I'd never have refused to put you up. You didn't stay long, did you? You'd probably imagined, I don't know, that things would be as they are in your country now, with people constantly blathering on about 'opening up,' 'asking for forgiveness,' inventing all sorts of problems and banging on about how much they love each other, but I had work to do in Dara Salam and in any case it's just not my thing to bare my soul. No, you didn't stay long, you must have been disappointed. I don't know. And Sony wasn't exactly in top form at the time so perhaps he disappointed you too."

Norah didn't budge, so concerned was she not to let on just how wretched she felt.

She raised her feet and held them above the little puddle under her chair.

Her face and her neck were burning.

She said nothing, kept her eyes lowered, and remained seated until everyone had left the table. Then she went to the kitchen to fetch a rag.

That evening before dark she went outside and stood in the doorway, knowing she'd find her father there, waiting patiently as always for the moment he could make the leap.

In his grubby shirt he shone as never before.

He looked at the beige dress she'd put on, pursed his lips, and said, almost kindly, "You peed yourself just now. It doesn't matter, you know."

"Sony told me you strangled your wife," Norah remarked, ignoring what he'd just said.

He didn't jump, nor even shoot a sideways glance at her; he was already somewhat absent, absorbed no doubt by his awareness of night's approach and his eagerness to regain his dusky perch in the poinciana.

"Sony acknowledges that he did it," her father said at last, as if dragged back to a tedious present. "He's never said, and will never say, anything different. I know him. I've every confidence in him."

"But why all this?"

"I'm old, my girl. Can you see me in Reubeuss? Come on. Besides, you weren't there, so far as I'm aware. What do you know about who did what? Nothing. Sony confessed, they've wound up the investigation, so that's that."

His thin, dreamy voice became fainter and fainter.

"My poor dear boy," he whispered.

In the bedroom turned into a temporary office she read for the umpteenth time the file on Sony's case.

Jakob and the girls had gone back to Paris as she was moving herself into the little house with the pink walls and the blue corrugated-iron roof. She'd reached an agreement with her colleagues at the firm that she could conduct Sony's defense.

She occasionally looked up from the file to gaze with pleasure on the small, white, bare room. She accepted the idea that she had perhaps, ten years earlier, slept in this same room, because it was now much simpler to freely acknowledge that possibility than to deny it in fear and anger. As a result she no longer feared being overwhelmed by a feeling of déjà vu, which could just as well have been provoked by a dream she'd had as by what she was currently living through.

There she was, alone in the intense brightness of a strange house, sitting on a cool, hard, shiny metal chair. Her whole body was at peace and her mind was equally calm.

She understood what had happened in her father's house, understood all those involved as if she were the devil gripping each one of them.

For this is what Sony had told the examining magistrate:

"I hid in my stepmother's bedroom. I stood in a corner between the wardrobe and the wall. I had in my pocket a bit of cord I'd taken from the cupboard under the kitchen sink, a piece left over from the clothesline in the garden. I knew my stepmother would enter the room alone after putting the twins to bed because that was what she did every evening. I knew my father would not be joining her because he'd stopped sleeping in that room, I can't say where he sleeps, I know but I can't tell you. That means I acted with premeditation throughout, because I knew that my stepmother would go toward the wardrobe and that it would be easy to slip the cord around her neck. She was on the tall side, but quite slim and not particularly strong. Her slender arms were not very strong, so I knew she wouldn't put up much of a struggle. I'd hugged her often enough in that same room, I'd put my arms around her often enough, to know that I was a great deal stronger than she was. She was so delicate that my hands almost touched my shoulders when I hugged her. Then everything went as planned. She came in, closed the door behind her, walked to the wardrobe, I reached out to her and did it. Her throat gurgled, she tried to grip the cord around her neck, but she was already too weak. She slumped a little, I lifted her up again and put her on the bed. I left the room and closed the door. Back in my own bedroom I pumped up all my basketballs. I knew that no one was going to pump them up for quite a while and I feel better if they're correctly inflated. I went to bed and slept soundly. At six I was awoken by the twins screaming. They'd gone to see their mother and it was their screams that aroused me. A little later the police arrived and I told them what had happened, just as I'm telling you today. I did it because my stepmother and I were involved in a love affair that had been going on for three years. She was my age and it was the first time I'd ever been in love. I loved her more than anything or anyone in the whole world. When my father married and brought her home, it was love at first sight. It was very hard, I felt guilty, I felt dirty. But she had fallen for me too and we started making love. It was my first time, I'd waited until then, I'd never dared before. I found her carefree and beautiful, I was very happy. She got pregnant and I became very fond of the twins: I was sure they were mine. I was happy with the situation because my father didn't suffer at all, I wasn't afraid of him anymore and he took no interest in me. But she began to tire of me. She wasn't capable of loving me for the rest of her life as I was capable of loving her for the rest of mine. She was unhappy and started hating me. She said I had to leave the house and make my life elsewhere. But where could I go and what could I do and who else could I love? My home was in my father's house and I was irrevocably married to my father's wife and my father's children were my children. As a result my father's secrets were my secrets, too, which is why I can't speak about him even though I know everything about him."

And the young Khady Demba, eighteen, had said:

"I was in the kitchen and I heard the two little girls screaming. I left the kitchen and went to the bedroom where the girls were. They were standing close to the bed and their mother was stretched out on it. I saw that her eyes were open and her face wasn't its normal color."

And the father had said:

"I'm a self-made man and I think I'm entitled to take some pride in that. My parents had nothing, no one around me had anything, we lived by our wits and survived thanks to various schemes, but each day's gains never equaled the amount of mental effort expended. I was a clever boy so I went to study in France. Then I returned with my son Sony, who was age five at the time, and I went into business. I bought a half-built holiday village in Dara Salam and I managed to turn it into a popular resort and make it profitable. But times changed and I had to sell Dara Salam. As you see me today I have to make do with very little, but I don't care, I haven't much pride left. When I entered the house I was greeted by all that screaming. If my son Sony affirms that he did this, I accept that, and I forgive him because I've always loved my son the way he is, even though people sometimes tell me, 'Your son has never made good use of his intelligence,' but he's made what use he could of it, he's done what he wanted, it's not my concern. My wife betrayed me, he didn't. He's my son and I accept and understand what he's done because I see myself in him. My son Sony is better than me, his generosity of spirit is greater than that of anyone else I've ever known, nevertheless I can see myself in him and I forgive him. I accept what he's affirmed, I've nothing to add, nothing else to say, and if he were to withdraw his confession I'd accept that likewise. He's my son and I raised him, that's all. My wife, I didn't raise her. I don't know her and I can't forgive her and my hatred of this woman who cuckolded me in my own house and didn't care a fig for me will never fade."

At afternoon's end, when the shade made the heat less oppressive, Norah went to see Sony.

She left each day at the same time, walking slowly so as not to sweat too much.

And she went over in her mind the questions she would put to

Sony, well aware that he would only answer with a smile, never going back on his resolve to protect their father, but she wanted to show him that she at least was determined to save him and was therefore prepared to confront him fair and square.

She walked joyfully along the familiar street. She was at peace with herself and her body was behaving itself.

She said hello to a neighbor who was sitting at her door and thought, What good neighbors I have, and if one or another of them, the Lebanese baker or the old woman who sold sodas in the street, piped up, claiming to have known her ten years earlier, it didn't upset her.

She accepted it humbly, without reason, as a mystery.

In the same way she'd stopped wondering why she no longer doubted that her love for her child would be rekindled once she'd done all she could for Sony, once she'd delivered them both from the devils that had sunk their claws into them when she was eight and Sony was five.

That's the way it was.

And she was able to contemplate with equanimity and gratitude the way Jakob was taking care of the children. His way of doing it was perhaps no worse than her way, and so she was able to think of Lucie without worrying.

She was able to think of her brother Sony's radiant expression when, in the old days, she used to throw him playfully on the bed. She could think of it now without suffering the torments of the damned.

That's the way it was.

And she'd watch over Sony and bring him back home.

That's the way it was.

COUNTERPOINT

HE SENSED near him a breath not his own, another presence in the branches. For some weeks now he'd been aware that he was not alone in his hideout, and patiently, without irritation, he was waiting for the stranger to reveal herself, even though he knew what was going on since it could be nothing else. He wasn't annoyed, and in the tranquil darkness of the poinciana his heart was beating languidly and his mind was lethargic. No, he wasn't cross: his daughter Norah was there, close by, perched among the branches now bereft of flowers, surrounded by the bitter smell of the tiny leaves; she was there in the dark, in her lime-green dress, at a safe distance from her father's phosphorescence. Why would she come and alight on the poinciana if it wasn't to make peace, once and for all? His heart beat languidly, his mind was lethargic. He heard his daughter breathing, and it didn't make him angry.

PART

II

*T*HROUGHOUT THE MORNING, the thought kept coming back to him, like the vestiges of a troubling, rather degrading dream, that it would have been better, for his own sake, not to have spoken to her like that. Going around and around in his unquiet mind the idea soon became a certainty, even though he could no longer remember the precise reason for the quarrel—that painful, degrading dream of which there remained only a bitter aftertaste.

He ought never, never, to have spoken to her that way. That was all he knew about their argument, and what made it now impossible for him to concentrate, or in any way gain an upper hand, anything that could prove useful when he returned home and found himself face-to-face with her again.

Because, he thought confusedly, how was he going to assuage his own conscience if his truncated memories of their disputes served to highlight nothing but his own guilt, over and over again, as in those troubling, degrading dreams in which whatever you say, whatever you decide, you're always the one who's irrevocably to blame?

And—he also wondered—if he couldn't manage to assuage his own conscience, how could he calm down and become a proper father? How could he get people to love him again?

He certainly shouldn't speak to her like that; no man had the right.

But what had pushed him to let slip those words that ought never to be uttered by a man who passionately desired to be loved as he had always been, that was what he couldn't recall, as if the terrible phrases (but what were they, exactly?) had exploded inside his head, obliterating everything else.

So was it fair that he felt so guilty?

If only, he thought, he could prove before his inner tribunal that he'd had good reason to get so terribly angry, he'd be in a better position to regret his behavior and his whole nature would be improved thereby.

As for his present swirl of agitated, chaotic shame, it only served to anger him.

Oh, how he longed for clarity, for some peace and quiet!

Why did he feel, as the years drifted by, his fine younger days slipping away, that only the lives of others—the lives of almost everyone around him—were proceeding naturally, gliding along an increasingly unencumbered path, already illuminated by the warm, gentle rays of the light shining at the end? It was a fact that made it possible for all the men in his acquaintance to let their guard down and adopt a relaxed, subtly acerbic attitude toward life, an attitude inspired by a discreet awareness of having acquired wisdom at the price of perfect health, a supple, flat stomach, and a full head of hair.

Being plunged in grief, I find myself mightily dejected.

He, Rudy, could see what this wisdom consisted of, even if his own progress seemed painfully slow, his path choked with tangled undergrowth that no light could penetrate.

From the depths of his chaos, his fragility, he felt he understood the fundamental insignificance of his suffering, and yet he was incapable of deriving any advantage from this awareness, lost as he was on the fringes of the true existence that everyone has the power to influence.

So—he said to himself—despite his forty-three summers, he, Rudy Descas, seemed yet to have acquired that knack, that easy levelheadedness, that sardonic tranquillity that he saw informing the simplest actions and the most routine utterances of other men, of people who spoke calmly and with unstudied sincerity to their children, who read newspapers and magazines with wry interest, who looked forward to a pleasant lunch with friends the following Sunday, whose success they could cheerfully make every necessary effort to ensure, never being obliged to conceal the fact that they were only just emerging from yet another squabble, from a painful, degrading dream.

I find myself mightily dejected.

He was never, ever, granted any of that.

But why, he wondered, why?

That he'd behaved badly at such-and-such a moment and in such-and-such a situation where it had been important to measure up to the attendant joy or the tragedy, *that* he was perfectly happy to acknowledge, but what constituted the tragedy, where was the joy, in this diminished life with his family, and what were the particular circumstances he'd been incapable of confronting as a fully formed person?

Exactly. It seemed to him that his immense fatigue—though his fury was no less considerable, Fanta would say with a snicker, adding that it was just like him to claim to be consumed, even as the perpetual muted rage he inflicted on his nearest and dearest was far more wearing on them: isn't that right, Rudy?—that his great fatigue resulted from his efforts to steer their poor tumbrel, that load of painful, degrading dreams, in the right direction.

Had his desire to do the right thing ever been rewarded?

No, not even—no—not even acknowledged, let alone praised or honored.

In defense of Fanta, who always seemed to be blaming him silently for all their setbacks and misfortunes, he had to acknowledge that he was quick to preempt any such judgment by cultivating the feeling that he himself was vaguely accountable for all the bad luck that came their way.

As for the rare strokes of good fortune, he'd gotten into the habit of greeting them with considerable skepticism, and his mistrustful face eloquently expressed his expectation that no one would think of showing him any gratitude for the brief moment of happiness in their house since he'd had nothing to do with it.

Oh yes, Rudy was well aware of that.

He felt this look of almost nauseous suspicion starting to show on his face the moment he suggested to Fanta, for example, or to Djibril, that they go to a restaurant, or out to the canoe club for a spin, then only to see in return (as the child, unable to fathom his father's secret intentions, turned to catch his mother's eye) a look of anxiety or slight dismay sweep across those two beautiful faces, so similar, his wife's and his son's, at which sight, unable to suppress his resentment, he'd get very cross, saying to them, "What? Aren't you ever pleased?" whereupon the two beautiful faces of the only creatures he loved on this earth became expressionless, now revealing nothing more than a dismal indifference toward him and all his suggestions for making them happy, and a will to banish silently from their lives, their thoughts, and their feelings this surly and erratic man whom malevolent fate had obliged them to suffer for the time being, like the aftereffects of a bad, shameful dream. *Everything that was going to happen to me has happened.*

He pulled up sharply on the verge of the little road that every day led him straight to Manille's headquarters as soon as he'd passed the big rotary at the center of which there now stood a curious statue of white stone, a naked man whose bent back, lowered head, and outstretched arms seemed, with terrified resignation, to be waiting for the fountain to drench him with its water when summer came around again.

Rudy had followed every stage of the fountain's construction as he drove slowly past the rotary every morning in his old Renault Nevada before turning off toward the Manille offices, and without his noticing it, his mild curiosity had changed into embarrassment, then into a deeper unease when he thought he discerned a close resemblance between the statue's face and his own (the same flat, square forehead, the straight but rather short nose, prominent jaw, big mouth, and angular chin so typical of proud men who know precisely where each one of their resolute steps is leading, something more comic than pathetic when one was still happy to slave away at Manille's, huh, Rudy?), and his distress only grew at the sight of the monstrous genitalia that the artist, a certain R. Gauquelan, who lived nearby, had carved on his hero's crotch, causing Rudy to feel himself the subject of a cruel mockery, so pitiful was the contrast between the statue's weak, spineless posture and its enormous scrotum.

He tried now to avoid looking at the statue as he drove past the rotary in his worn-out Nevada.

But a malevolent reflex sometimes caused him to glance at the stone face that was his own, at that large, pale figure stooping with fear, and at the testicles out of all proportion with the rest, until he'd come to resent and almost hate Gauquelan, who'd managed, Rudy read in the local paper, to sell his sculpture to the municipality for around a hundred thousand euros.

That bit of news had caused him considerable anguish.

It was, he said to himself, as if while he was still an innocent or just asleep, Gauquelan had taken advantage of him and gotten him to pose for some ridiculous pornographic photo that had made Gauquelan richer as it made Descas poorer and more grotesque—as if Gauquelan had yanked him from a tiresome dream and plunged him into a degrading one.

"A hundred thousand euros, I can't believe it," he'd said to Fanta, snickering to mask his distress. "No, I really can't believe it."

"What's it matter?" Fanta must have replied. "How does the fact that others are doing well diminish you?" she asked, with that irritating habit, recently adopted, of appearing to look at every situation with a lofty, magnanimous detachment, abandoning Rudy to his petty envies, which, no more than the rest of it, did she care any longer to share with him.

But she couldn't stop him from recalling the good years not so long ago—nor reminding her of them, beseechingly—when it was one of their fondest pleasures to sit cross-legged, side by side, like two old chums in their darkened bedroom, sharing the same cigarette, and dissecting with brutal frankness the habits and personalities of their acquaintances and neighbors, and deriving from the very harshness they shared, along with a quite conscious bad faith, laughs they could never—would have never dared—share with others, but that were appropriate enough to two old friends, which, in addition to being man and wife, they genuinely were.

He wanted her to remember this, she who now affected to think that she'd never enjoyed a moment's fun with him; but (given the groveling manner he'd been reduced to in spite of himself) it was hardly the best move he could have come up with: begging her to notice that, however it had come about, what had been was no more, that the amusing companion he might have been, once, was now probably dead and gone for good, and that it was all his fault, and his alone.

And he always came back to this intolerable aspect, the unspoken accusation grabbing him by the throat—that it was, eternally, his fault—and the more he struggled to free himself from what was strangling him, killing him, the more he shook his heavy head, the angrier he got, and the worse his crimes became.

Indeed, they'd not had any friends for a long while, and the neighbors avoided him.

Rudy Descas couldn't care less, thinking he had enough to

worry about without troubling himself to wonder how his attitude might be putting people off, but he could no longer make fun of them with Fanta, even if she'd been inclined to want him to.

They lived isolated lives, very isolated, that's what he had to accept.

It seemed that their friends (who were they exactly? what were their names? where had they all gone?) had drifted away as Fanta started to turn her back on him; it was as if the love she'd felt for him had, like some dazzling outsider in their midst, been the only thing they both liked and took interest in, and that once this beautiful witness had vanished into thin air, Fanta and he—but he most of all—had finally come to be seen, by all those friends, in the starkness of their banality, their poverty.

But Rudy couldn't care less.

He had need only of his wife and of his son—and, as he had already admitted to himself with some embarrassment, he had a lot less need of his son than of his wife, and less need still of his son per se than as some mysterious and seductive extension of his wife, as a fascinating, miraculous development of the personality and beauty of Fanta.

As for these formless shadows, those who'd acted the part of friends, all he missed were their warm, kindly looks assuring him that Rudy Descas was a nice guy, a pleasant man to be with, whose wife from a far-off place loved him unreservedly—in that gaze he was then truly himself, Rudy Descas, just as he saw himself, present in this world, and not the unlikely, discordant figure emerging from some tiresome, shameful dream that no dawn would manage to chase away. *What has become of my friends whom I loved so much and was so close to?*

He looked at his watch.

He'd only five minutes before the workday started at Manille's.

He'd stopped in front of the only telephone box around, by the side of the little road that boldly and cheerfully opened up a route between the expanses of vines.

The sun was already beating down.

Not a breath, not a scrap of shade until you got to the tall green oaks far off that surrounded the wine-producing chateau, an austere dwelling with closed shutters.

How proud he'd been when he introduced Fanta to this region where he was born, where they were going to live and prosper, and particularly to this building, the owners of which his mother knew slightly, people who made an excellent Graves that Rudy could no longer afford to drink.

He was obscurely aware that his proud delight in showing Fanta the small dark winery, almost dragging her up the drive and to the gate, up to the evergreen oaks, approaching with a confident air on the pretext that his mother knew the owners slightly (she must have substituted for their usual cleaner for a few weeks at the outside)—he was obscurely aware that this proud delight came of his having convinced himself, with no reasonable hope, that one day the property would belong to them, to Fanta and to him, that it would be passed on to them in some way, by some means as yet unknown.

This certainty had been unaffected by the three enormous dogs that had shot out from the back of the dwelling and rushed toward them, even given the sensation of pure horror that then seized him—Rudy Descas wasn't *that* courageous a man.

Those friends have really let me down.

Hadn't the unleashed Dobermans wanted to punish him for his

presumptuous and absurd desires, for the heavy possessive hand he'd laid on the property, if only in his mind?

The invisible master whistled to the dogs and stopped them in their tracks. Rudy all the while was slowly backing away, holding his arm out in front of Fanta as if to dissuade her from leaping at the three monsters' throats.

How useless and futile he'd felt on this warm spring day in the bright, tranquil silence that had followed the dogs' retreat and their own return to the car, how pale and trembling he'd felt beside Fanta, who'd hardly batted an eyelid.

She doesn't bear a grudge for my putting her in harm's way, he thought, not because she is a good person, though she is, but because she'd never had an inkling that she might be in danger. Is that, he wondered, what it is to be courageous, whereas all I am is foolhardy?

For, while God was assailing me, I never saw a single one at my side.

Out of the corner of his eye he glanced at his wife's impassive face and at her big brown irises as she looked down at the gravel path, prodding at it absently with the end of a stick, a hazel twig she'd picked up just before the dogs came charging at them.

Something, something in the natural placidity shown by a woman who was above all an intellectual, something in the seeming unawareness of her own composure on the part of a woman who usually got to the bottom of everything: something in her appeared to defy all understanding, he thought almost admiringly, but also a trifle unnerved.

He gazed at the broad, high plane of her smooth cheek, her thick black eyelashes, her not particularly prominent nose, and the love he felt for this unfathomable woman put the fear of God in him.

Because she was strange—too strange for him, perhaps—and he was wearing himself out trying to prove that he was a lot more than he seemed, that he wasn't simply an ex-schoolteacher who'd come back to live in the region of his birth, but a man chosen by fate to bring something truly original to fruition.

For Rudy Descas, to be charged with no other duty than that of loving Fanta would have sufficed, indeed he would have welcomed such an obligation with open arms.

But he had the feeling that it was too little for her even if she didn't realize it, and that, having dragged her from her familiar surroundings, he owed her a lot more than a heavily mortgaged shabby little house in the country and everything pertaining to it, all the pettiness that left him quite beside himself.

And now here he was, standing on the edge of this same cheerful little road, several years after the dogs had nearly torn them both apart (but hadn't Fanta's coolness stopped them in their tracks, hadn't they retreated, perhaps with a growl, intimidated by a vague awareness that she wasn't like other human beings?), on a balmy May morning very much like this one, except that his discomfiture on that occasion had barely dented his confidence in the future, in their chances of success, in their amazing good fortune, whereas now he knew that nothing would ever turn out right.

They'd driven off in the same old Nevada from which he was now extricating himself, because, yes, it was even then a nasty out-of-date car, painted grayish blue in accordance with the prudent taste of Rudy's mother, from whom he'd bought it when she'd abandoned it for a Clio, and since he'd been sure at the time of soon being able to get himself something much better (an Audi or a Toyota), he'd encouraged Fanta to view their car as a rather treacherous dirty beast, sad and weary, whose last days they were patiently seeing out, never starting it up except to have it serviced.

He'd treated the poor Nevada with casual disdain, but wasn't it now a veritable loathing he felt for its very sturdiness, the unfailing courage typical of a good old uncomplicated car, its decency almost, its selflessness?

Nothing could be more wretched, he thought, than to hate one's car, how did I come to this and can I sink any lower? Oh yes, I can, he told himself, since that was nothing compared to what he'd said to Fanta that morning before leaving for work at Manille's, taking the very same route that once used to cut a merry path through the vines . . .

What had he said to her exactly?

The wind was blowing in front of my door and it bore them away.

He left the car door open and stood there, his knees knocking, stunned by the extent of the damage he'd very probably caused.

You can go back where you came from.

Was it possible?

He smiled weakly, nervously, unamused—no, Rudy Descas wouldn't speak like that to the woman he so ardently wished to be loved by once again.

He raised his eyes and shielded them with his hand. Sweat was already dampening his forehead and the fair hair covering it.

Fair too was the world around him on this mild, clean morning, likewise the walls of the small chateau over there, which some foreigners (Americans or Australians, thought Mummy, ever alert for news that would feed her penchant for voluptuous lamentation) had recently bought and restored, and so too the patches of light that danced beneath his eyelids whenever he blinked—if only they would flow at last, those tears of anger he felt weighing heavily within, pressing against his eye sockets.

But his cheeks stayed dry and his jaw remained clenched.

He heard behind him the roar of a car approaching. He crouched down at once behind the door of his own car, not keen to acknowledge the driver, who—given the setting—was very likely an acquaintance, but he straightaway succumbed to a rather doleful fit of the giggles at the thought that he was the only person in these parts who drove a blue-gray Nevada and that the vehicle betrayed the presence of Rudy Descas as surely as the silhouette of Rudy Descas himself would have done, indeed even more so, since at a distance Rudy Descas could well have looked like someone else.

For it seemed that everyone could afford to buy a car less than ten to twelve years old, everyone except him, and he couldn't understand why.

When he stood up he realized he couldn't now avoid being late for work, so he'd have to come up with a fairly fresh excuse as he passed through Manille's office.

That thought was vaguely satisfying.

He knew that Manille was tired of him, of his frequent lateness, and of his grumpiness—at least that's what Manille, a naturally affable and commercially astute man, called it whenever Rudy made it clear that keeping his own counsel figured among the basic rights that he as a poorly paid employee was prepared to defend fiercely, and although in some ways Rudy thought quite highly of Manille, he was actually glad that Manille, one of those typically pragmatic, narrow-minded men who were astonishingly gifted, almost talented within the extremely narrow limits of their faculties, didn't think particularly highly of him.

He knew that Manille would have liked and respected him, and even excused his difficult personality, had Rudy shown some skill at getting customers to purchase new kitchens; he knew that Manille would not have considered a capacity to generate income for the firm as anything more than simple competence in a particular field, just as he knew that in Manille's eyes he was neither skilled nor clever nor committed, nor even—as if by way of compensating for his utter uselessness—merely pleasant.

Manille only kept him on, Rudy thought, out of a peculiar form of indulgence, a complicated sort of pity, because why, really, would Manille pity him?

What did he know about Rudy's precise circumstances?

Oh, very little, since Rudy never confided in anyone, but a wily, amiable, if unpolished sort like Manille must have realized that in his way Rudy was just a square peg in a round hole and that in a crunch it behooved people like him—people who felt perfectly happy with their place in the world—to protect someone like Rudy.

So Rudy understood Manille's reasoning even if Manille would never have put it quite like that.

Though grateful, he felt humiliated by the situation.

Go to hell, I don't need you, you crummy little man, to hell with your country kitchens business.

But what'll become of you, Rudy Descas, when Manille, genuinely upset and sincerely sorry but unable to conceal the fact that you brought it all upon yourself, finally shows you the door?

He was sure it was his Mummy that he owed his job to, though she would never have admitted having gone to talk to Manille (or that she'd had to beg him, the corner of her drooping eyelids damp and pink, her long nose red with shame at what she was asking of him), or confessed that the reason Rudy had had to seek work in the first place was so painful he couldn't summon up the courage to raise the issue with her.

Yeah, I couldn't care less about Manille.

How could he waste time thinking about Manille when he couldn't recall his exact words to Fanta that morning, which he should never have uttered in the first place, because it was clear that if she decided to take them literally, they would rebound on him in the most terrible way imaginable, and that he would achieve the precise opposite of what for some time now he'd been striving for.

You can go back where you came from.

He was going to phone her and ask her to repeat the exact words he'd used during their furious quarrel and to tell him what had sparked it.

It wasn't possible he'd said that to her.

His belief that he had, in fact, came from his tendency to feel guiltier than he really was, to accuse himself where she was concerned of the worst, because she was incapable of nasty thoughts or duplicitous designs, being so helpless and—quite rightly—so disappointed, so disappointed!

The sweat poured down his face and neck at the very thought that she might indeed do what he'd so horrendously proposed.

Then, almost immediately, he began to shiver violently.

With a feeling of childlike despair he then sought to extricate himself from that cold, interminable, monotonous dream in which

Fanta was about to leave him because he had in a way—even if he couldn't remember the exact words—ordered her to, and in which nothing more horrible could now befall him. He knew that, didn't he, because she'd already done so, already tried to do so: isn't that true, Rudy Descas?

He hastily banished the thought, the intolerable memory of Fanta's flight (as he called it, to soften the blow of what had been nothing less than an act of betrayal), in favor of the monotonous cold of the interminable bad dream that, to his great surprise, his life had become, his poor, poor life.

He opened the door of the phone booth and slipped in among the walls covered in scribbles and graffiti.

In much the same way as he was reduced to driving around in a worn-out Nevada, he'd recently had to cancel his cell-phone contract, and this decision, which—given the tightness of his monthly budget—he should have been content to deem a not unreasonable one, seemed to him inexplicable, strange, and unjust, a form of self-inflicted cruelty, because apart from himself he knew of no one, and had never heard of anyone, who'd had to give up their cell phone.

Even the Gypsies, who lived in a permanent encampment they'd set up below the little road, just beyond the vines planted along the slope, the green mossy roofs of whose caravans were surely visible—Rudy mused—to the new inhabitants (American or Australian) of the small chateau, even those Gypsies who were often to be seen loitering in front of Manille's shopwindow, gazing intently and scornfully at the model kitchen displays, even they didn't have to do without a cell phone.

So how come—he wondered—all those people manage to have lives so much better than his?

What kept him from being as smart as the others, when he was no stupider than they were?

He, Rudy Descas—having long believed that his lack of shrewdness and cunning was amply compensated for by his unique sensibility, the spiritual, idealistic, and romantic scale of his ambition, by its very imprecision—was now beginning to wonder if such singularity had any value, if it wasn't ridiculous, secretly contemptible, like a virile man confessing to a penchant for spanking and cross-dressing.

He was trembling so much he had to have three goes at dialing his own number.

He let it ring for a long time.

Through the glazed walls of the phone booth his eyes wandered over the small, blond, tranquil chateau nestling in the cool shade of the dark oaks and their dense, well-kept foliage. Then his gaze returned to the glass panel, in which he contemplated his own transparent, sweaty face, as if it were imprisoned in matter, the wild stare, the blue of his eyes darkened by anguish, and in his mind's eye he saw clearly the room in which the telephone was vainly ringing, ringing, the undecorated living room of their small house frozen in its hopeless, unfinished state, with its unpointed wall tiles, its ugly brown flooring on which stood their poor furniture: an old assortment of varnished wood and flowered upholstery (a hand-me-down from one of Mummy's bosses), the garden table covered with a plastic tablecloth, a pine dresser, the small bookcase overflowing with books, all the sad

ugliness of a place that neither an indifference to one's surroundings nor the gay liveliness of its inhabitants could illuminate or
soften. It all constituted one big eyesore that was never meant to
be more than temporary, and Rudy loathed it; he was wounded
by it every day, and even now, just imagining it as he stood in the
phone booth, he was pained and angered by it, trapped as he was
in an interminable nightmare, the unending discomfort of a cold,
monotonous dream.

Where could she be at this hour?

She'd no doubt, as every morning, walked Djibril to the school
bus stop, but she should have been back long since, so where was
she, why wasn't she answering the phone?

He hung up and leaned against the wall of the phone booth.

His pale blue short-sleeved shirt was soaked. He could feel it,
warm and damp, against the glass.

Ah, how tiresome, unsettling, and humiliating it all was, how he
yearned to hide away and weep once his anger had cooled.

Could it be, could it be that she'd . . . taken to heart the words
he wasn't even certain of having uttered and which in any case he
was certain of never having formulated inside his head?

He picked the receiver up again so abruptly that it slipped
through his fingers, struck the glass, and dangled at the end of its
cord.

From the pocket of his jeans he pulled out his ancient dog-eared
address book and looked up Madame Pulmaire's number, even
though he was sure he had phoned the old bag often enough to
know it by heart.

She wasn't actually all that decrepit, hardly older than Mummy,
in fact, but she put on a *vieille dame* act and had a conspicuous

way of deigning to oblige the complicated and slightly disgusting favors that ever since they'd become neighbors Rudy was wont to request—even while she, no doubt, made it a point of honor never to ask them for anything.

As he expected, she answered straightaway.

"It's Rudy Descas, Madame Pulmaire."

"Ah."

"I just wanted to know whether . . . whether you could go and have a peek next door and check that all's well."

He felt his heart thumping madly as he tried to sound casual and relaxed. Madame Pulmaire wouldn't for a second be fooled by that, and he was prepared to pray, weeping and wailing, to Mummy's god, that nice little god who seemed to have heard his mother's prayers and eventually answered them, but instead he simply held his breath, sweating, chilled to the bone despite the stifling atmosphere in the phone booth, feeling suddenly isolated in a static interval (for everything round about him—the foliage of the holm oaks, the leaves on the vines, and the fluffy clouds in the petrified blue sky—seemed frozen in time, in anguished suspension). In this immobility, the only thing that could propel him forward again would be the news that Fanta was happily at home, was still in love with him, and had never stopped loving him.

That, though, Pulmaire wouldn't be reporting, would she?

"What's the matter, Rudy?" she murmured, in an affectedly gentle tone, "is anything wrong?"

"No, nothing in particular, I was just wondering . . . seeing as I don't seem to be able to get hold of my wife . . ."

"Where are you phoning from, Rudy?"

Knowing that she'd no right to ask, knowing too that he

wouldn't dare tell her to get lost before she'd deigned to heave her useless imposing mound of flesh as far as the Descas household and look through the bare windows or ring the doorbell to prove that this peculiar wife he had, this Fanta, who'd run away once before, had neither run off nor collapsed in a corner somewhere of this sad little half-done-up house—oh, how weary he was of understanding Pulmaire so well, how sullied he felt by acquaintances of that sort.

"I'm in a phone booth."

"Aren't you at work, Rudy?"

"No!" he shouted. "What has that got to do with it, Madame Pulmaire?"

There was a silence; it was protracted, but it betrayed neither offense nor surprise. Old Pulmaire was above such childish reactions, being invested with a weighty dignity that, if Rudy had an ounce of respect, would soon make him contrite.

He could hear her panting into the receiver.

And once again, as on that morning when Fanta defied him either by her words or her silence, he couldn't remember which (but it made him wonder whether he wouldn't at last tell her that a man can only struggle so long to preserve his manly honor as a father, a husband, and a son, striving every day to prevent the collapse of everything he's built, endure only for so long the same old reproaches, whether verbal or in the form of a pitiless, bitter look, and smile through it all, not batting an eyelid, as if saintliness too were one of his obligations, would he finally tell her that, he who'd been abandoned by all his friends?), he felt welling up inside him, that warm, almost sweet anger he knew he ought to resist, but that felt so good, so comforting, to let flow, that he sometimes had to wonder: Wasn't that warm familiar anger all he had left now that he had lost everything else?

He clamped his lips onto the damp plastic.

"Would you please just move your fat ass, and go do what I ask!" he shrieked.

Madame Pulmaire hung up at once, without a word or a sigh.

He slammed his hand two or three times on the cradle, then once again dialed the telephone number of his home.

He'd now learned to call it that—"my home"—however annoying and painful that was, but the expression only matched what Fanta clearly felt, what her whole attitude betrayed, that she no longer considered the poor ramshackle house their home but solely his, and not because of its disrepair, he knew, not because of its irremediable ugliness, about which at bottom he knew she couldn't care less, but because he'd chosen the house, given it its name, and, in a sense, had created it.

This building, he'd decided, was to be the temple in which their happiness would dwell.

Fanta was now withdrawing from the house, taking along with her the child, seven-year-old Djibril, with whom Rudy had never felt very comfortable (because he realized, without being able to do anything about it, that he frightened the little guy).

Fanta was there, having no choice but to be there, but—Rudy thought—she felt no warmth for the house, she refused to lavish any care and affection on her husband's home, to enfold her husband's wretched house in an anxious, maternal embrace.

Taking his cue from her, the child also occupied the house in a noncommittal way, gliding lightly over the floor, sometimes seeming to float above the ground as if wary of all contact with his father's house, or, for that matter—Rudy thought—with his father.

Oh—he wondered, dizzy with pain, all his anger spent, the sound of the line ringing in his ear, and beyond the glass the vines and oaks and little baby clouds coming back to life in a negligible wind—what had happened to the three of them that his wife and his son, the only people he loved in the whole world (for he felt only a vague, formal, inconsequential tenderness for Mummy), should look upon him as their enemy?

"Yes?" Fanta asked, in a tone so flat, so sullen, that at first he almost thought he'd phoned Madame Pulmaire again by mistake.

He was so taken aback that his heart missed a beat.

So that was what Fanta sounded like when she was alone at home and didn't think he was around (whereas whenever she talked to him it was in a voice so full of hardness and rancor that she trembled), so that was how, when she was herself and not with him, Fanta spoke: with such sadness, such glum disappointment, such a melancholy that the accent she'd lost was revived.

Because, as far back as he could remember, she'd always tried to conceal it, though he never quite approved of her desire to appear to come from nowhere, finding the wish even a little absurd since her features were obviously foreign, not to mention that he found the accent endearing, always connecting it with Fanta's energy, a vitality greater than his, and with her courageous struggle since childhood to become an educated and cultured person, to escape the never-ending reality—so cold, so monotonous—of poverty.

What a cruel irony it had been that he, Rudy, had been the one to pull her back into what she, all on her own, had so courageously managed to escape, that he should have been the one to save her from all that, helping her seal her victory over the misfortune of having been born in the Colobane district, not to have buried her alive—still young and beautiful—in the depths of . . .

"It's me, Rudy," he said.

"Hold on a moment, there's someone at the door."

Now that she knew who she was speaking to, her voice became a little less sullen, as if some wary reflex had reset her reaction mechanism to prevent her from letting slip any word that he could use against her in the next bout, although to tell the truth, it was his impression that Fanta never talked back but simply met his attacks with a stubborn silence, a distant, rather sulky look, her lips swelling and her chin drooping; he, Rudy, was well aware that she chose only too carefully the little she said, knowing any word of hers could provoke his outburst, just as he knew only too well that what truly angered him was the very indifference—so deliberate, so studied—of her expression, and that the crosser he became the more Fanta walled herself off and the more he got bogged down in his fury at her disingenuous nonchalance, until he couldn't help spitting in her face those words he would later regret so desolately even if, as on this morning, he couldn't be sure he'd really uttered them.

How hopeless it was, he thought, didn't she understand that a few innocent, simple words from her, spoken with the requisite warmth, would have been enough to make him once more the good, calm, affable Rudy Descas that he'd still been, it seemed to him, two or three years earlier, not very practical minded, perhaps, but curious in outlook and pretty energetic for all that, did she not understand . . . ?

"I love you, Rudy," or "I've never stopped loving you," or even—good enough—"I'm fond of you, Rudy."

He felt himself blushing, ashamed at these thoughts.

She understood, all right.

No entreaty, no fit of anger (but weren't the two of a piece where he was concerned?), would ever make her say anything like that.

He was convinced that even if he beat her up and smashed her face down on the rough floor she would still say nothing, being quite incapable even of telling a white lie just to get herself off the hook.

Through the receiver he could hear Fanta's footsteps, dragging a little as she made toward the door, then Madame Pulmaire's high-pitched, anxious voice followed by Fanta's murmuring. Could he, even at that remove, discern an immense weariness in his wife's voice, or was it merely the effect of distance and his own shame?

He heard the door slam, then the lethargic progress of Fanta's feet once again, that weary, exhausted gait evident these days from the moment she got up, as if the prospect of another day in the house she refused obstinately to concern herself with ("Why do I have to do everything around here?" he often shouted in exasperation) hobbled her slender ankles with their dry, glossy skin, those same ankles that used to dash indefatigably in their dusty pumps or sneakers through the alleyways of Colobane toward the lycée where Rudy had first set eyes on her.

Back then those ankles had seemed winged, for how else could two slender, rigid, valiant reeds covered in gleaming skin so swiftly and nimbly transport Fanta's long, supple, youthful, muscular body, how could they, he'd wondered rapturously, but for the help of two invisible little wings, much like those that made the skin between Fanta's shoulder blades quiver gently below the neckline of her sky-blue T-shirt as he stood behind her waiting his turn in the teachers' line at the cafeteria of the Lycée Mermoz, how, he'd wondered, as he gazed at the bare nape of her neck, her strong dark shoulders, her delicate tremulous skin . . .

"That was the neighbor," she said laconically.

"Ah."

And since she didn't add anything, since she didn't specify, in that tone of gloomy sarcasm she was apt to use, the reason why Madame Pulmaire had called, he surmised that the old girl had covered for him, after a fashion, by saying nothing about his telephone call, probably inventing some mundane excuse, and he felt relieved, though at the same time embarrassed and annoyed, at becoming complicit with Madame Pulmaire, in a way, behind Fanta's back.

Suddenly he felt deeply sorry for Fanta, because wasn't it, if not his fault exactly, at least his doing, that the ambitious Fanta of the winged ankles no longer flew over the reddish muddy streets of Colobane, she who, though still poor, certainly, and held back by many constraints at home but, in spite of all, on her way at the lycée as a full-fledged French literature teacher, wasn't it his doing, with his lovesick gaze, tanned features, fair hair (a lock of which always kept falling over his eyes), his fine words and serious manner, his promise of a comfortable, intellectual, altogether elevated and attractive way of life, wasn't it his doing that she'd given up her neighborhood, her town, her homeland (so dry, red, and very hot) to end up unemployed (he should have known

that she wouldn't be allowed to teach French literature here, he
ought to have made inquiries and found out what the deal was and
what the consequences would be for her) out in a quiet provincial
region, dragging her leaden feet through a house a little better,
to be sure, than the one she'd left but that she'd refused to grace
with a moment's thought, effort, or scrutiny (she whom he'd seen
so patiently, methodically sweeping the rundown two-room apartment with sea-green walls she shared in Colobane with an uncle, an
aunt, and several cousins, so patiently, methodically!): if it wasn't
his fault, wasn't it his doing, Rudy Descas's, if she seemed trapped
and lost in the icy mists of a perpetual, monotonous dream?

He, with his tanned face, the tremendously persuasive force of
his wooing, his suave manners, and the unusual splendor attributed
over there to his blondness, that particularly striking quality . . .

"Don't you want to know why I'm calling?" he asked at last.

"Not really," she said after a moment, her voice no longer
imbued with the listless utter disillusionment that had moved him,
but now with something that was almost the opposite, the controlled, metallic, perfect mastery of her French accent.

"I'd like you to tell me why we had an argument this morning.
Listen, I don't know what started that off, all that . . ."

That particularly striking quality of his, he recalled in the ensu-
ing silence, a weakly panting silence that sounded as if he were
phoning a far-off country with rudimentary communications, his
words needing all these slow seconds to arrive, though it was only
the echo of Fanta's anxious breathing as she pondered the best way
of answering his question so as to safeguard he knew not what—he
dared not imagine—future interests she might have (a bubble of
anger suddenly exploded in his head: what possible future could

she envisage that didn't include him?), yes, he recalled, as he let his eyes wander over the green vines with their tiny bright green grapes, over the green oaks beyond them that the property's new owners, those Americans or Australians (who fascinated and upset Mummy because she believed the vineyard should have stayed in French hands), had pruned so savagely until the trees looked humiliated, punished for daring to let their shiny, unfading foliage grow so dense as to partially conceal the once grayish, now blond and fresh stonework of what was, after all, only a large house, though of the kind on which people in these parts bestowed the respectful name of "chateau," yes, that particularly striking impression that his own blondness, his own freshness, made over there . . .

"I don't know," Fanta said in a low, cold voice.

But he was convinced that she was only answering in the least compromising manner possible, and that to minimize the chance of committing herself to anything involving him in any way, be it by the merest exchange of words, had become the sole criterion of her frankness.

Besides, if he wanted (but did he really?) to be straight with himself, he thought, looking up again at the distant sunny outline of the chateau, which he sensed more than actually saw, knowing it so well that he often dreamed about it, in the course of those monotonous, cold, gray dreams he regularly had, full of precise details of which he could only have heard secondhand, though he'd no memory of doing so, from Mummy, who had perhaps filled in once or twice for the previous owners' cleaning woman (the maid who did everything, preparing and serving the meals, the vacuuming, the ironing), and passed on her observations in that tiresome and degrading way Mummy had of feigning to scorn everything she described (the many unused fully furnished rooms, the fine china, the silver) while her droopy little pinkish eyes shone clear with frustrated longing—and now his own limpid pale eyes were once again raised toward the outline of the chateau as if that large, drab, cold house (no longer gray, perhaps . . .), as if it ought to be sending him any moment some resounding and definitive answer, but what could the property possibly have to tell him except that it would never be his or Fanta's or Djibril's, so, if he wanted to be straight with himself . . .

"By the way," he said, "what if I picked Djibril up from school this evening?"

"If you like," she replied, with an undertone of disquiet in her bland, cold voice that immediately set his teeth on edge.

"It's been a hell of a while since I last picked him up from school, hasn't it? He'll be pleased not to have to catch the school bus for once."

"Oh, I don't know, but yes, if you like." Her voice was wary, constrained by anxious calculation. "Make sure you get there early, otherwise he'll already have gotten on the bus."

"Yes, yes."

. . . straight with himself, but if he'd really wanted to be straight with himself, he had to admit he wouldn't have believed in Fanta's sincerity, even having suddenly noticed in her voice those honest, genuine former tones of the young woman with winged feet and passionate, focused aspirations whose determination and intelligence had already taken her from the small peanut stall that as a little girl she set up every day in a Colobane street to the Lycée

Mermoz, where she went on to teach French literature and prepare the children of diplomats and wealthy businessmen for the baccalaureate, this tall, upstanding woman with a domed head and close-cropped hair who'd looked him straight in the eye with completely uninhibited ease when, on an impulse, very unusual for him, he'd stroked the delicate, quivering skin between her shoulder blades lightly with the tip of his finger, something that he'd never before even . . .

"Fanta," he breathed, "is everything all right?"

"Yes," she said, cautiously, mechanically.

It wasn't true. He knew it, he could feel it.

He couldn't believe what she said anymore.

He nonetheless persisted in asking questions that to his mind demanded honest answers—intimate questions, questions about feelings—as if the stubborn frequency with which he conducted these interrogations might one day wear down Fanta's current determination not to let anything slip and drop her guard.

"I'm taking Djibril to sleep at Mummy's place tonight," he said abruptly.

"Oh no," she moaned, almost sobbing, unable to contain herself. Rudy felt pain gripping his heart for having made her so upset, but what else could he do?

Should he deprive Mummy of the company of her only grandchild simply because Fanta couldn't stand being separated from him?

What else could he do?

"She hasn't had him over much for quite a while now," he said in a kindly, comforting tone that sounded in the earpiece so deceitful to him that he pulled the receiver away from himself in embarrassment, as if someone else, who ought to be ashamed at disguising his hypocrisy so badly, had said it.

"She doesn't like Djibril!" Fanta blurted out.

"What? You're completely mistaken, she adores him."

He was speaking cheerfully and forcefully now, even though he didn't feel in the least cheerful or forceful, not in the least bright eyed and bushy tailed, having emerged from the melancholy, depressing, and painful dream (but a dream curiously not without a glint of hope) that every conversation with Fanta now resembled.

The sonorous tones of cheerful prattle from times past floated around them.

He could discern their obscure chirping and—as his skull throbbed and the hair stuck to his forehead in the stifling heat of the phone booth—it made him nostalgic, as if he had happened to hear a recording of deceased old friends, loving, very dear friends of old.

"Oh god of Mummy's, oh good little father who's done so much for Mummy, if she's to be believed, grant that Fanta . . ."

Even if he'd never paid much attention to Mummy's pious enthusiasms—greeting her professions, prudent signs of the cross, and muttered invocations with a perpetually irritated, ironic smirk—he'd retained, almost in spite of himself, as a result of hearing it said so often, that the moral rectitude of a prayer was the necessary, if insufficient, condition of its fulfillment.

Where was that quality in what he was asking for?

"Mummy's nice little god, compassionate father, I beg you . . ."

Where was it, his honesty, he wondered, from the moment he

knew (or a second Rudy within him did: a younger, sterner, more scrupulous Rudy, a Rudy as yet unspoiled by setbacks, by want of understanding and compassion, and by the need to cobble together good reasons and poor excuses for himself), where was it, the truth of the soul, he wondered, knowing full well that in proposing to take Djibril to Mummy's for the night, he wasn't thinking about Mummy, that uppermost in his thoughts wasn't any concern for her pleasure and happiness, but solely his own peace of mind in thereby preventing Fanta . . .

Because, surely, she'd never run away without the boy—or would she?

He could only judge from what she'd done before, but if, that first time, she'd taken Djibril with her, had Manille asked her to?

Why would Manille have wanted to be saddled with the child if there'd been any chance that Fanta would have abandoned Djibril to his father's custody?

No, no, she wouldn't leave without Djibril. Besides, the boy was afraid of his father, and Rudy, in a sense, was afraid of him too, because the child, his own son, didn't like him, even if, in his young mind, he was unaware of the fact, and furthermore he didn't like the house, his father's house . . .

A fresh surge of anger was threatening to drown out all rational thought. He wanted to shout into the receiver, "I'll never forgive you for what you've done to me!"

He could just as well have shouted, "I love you so much, there's no one else I love in the whole wide world, everything must go back to what it was before!"

"Okay, see you this evening," he said.

He hung up, downcast, exhausted, and feeling stunned, as

if—after a long, melancholy, agonizing dream—he had to adjust his consciousness to the ambient reality, a reality that for him, he thought, was itself frequently just a cold, interminable, unchanging nightmare; it seemed to him that he moved from one dream to another without ever finding the exit, some sort of awakening that he modestly saw as putting things in order, as organizing rationally the scattered elements of his existence.

He left the phone booth.

It was already the hottest hour of the morning.

A glance at his watch informed him that he'd be later than he'd ever been before.

So what, he said to himself, annoyed, though slightly anxious at the prospect of finding himself once again face-to-face with Manille.

If Manille had been unable to show him an iota of compassion, merely irritation and impatience, everything would have been much simpler.

Should he not detest Manille?

Wasn't it shameful and deeply regrettable that the kindness, the pity, and (albeit barely perceptible, despite it all) the arrogance that he read in his boss's eyes prevented his feeling the hatred he thought any normal person would have cultivated toward the man who . . .

Still dumbfounded, even though it had all happened two years earlier, he shook his head slowly, pondering the retribution a normal man would have formulated in his mind. It wasn't as if he was there at Manille's place, biding his time, just waiting for the ultimate moment to bring down an avenging fist on Manille's head, and Manille knew this perfectly well too, so he had no fear of Rudy, had never feared him.

"So that's how it is, eh?" Rudy wondered.

Was it admirable or was it degrading? Who knows?

He thought he could smell the holm oaks in the distance.

It was probably only the memory of that rather sour scent of their tiny silky leaves, but he thought if he breathed in gently he could indeed smell them. It cheered him up and made him almost happy to imagine himself over there, in the chateau, opening the shutters on a clear bright morning and sniffing his holm oaks, smelling the tart odor of the tiny silky leaves, every one of which belonged to him, Rudy Descas—but he would never have scalped those poor old trees as they had dared to do, those Americans or Australians who'd had the impertinence, according to Mummy, to believe themselves sufficiently French to produce the same excellent wine that . . .

The thought of Mummy, of her pale, bitter face, snuffed out his cheerfulness.

He was tempted to go back into the phone booth and ring Fanta again, not to check that she was still in the house (Though come to think of it, he thought, suddenly anxious), but to promise her that everything would be all right.

There, in the heat heavy with the smell of the holm oaks, he felt carried away by love and compassion.

Everything would be all right?

Based only on some vision of himself opening the shutters in their bedroom on the first floor of the chateau?

No matter, he would have liked to talk to her, to inspire her with the confidence filling his heart at this moment, as if, for once, the reality of existence coincided exactly with his daydreams, or was just about to do so.

He made as if to go back to the phone booth.

He was upset at the thought of getting back into the stifling Nevada, which smelled vaguely of dog (it sometimes seemed to him that the vehicle's previous owners had used it as a kennel for their dog, many of whose hairs remained trapped in the felt of the seats).

He decided, however, against calling Fanta again.

He no longer had the time, did he?

And if, once again, she failed to answer, what conclusions could he draw from that, and what good would it do?

And anyway he no longer really had the time.

But she wouldn't run away without Djibril, and the child was out of reach for the moment, wasn't he?

He cursed himself for working that out.

He almost felt then like defending Fanta against himself and his nasty calculating ways.

Oh, what could he do, considering that he loved her?

"What else can I do, dear God, good little father, good, kind little god of Mummy's?"

He was convinced that the flimsy, very flimsy and unstable, armature of his existence held together and only barely because, after all, Fanta was present, present more like a small hen whose clipped wings prevented her from flying over the lowest fence than like the brave independent human being whom he'd met at the Lycée Mermoz. He could hardly bear that thought, it made him feel ashamed, and he only managed to countenance it because this dreary state of affairs was merely provisional in his eyes.

It wasn't just the lack of money—was it?

To what extent did his monthly salary of a thousand euros make him less alluring than someone like Manille?

Yes, yes (standing all alone in the ten o'clock sun, near the scorching hood of his car, and shrugging impatiently), that was true to a large extent, certainly, but what he lacked above all was faith in his own talents, in his good fortune, and in the infinitude of his youth, which once shone in the clear blue eyes he'd inherited from Mummy, which caused that hand, at once caressing and indifferent, to sweep back the lock of fair hair on his forehead, and which . . .

All that he'd well and truly lost, even though he wasn't old, even though compared with others he was still almost young, all that he no longer possessed since his return to France: all that must have played an essential part in making Fanta fall in love with him.

If only—he said to himself—he could slough off this harsh, depressing, painful, degrading nightmare and rediscover, even if it only meant moving from one dream to another, the vision of Fanta and himself, bathed in golden light, walking side by side in the streets of Colobane, their naked arms brushing against each other at every step, he, Rudy, tall and tanned, talking in his strong, cheerful voice, striving already, even though he was unaware of it, to ensnare in his web of tender, flattering, bewitching words this young woman with the small shaven head, with the discreetly ironic, direct gaze, who'd pulled herself up to the level of the Lycée Mermoz, where she taught French literature to the children of army officers and prosperous businessmen; those adolescents had no idea, Rudy declaimed in his strong, cheerful voice, of the frightening determination it had required for this woman to be able to stand before them, this woman with the winged feet and the delicate quivering skin on her forehead, no idea of the time and trouble it took her to maintain the only two cotton skirts she possessed, one pink and the other white, always beautifully ironed, which she wore with a tank top, between the straps of which the delicate skin of her back, quivering as if two tiny wings . . .

He, Rudy Descas, had really been that charming, lighthearted, smooth-talking young man whom Fanta had eventually taken home, to the apartment with green walls where they all lived.

He remembered how his heart skipped a beat when he entered the room suffused with shimmering, vaguely funereal light.

He'd first climbed a cement staircase behind her and then walked along a gallery entered through doors with peeling paint.

Fanta had opened the last one and the greenish half light, accentuated by the window shutters, had seemed to engulf her.

He'd seen nothing but the white patch of her skirt as she'd entered the room before coming back and inviting him in, having checked, he'd supposed, that the apartment was in a fit state to be seen.

And he'd moved forward, not without shyness and some embarrassment, but chiefly it was gratitude that suddenly rendered him speechless.

Because in the greenish half light Fanta's calm expression said, Here's where I live, this is my home.

Her expression accepting the judgment of a foreigner with a white face (in that respect his tan made no difference!), blond hair, and smooth white hands on her well-kept but very humble home—accepting it, and together with it, the potential effects, the possible feelings of uneasiness or condescension.

Rudy could sense, could almost hear, how this woman took in everything, how shrewd, lucid, and immensely perceptive she was, but also how profoundly indifferent, out of pride, to how a man with such a white forehead, such white, smooth hands, might view her home.

She must have taken him, with his blond hair and fine words, for a wealthy, spoiled young man.

But she'd invited him home, and now, with a gesture and a word or two she was introducing him to her uncle, to her aunt, to a neighbor, and to others as well, all of them gradually revealed by the pale light, sitting at the back of the room on bare seats or threadbare velvet armchairs, silent, motionless, with a vague nod acknowledging Rudy, who felt out of place, not knowing what to do with his big hands, their pallor conspicuous in the dim light as his white forehead and long, smooth forelock must have been too.

He longed to fall at Fanta's feet and swear to her that he wasn't what he seemed—the tanned and ultra-confident type who spent every weekend at his Somone villa.

He longed to fall on his knees and embrace Fanta's slender legs and tell her how grateful he was and how much he loved her for having allowed him to see what he had just seen: this austere room, these silent people who didn't smile or pretend to be thrilled to meet him, this difficult, frugal life of hers, of which people at the Lycée Mermoz, where she arrived every day on her winged feet, in her clean, starched pink skirt, or in her white one, probably knew nothing, and of which the children of diplomats and the children of entrepreneurs, who went water-skiing in Somone every weekend—that whole group of people, who, he longed to tell her, he couldn't abide, even though occasionally he envied them in secret—no doubt knew even less.

Oh, they certainly knew nothing about her or about the verdigris room with its heavenly glow.

The midday light now shone through the shutters on the face of the aunt, the clasped hands of the uncle, both of whom seemed to be waiting for Rudy to leave so that they could go back to what they'd been doing.

And he, Rudy, saw all that without knowing how to convey it to Fanta.

He contented himself—rather stupidly, he felt—with bowing to each person present, stretching his lips to form a little, quivering, awkward smile.

He knew at that moment, with a kind of surprised wonder, that he loved her, loved her beyond measure.

Now he was opening the door of his car and slipping inside, holding his breath.

It was even hotter, stuffier inside the car than in the phone booth.

Was he right not to call Fanta again?

And suppose that she was trying, not to leave but, in her utter misery at his decision to take Djibril to Mummy's for the night, she was trying to . . . ?

No, he couldn't bear even to think of the word.

"Oh, good little god of Mummy's, kind little father, help me to see things clearly!

"Help us, dear God."

Couldn't he just—only for a minute—phone her, wasn't that, actually, perhaps what she was expecting him to do at this moment?

No (a small snickering voice murmured), actually she doesn't care to hear the sound of your voice again until this evening, and what's more she understands that you feel guilty and are trying somehow to make amends, even though you were only trying to stop taking the blame for all the wrangling on your own frail shoulders, an effort that has no doubt failed to win you any more respect and perhaps has even made her despise you a little more for acting tough only then to lose your nerve and come seeking her forgiveness and consolation after having offended her by telling her—is it conceivable?—to go back where she came from—can you really imagine that . . .

As he switched on the ignition he shook his head in denial.

Such a thing he, Rudy Descas, just couldn't have said.

Just couldn't.

He couldn't restrain a little dry laugh.

Might he have meant—ha! ha!—that she should go back to Manille?

He was sweating profusely.

The sweat was falling on the steering wheel and on his thighs.

When he tried to put the car into first gear, the stick shift jammed.

The engine stalled.

He found himself once again wrapped in the silence that had been shattered briefly by the roar of the Nevada's engine, and he now saw himself as forming a necessary, indisputable, and perfect part of this section of the countryside.

He was disturbing nothing and no one, and there were no restraints on him.

He leaned back against the headrest.

Although he was still sweating, his heart beat less fiercely.

He had to admit that Manille was, in his rather discreet, provincial way, a successful businessman, and that, even if he'd never gone in for water-skiing or owned any other house but the big villa he'd had built behind the firm's premises, his manly, but sober, rather elegant, and reserved self-assurance, that particular gentleness he possessed, that of someone who could afford to be gentle because nothing threatened or frightened him, could still attract an upset, confused woman with nothing to do all day, a woman as lost as Fanta was now.

It's strange, he said to himself, or perhaps it's on account of love, that I can't forgive her, whereas with him, it was as if I understood.

But stranger still, to tell the truth, I understand her side, too, so much so that were I a woman I could imagine yielding joyfully and easily to Manille's uncomplicated charm—oh, how well I understand her, and how I hold it against her.

He was caught unawares by a feeling of panic, by a sort of hallucination, and his heart stopped as he tried to envisage Manille's bedroom, which he imagined was like the rest of the villa, vast and conventional, filled with the usual expensive trappings of contemporary interior design, and when he gently pushed open the door of this unfamiliar bedroom and saw on the huge bed, in a dazzling light, Fanta and Manille, Manille stretched out on Fanta, Rudy Descas's wife, Manille groaning softly while his powerful haunches, his centaur's buttocks, moved in a calm, slow rhythm that brought out the dimples in his hairy flesh, and his head rested on the neck of Fanta, Rudy Descas's wife, the only woman Rudy Descas had ever truly loved.

Or he could see on this bed the hindquarters of a no less vigorous man with a horse's head panting as he lay on top of Fanta—should he kill this monster, shouldn't he at least despise him?

And, under Manille's much more considerable bulk, what novel and mysterious things could she be feeling, of which he'd never know?

Rudy was a lean, delicate man, narrow shouldered yet robust, he liked to think, but Manille—he shook his head—he didn't want to know anything about that.

And he shook his head again, alone at the wheel of his stationary vehicle, in the silence throbbing with heat, and he felt trapped, torn by the same deeply frustrating fear that had left him transfixed, mesmerized, able to reply with only a hideous, weird little smile when someone (Madame Pulmaire, or Mummy, perhaps) had in the drawing room of some house he was visiting (so wouldn't it have been a client's, then?) revealed to him in a whisper what Fanta and Manille were up to, this nasty suggestion wiping the silly smirk off his face, as he could see in the mirror of the unidentified drawing room in which he stood with his legs apart, riveted now by how silly and bizarre he looked, but anything was preferable to the sight of that nasty mouth with its acrid breath that took pleasure in robbing Rudy Descas's innocence, his lover's credulity, anything was preferable to the spiteful tone of impotent anger (well, it must have been Mummy, because neither Madame Pulmaire nor a customer could have discussed the affair with as much animosity) summoning him to action, to spurn a woman like that.

What else could this indignant person, in a tone of such sweet reason, be suggesting (oh, it was certainly Mummy), except that any man with a remaining shred of dignity should not, could not, penetrate the very body in which there still reposed a sacred liquor, the centaur's sperm?

He could have answered, with a snicker, "No risk of that, I haven't been sleeping with Fanta for a long time, or, rather, she's not been sleeping with me."

But he could also have replied, with a cry of despair, "But it was you, Mummy, who got me taken on at Manille's, it was you who went and begged him to give me a job! Had it not been for that, he'd never have met her!"

But he had no recollection of having opened his mouth, frozen as it was in a slack, feeble rictus.

He could see himself again, his own impassive face in the mirror, and just under it the back of the head of this woman who was still talking, still trying to drown him in vile, sneaky appeals to his male honor, and hadn't he then thought that a simple blow to that head, with its short, dyed blond hair, would free him from this torment, hadn't he seen himself striking Mummy to shut her up, shouting at her perhaps, just before she lost consciousness, "What do you know of honor, eh, and Dad, what did he know of it?"

But he didn't want to think about it anymore.

It was humiliating and pointless and made you feel grubby, as if you were emerging from a recurring, interminable, stupid dream: you're only too familiar with every painful stage of it, and even while plunged in it you know that you're not going to be allowed to skip a single episode.

He didn't want to think about it anymore.

He switched on the ignition again and put the car straight into second gear.

The engine protested and spluttered, then, slowly, the Nevada began to move forward, with fits and moans from every part of its ancient carcass but, he said to himself with some satisfaction, rather spunky, all things considered.

He wouldn't think about that anymore.

He lowered the window and, steering with one hand, let his left arm hang over the hot side of the car. He could occasionally hear the melting surface of the asphalt crackling under his tires.

How he loved that sound!

He was now experiencing a gentle, delightful feeling of euphoria.

No, by Mummy's good little god, our kind little father, he wouldn't think about the mortifying past anymore but only about making himself worthy of the love Fanta would feel for him again if he cared to make the effort, and didn't he just, as heaven was his witness, high, bright, and scorching hot this very morning. Why, for once, shouldn't the best be Rudy Descas's for the asking, the finest and the most certain of the innumerable promises offered by the sun this fine spring morning?

He suddenly burst out laughing.

The sound of his own voice enchanted him.

After all, he thought, almost surprised, he was alive, still young, and in perfect health.

Could Gauquelan himself, that crook whose loathsome sculpture he was circling around at that moment (and today he found the strength not to look at it), with his ill-gotten gains, could he claim as much?

Certainly not.

Alive, alas yes, but the photo Rudy had seen in the paper showed a man with a rather puffy, scowling face, a receding hairline, a tuft of graying hair on top, and, curiously, a gap in his front teeth, and it had occurred to Rudy then, as he now recalled, feeling slightly ashamed, that a man who got paid a hundred thousand euros for a hideous piece of sculpture should surely have been able to avoid the cameras until he got his teeth fixed.

The manner of Gauquelan's existence was as nothing compared with Rudy's own impressive vitality, which he—Rudy—felt throbbing in his every muscle as if he were a horse (or a centaur), a big, proud, young beast, the whole purpose of whose existence was in being a superb specimen, his spirit never again to be seized by those dreams that leave you with a pasty mouth and stale breath, any more than the spirit of a horse (or a centaur) would be.

Was Mummy alive?

After the rotary, without intending to, he accelerated sharply.

He'd no business thinking about Mummy at that moment, nor about his father; he (his father) was well and truly dead, and no one would ever remotely have thought of comparing him to a horse (or a centaur) with rippling muscles under his damp skin—damp as Rudy's cheeks, neck, and forehead were in the un-air-conditioned car, a reaction of his system, he recognized, to his having evoked, however briefly and insignificantly, his long-dead father, the terror and astonishment always provoked in him by the thought of that white-boned skeleton formerly called Abel Descas, its very white bones and the hole neatly drilled through its skull, lying, Rudy imagined, in the hot sandy soil of the cemetery at Bel Air.

He parked the Nevada in the parking lot of Manille & Co.

Before getting out, he carefully mopped his face and neck with the towel that he kept on the backseat for this purpose and that had eventually absorbed the smell of the car.

Each time he promised himself he'd change it, then he'd forget, and so his annoyance was intense when he reached for the towel and found this nauseating rag once again, because it seemed to him that this minor testimony to his own negligence, obliging him to wipe his face with a dubious piece of cloth, represented his whole current existence in its vaguely grimy disorder.

But this morning, just as he hadn't managed to suppress a reflex of irritation in wiping his face, he succeeded in forcing himself to let his eyes wander over the different cars parked around him and evaluate them in the most neutral manner possible, without succumbing, as he usually did, to the bitter, violent feelings of envy that he found so degrading.

So that's what my colleagues and customers drive, he said calmly, almost ritually, to himself, as he itemized the black and gray Audis, Mercedeses, and BMWs that made the parking lot of a kitchen showroom on the outskirts of a small provincial town look like a grand hotel.

Where do they get so much money?

How are they able to extract from their hardworking existence the sums needed to buy such cars? I've not the slightest idea.

What's their scheme, what knack do they possess, what's the trick? I'll never figure it out.

And other pointless questions like that swirled around in his furious mind as he slammed the door of the Nevada.

But he'd been able, this morning, to resist the monotonous surge of covetousness.

With a light step he crossed the lot and dimly recalled feeling much the same during an earlier time in his life when he always walked like that: light of foot and at peace with himself—yes, always like that, and looking serene and benevolent—that was the face he always showed to the world.

It all seemed so remote to him that he almost doubted it had anything to do with him—him, Rudy Descas—and not his father or someone else he'd dreamed about.

How long ago was all that?

He thought it must have been when he returned to Dakar alone, without Mummy, who'd stayed in France, shortly before he met Fanta.

He thought too, with a start, because it was a detail he'd forgotten, that for him, then, it used to seem natural, that inclination to be good and kind.

He stopped suddenly in the sun-drenched parking lot.

The smell of hot tar filled his nostrils.

He had quite a surprise when he looked not at the sky but at the bitumen under his feet.

Had he really been that lighthearted man, at peace with himself, who strode along the placid streets of Le Plateau, where he'd rented a small apartment, looking, with his fair hair and pleasantly regular features, hardly any different from the other white-faced types who he passed in the neighborhood but whose business ambitions and drive he in no way shared?

Could he really have been that man, Rudy Descas, who aspired, with calm self-scrutiny, to show himself good and just, and even more (oh, how that made him blush with surprise and embarrassment) to always distinguish good from evil in himself, never favoring the latter even when it appeared under the mask of good as happened all too often here when one was a white man with deep pockets and could for very little buy any kind of labor involving great patience and endurance?

He started walking again, slowly, toward the double glass doors of the building, adorned by the name "Manille" lit up in huge letters.

His legs had stiffened, as if suddenly robbed of the gift of lightness.

Because he wondered for the first time whether, in persuading Fanta to follow him to France, he hadn't knowingly looked the other way and allowed evil every latitude to take possession of him, and whether he hadn't indeed savored the feeling of acting wickedly while not appearing to do so.

Until now he'd only asked himself the question in practical terms: Had it been a good idea or a bad idea to bring Fanta here?

But oh no, it wasn't that, it wasn't that at all.

Put like that, the question was a ploy used by the evil comfortably lodged in him.

And, in that radiant period of his life when every morning, with an innocent heart, he left his small modern apartment in Le Plateau, he was still able to recognize the bad impulses and deceitful thoughts that sometimes entered his mind and to shoo them away by thinking the opposite, by which effort he was able to find relief and happiness, since he had only one profound desire, to be capable of loving everything around him.

But now, now—the extent of his bitterness almost made his head spin.

If he had been that man, what had happened to him, what had

he done to find himself now inhabiting such an envious and brutal personage, his disposition to universal love having shrunk to encompass only the person of Fanta?

Yes, what, indeed, had he done to himself to unload, now, all this untapped, unbidden love upon a woman who had gradually wearied of his incompetence, at an age, his mid-forties, when such faults (a certain unfitness for sustained work, a tendency to entertain fantasies and to believe in schemes that were hazy at best) can no longer hope to be met with indulgence and understanding?

Not only, he said to himself as he pushed open the glass door, through which, with a cowardly sense of relief, he could discern Manille's imposing shape, surrounded by a couple of people, customers probably, to whom Manille was demonstrating the main features of a floor model of one of his kitchens, not only had he willingly connived in the lies and corruption entering and taking possession of his soul, but on the pretext of caring for her he'd enclosed Fanta in the cold, gloomy prison of his love—for such was his love at present, endless distress, like a dream from which you struggle in vain to awake, a rather degrading and pointless dream, wasn't that what Fanta must be enduring, and wasn't that how he himself would feel as the victim of such a love?

Once inside he walked purposefully toward the staff offices, even though he couldn't stop his upper lip from trembling.

He knew that this tic made him look unpleasant, almost nasty, and that it was always fear that provoked it.

At such moments his lip curled back like a dog's.

And yet he had no need to worry about Manille—did he?

Out of the corner of his eye he watched the slow progress of the little group, and worked out that he could reach the back offices before Manille and his customers got close.

Afterward, he said to himself, Manille will have forgotten seeing me arrive so late.

All he had to do was keep out of Manille's way for an hour or so, and all would be well.

He had time to notice that Manille looked good this morning, in his neatly ironed black T-shirt and well-cut pale jeans.

His thick gray hair was combed back, and his complexion was dark, almost golden.

Rudy could hear Manille's slightly husky voice as he opened and shut a cupboard door, and he was sure that the customers, a drably dressed middle-aged couple with thick legs, were without realizing it succumbing to Manille's insistent charm as he fixed his dark eyes intently on theirs, as if on the verge of passing on an important piece of personal information or making a flattering comment that he was only holding back for fear of embarrassing them.

He never gave the impression, Rudy had often observed, of trying to sell something.

Without seeming to make any effort in that direction, he managed to create the illusion of a friendly, intimate relationship that would last well beyond the eventual sale of the kitchen, which had merely been the fortuitous pretext for the birth of a friendship, and often it turned out that the tactic was quite sincere: Manille went on visiting his customers just for the pleasure of their company, and as they chatted he never abandoned the subdued tone of ardor, so delicate and restrained, that had led to the sale in the first place, so that, Rudy thought, the manner Manille adopted to overcome a client's resistance ended up being his true way of speaking, the only one ever heard—that smooth, slightly hoarse timbre and that restrained fervor that, it must have seemed to people, would have moved him, if he couldn't control himself, to sing their praises, to share secrets with them, even to hug them.

Rudy couldn't help admiring Manille even if he despised his trade.

How was it that the same jeans and T-shirt or short-sleeved top, the same sort of canvas shoes, as the boss wore, always made Rudy look like some broke overgrown adolescent, even though Rudy was taller, younger, and slimmer than Manille: that he just couldn't understand.

He would never possess Manille's relaxed elegance . . . No, he said to himself at the sight of his reflection in the second glass door, the one separating the showroom from the offices, don't even think about it.

It occurred to him that he had a stingy, crumpled, almost needy appearance.

To whom could such a man, however kind, ever appeal?

How would anyone ever notice his love of life and of others, even if he could find it again?

How would people see it?

He had to admit that in someone like Manille, however hardened he was by a life in business, by the unremitting calculations and the pragmatic maneuvering it required, and despite the stylish sportswear and Chaumet watches and the villa at the back of the shop—despite, that is, everything that had transformed Manille, a farmworker's son, into a dreary provincial parvenu—one could still at once discern the amiability, kindness, and capacity for discreet compassion in his gentle, modest expression.

And then Rudy wondered for the first time if it hadn't been precisely that which had attracted Fanta, something he'd lost long ago, the gift for . . .

He went into the office and closed the door quietly behind him.

He felt himself turning red.

But it was certainly that, and even if the term was pompous, there was no other word for it: the gift for . . . compassion.

He'd never thought, even in the depths of his anger and grief, after Mummy (wasn't it?) had told him about the liaison between Fanta and Manille, he'd never thought, no, that it was Manille's wealth, and the respect and the power that went with it, that could have seduced Fanta.

He'd never thought that.

Now—oh yes—he understood what it was all about, and he understood it in the light of what he no longer had, for he finally understood what he no longer had, whereas he had been suffering without knowing the reason.

The gift for compassion.

He went to his desk and dropped down onto his swivel chair.

Around him, in the big glass-walled room, all the desks were occupied.

"Ah, there you are!"

"Hi Rudy!"

He replied with a smile and a little wave of the hand.

On his cluttered desk, next to the keyboard, he saw a pile of leaflets.

"Your mother brought them a little while ago."

Cathie's voice, cordial but a shade anxious, reached him from the next desk, and he knew that if he turned his head his eyes would meet hers, with their questioning, slightly perplexed look.

She would ask him in a low voice why he was three quarters of an hour late and perhaps, too, why he didn't simply forbid Mummy to set foot in Manille's workplace.

So he contrived to mumble some answer that didn't require him to look her in the eye.

In the dazzling glare of the room the vivid pink of Cathie's blouse shone brightly around her.

Rudy could see it reflected in the white surface of his own desk.

He knew too that if he turned toward Cathie he'd clearly see past her small, pale face to the other side of the picture window looking out over Manille's villa, a big building with blue shutters, pale pink roughcast walls, and a roof of Provençal tiles, separated from the commercial premises by a simple lawn, and he couldn't help wondering, for the nth time, painfully and fruitlessly, whether Cathie and the others, Dominique, Fabrice, and Nathalie, had watched Fanta's comings and goings at the boss's dream house, noticed how many times she'd entered, and why he, Rudy, had never seen her there, even though, during that terrible period when he "knew" without "really knowing" (no need to believe everything Mummy said, after all), he'd never ceased glancing at the picture window, past Cathie, who felt sorry for him and showed sympathy (so was everybody privy to his troubles?), at the villa's fussy double doors with their wrought-iron fittings.

How he'd suffered then!

How ashamed, how furious he'd felt!

All that was now long past, but he still couldn't speak to Cathie without feelings of rage boiling up in him as he glanced at Manille's house.

He suddenly felt like saying to her in a dry tone that would make her uncomfortable, "But that's pretty well the only consolation Mummy's got left in life, distributing left and right her bundles of pathetic leaflets in support of poor cretins as lonely and idle as she is, how do you expect me to tell her to stop coming here and, really, who's bothered by it, eh?"

But he said nothing.

He remained conscious of the aura of fuchsia that surrounded her and it annoyed him, because he couldn't forget her presence.

He pushed to one side the packet of leaflets held together with a rubber band.

"They are in our midst."

The clumsy, almost laughable picture of an adult angel sitting down at a table with members of an ecstatic family, and the angel's silly smirk.

"They are in our midst."

Such inanities that kept Mummy from drowning in melancholy and antidepressants were, literally, her salvation.

He was outraged that a Little Miss Nobody like Cathie, in the guise of trying to be helpful, would dare to suggest that he deprive Mummy of the pleasure of bringing her brochures to Manille's place.

What did she know about Mummy's sad life?

"Hey, tell me, does Manille want my mother to stop coming here?" he asked suddenly.

He looked at Cathie, dazzled by the absurd intensity of her pink blouse. It was such an effort keeping his eyes fixed upon her face, to resist their tendency to wander, that his head started aching violently.

Meanwhile he felt as if a hot poker was being pushed up his anus.

"Not at all," said Cathie, "I'm not even aware if he noticed your mother coming in."

She smiled, surprised he could think such a thing.

Oh no, he thought, downcast, it's starting again.

He raised his buttocks feebly from the chair and balanced on the edge of the seat so that only the top of his thighs remained in contact with it.

But the mild relief he'd hoped for failed to materialize.

He then heard, through the fog of pain that had suddenly enveloped him, Cathie's muffled voice.

"It's not like Manille to stop your mother coming, is it?"

Rudy couldn't now remember what he'd said or what he'd asked.

Ah, Mummy. It wasn't like Manille to show the slightest harshness, or to try to shoo away this ridiculous woman who really believed she could, by means of tracts written and printed in her living room—tracts that swallowed up a not inconsiderable part of her meager pension—convince kitchen salesmen of the presence of angels all around them.

At the very most he'd . . .

That familiar itch, which had taken him by surprise, he was beginning to subdue in his mind.

He brought to bear all the old defense mechanisms (those he'd not used in quite a while, because for several months he'd been left in peace by the problem), the most immediate of which consisted in directing his thoughts toward topics having no connection with his own body, or with any other body, real or otherwise, so that, quite naturally, he started thinking intensely about Mummy's angels, and he reached out with his fingers to bring the packet of brochures nearer to him.

How would Mummy answer the question of whether angels ever suffered from piles?

Wouldn't she be happy and flattered to see him asking, with apparent seriousness, to hear him broaching . . .

Stop, stop, he said to himself, in a panic. That wasn't at all what he ought to be concentrating on.

The pain came back, more insistent, exasperating.

He had a terrible longing to scratch, no, to scrape off, to tear away, this goading, burning flesh.

He rubbed against the edge of the chair.

With a trembling finger he started up his computer.

Then he looked again at the picture of the angel, the clumsily drawn figure, the naive decor sketched by Mummy, and suddenly he discerned beyond all possibility of error what his eyes had been content to skim over without any attempt at interpretation a few moments earlier.

As he'd vaguely felt already, the three members of the small family seated at the table looked like Djibril, Fanta, and Rudy, and only the artist's lack of skill shielded them somewhat from the risk of being recognized, but more than that someone had afterward attached to the angel a vigorous penis that was clearly visible under the table and seemed to emerge from a specially fitted pocket in the long white robe.

Rudy flicked through the packet of fliers.

The angel had only been mocked on the first one.

He turned the packet over and pushed it toward a corner of his desk.

He glanced at Cathie.

At the same moment she raised her eyes and frowned anxiously.

"Anything wrong, Rudy?"

He grinned sardonically.

Oh, how it hurt, and how angry he felt that it hurt.

"Who put the brochures on my desk?" he asked.

"I told you, your mother came in this morning."

"So she herself put them there, in person?"

Cathie shrugged uncomprehendingly, slightly annoyed, and said, "I don't see who else it could have been."

"But you didn't see her?"

Cathie was smiling now, but coldly, conspicuously restraining her feelings of impatience.

"Listen, Rudy, I do know that your mother came in with her . . . brochures, or whatever. I saw her in the lobby, but it so happens that I wasn't at my desk when she dropped them off."

He leaped off his chair, suddenly intoxicated with rage and pain.

But a small sad voice whispered inside him, "How can you hope to be good when you suffer the torments of the damned?" It was the voice of the calm, cheerful, seductive Rudy Descas that Rudy wanted so badly to be again, with the pitiless moral standards he set himself and the less stringent ones he applied to others.

And it was with terror and dread that he noticed Cathie flinch slightly as he approached her chair.

He felt the others around him watching him silently.

Had he become the sort of man feared by women and despised

by other men, especially strong men capable of self-restraint, like Manille?

He suddenly felt terribly unhappy, craven, useless.

He grabbed the packet of brochures and flung it on Cathie's desk.

He hopped from one foot to the other, trying to calm the pain by rubbing his underpants against his inflamed skin.

"And that charming little joke, whose idea was that, then?" he exclaimed, indicating the angel's penis with his finger.

Cathie glanced warily at the picture.

"No idea," she muttered.

He picked the packet up again and went back to his desk.

One of his male colleagues, at the back of the room, clucked his tongue audibly.

"Hey! What's your problem?" Rudy shouted. "Go to hell!"

"Now you've gone too far, big boy," said Cathie drily.

"I just want my mother left out of it," said Rudy.

He was sticking to his guns that someone had wanted to humiliate Mummy by adding an obscene doodle to her drawing. Although he'd always hated her sanctimonious propaganda and consistently refused to talk about it, the diligent passion with which she drafted and illustrated her messages, taking a lot of trouble to produce the best result that her meager talent was capable of, laid an obligation upon him, he felt, to stand up for her.

As in those threatening, implacable, irresolvable dreams where a heavy, absurd, and insurmountable obligation is laid upon you, no one but he could defend that unreasonable woman, no one but he could do it.

He recalled confusedly when and how that feeling of obligation arose, and the memory was so embarrassing that he blushed violently. At the same moment, a pain even sharper than before pierced his anus.

"They are among us, these pure spirits, and they address us in thought, even at the table, if only to ask us to pass the salt or the bread."

Who's your guardian angel, Rudy, what's his name, and what's his position in the angelic hierarchy?

Rudy's father had neglected his angel—treating his dog better—which is why, Mummy hinted, he'd had to endure such a sad end, because his angel had lost touch with him or had worn itself out looking for him in the dark shadows of worldliness and indifference.

While all was going well for him Rudy's father had, out of spite or vanity, contrived to ditch his angel. Ah, men can be so arrogant!

So where—Rudy had wondered—was the guardian angel of his father's business partner when Rudy's father knocked him unconscious and ran over him?

Had he—the partner—been a foolhardy man, too cocksure for his own good, a person who'd delighted in giving his angel the slip? Or else did Africans in general have the misfortune of being poorly guarded, were their angels lazy and incompetent?

The dirty work of defending Mummy, no one but he could do it, nobody else could . . .

"You need to get a grip, Rudy," said Cathie, in a tone of disappointment and reproach. "No one's attacking your mother."

"Okay, okay," he mumbled, unable to ignore his physical pain, so wrapped up in it that he could scarcely breathe.

"You need to get a grip," she said again, in an emphatic, monotonous voice.

"Okay, okay," he repeated, almost inaudibly.

"If you don't, Rudy, you'll land yourself in serious trouble. Monsieur Manille is beginning to get fed up, you know, and so are we. You need to calm down and start doing your job."

"But who scribbled on my mother's drawing?" he whispered. "It's so . . . horrid!"

He heard the glass door open, and, a few moments later, there was Manille standing in front of him with his fists on the desk, as if restraining himself from leaping at Rudy, and yet his look was kindly, almost tender, though a bit weary.

And Rudy felt something slip between them, as palpable as a fine sheet of rain. It was their mutual embarrassment, a mixture of shame and resentment shared equally, it seemed, by the two of them: Manille, on the one hand, and Rudy himself—who to his advantage still had Fanta at his side, whereas Manille had lost her—on the other.

But more recently Rudy had sensed something else, scarcely less embarrassing but also more comforting, a remarkable, inexpressible communion born of an awareness of having both loved the same woman at the same time.

He saw Manille's eyes focusing on Mummy's drawing.

"You see that?" Rudy asked in a shrill, febrile voice that echoed horribly in his ears.

Hearing that acrimonious tone, didn't Manille wonder, incredulously, how it was that Fanta had finally chosen this sickly, narrow-hipped, gangly, bitter man over him, how she could have gone back to Rudy Descas, who'd long ago forfeited all honor and respect?

That was certainly, Rudy felt, precisely what he'd be thinking if he were in Manille's shoes.

Why had Fanta come back to him, in despair and completely benumbed, as if, held captive in an implacable, irresolvable dream, she'd inflicted upon herself the absurd obligation of spending the rest of her days in a house she didn't like, beside a man who she spurned and who had from the outset deceived her as to what he really was by passing himself off as a mild-mannered person of integrity whereas he'd always allowed untruth to reside in his heart?

Why, really, hadn't she stayed with Manille?

The latter gestured dismissively at the packet of brochures.

"I'd like to know who played this dirty trick on my mother," said Rudy, panting slightly.

"It's not a big deal," said Manille.

His breath smelled of coffee.

Rudy thought that nothing would have given him greater pleasure, at that moment, than a double espresso with sugar.

He wriggled about on his chair, gradually finding a rhythm that, without getting rid of the pain, brought some relief through strategic scratching.

"It wouldn't have been you, by any chance?" he asked as Manille was about to say something.

"If there's anyone I'll never make fun of, it's your mother," Manille murmured with a smile.

He took his hands off the desk and stuck his thumbs in his belt, a fine black leather strap with silver studs that seemed to Rudy to sum up Manille's personality, manly but restrained.

"You perhaps don't remember, you were too small at the time,"

Manille said in a voice low enough so only Rudy could hear, "but my recollection is clear. Your parents and mine were neighbors, we lived in the country, in the middle of nowhere, and on Wednesdays my parents left me alone at home while they went to work, and they asked your mother to pop in from time to time to check on me. Well, your mother came by as agreed and when she saw how sad and lonely I was she took me back to your place, she gave me a nice big snack, and I had a lovely afternoon. Unfortunately that all came to an end when you left for Africa. But whenever I meet your mother I always recall those happy times, so I'd never do anything, even behind her back, that could upset her, never."

"I see," said Rudy.

He affected a sneering tone, but he suddenly felt almost as jealous, wretched, and disoriented as he had been when, at the age of no more than three or four, he'd seen Mummy return every Wednesday with this bigger boy about whom he knew nothing and who—he hadn't realized until this moment—was none other than Manille. He'd had to put up with the giant shadow of the boy towering over him, with his golden legs emerging from his shorts like two pillars barring his path toward Mummy. So that was Manille!

He couldn't recall the boy's face, only the two strong legs at the level of his own face, and between them Mummy's barely visible features.

So why had it seemed that the atmosphere in the house always changed dramatically whenever the boy entered, that it became at once livelier and more effervescent, and that with barely contained excitement Mummy would start talking and moving faster, before proposing, as if suddenly inspired, to make pancakes? Why had it always seemed to him that this boy with the sturdy legs and deep voice could lift Mummy out of the boredom that the mere presence of Rudy failed to dispel and perhaps even exacerbated?

It was hard to escape from Rudy, and Rudy was sometimes a real drag, whereas the little neighbor of about nine or ten never asked for anything and saw Mummy as his salvation. She for her part failed to notice that the boy's firm legs were always in Rudy's face, how those same legs seemed to always move when Rudy did, thereby blocking his way to Mummy.

Ah, it was him, it was Manille!

Terribly shaken, Rudy was wriggling more and more in his seat.

The sunlight, still tinged with the shimmering glow of Cathie's pink blouse, shone directly on his face through the window.

He was hot, fearfully hot.

Manille seemed to be looking at him anxiously.

Was it not extraordinary that Mummy never reminded him of that period when a big boy, relentless but low key, filled the kitchen with his fateful presence every Wednesday afternoon? Wasn't it extraordinary that she'd never told him that the lad was Manille?

Behind his back Mummy and Manille had both shared this secret memory—why, for God's sake?

Manille was talking to him.

Rudy could be in no doubt that Manille represented for Mummy exactly the kind of son she would've wanted, but was that a reason for . . .

Ah well, what's it matter, after all.

He tried to understand what Manille was saying to him in his subdued, mellow voice, but a violent feeling of injustice gripped him at the thought that Manille had always blocked Mummy and that she, for her part . . .

Man, was he hot!

Manille was so positioned that he was in shadow, whereas Rudy was blinded by the sun.

He then became aware of frantically rubbing his bottom against the chair until it squeaked, causing colleagues at the back of the room to turn around.

So what was Manille saying about that customer, Madame Menotti?

Without understanding exactly why, he had a sense of foreboding and unease at the mention of this customer's name, as if he were aware of having let her down while being unable to guess in what way.

He thought he was done with Madame Menotti and her pretentious kitchen, the execution of which he'd followed from the outset, having sketched the plans himself, helped her choose the color of the wood, and discussed at length with her what kind of exhaust hood she needed. When it finally occurred to him to wonder why Manille had entrusted the whole Menotti project to Rudy's unskilled hands, it didn't take long to find out: Madame Menotti had phoned him at home in the middle of the night to say she'd awoken in a terrible fit of anguish—no, worse, in a hyperventilating fit such as she'd never before experienced—at the thought that the whole design project wasn't at all to her liking and why couldn't they simply go back to the original idea and line the walls with the main elements, why could they not go back to the drawing board regarding the entire conception of this kitchen, which, she admitted, spluttering with distress, she wasn't even sure she really wanted anymore, sitting there in her nightie in her beloved old kitchen, why not forget the whole thing, she felt so bad, so bad.

It had taken Rudy a good hour to remind her precisely why she'd gone to Manille in the first place: because she could no longer stand the mismatched, outdated furniture and fittings of her present kitchen; then, almost drunk with fatigue and boredom, he'd assured her that her secret longing to see her life transformed, brightened up thanks to the installation of ingenious cupboards and a retractable hood, was not an absurd hope—"Trust me, Madame Menotti," he'd said.

He'd hung up, exhausted, but too tense to sleep.

He'd felt a spasm of hatred toward Madame Menotti, not because she'd awoken him in the middle of the night but because she'd envisaged quite simply canceling weeks of tedious, disheartening work devoted to the attempt to adapt the woman's complicated, reckless desires to her limited budget.

Oh, the time he'd wasted in front of the computer seeking ways of including an American countertop or a trash bin that opened automatically into plans she'd approved only to have second thoughts on them, oh, the disillusionment he'd often felt realizing that he had to apply to such trivialities nothing less than his full intelligence, all his concentration and ingenuity!

It was at that point, perhaps, as he was offering Madame Menotti reassurances in the middle of the night, that he, for the first time—certainly never before so acutely and painfully—that he got the full measure of his world's collapse.

He'd gone over with Madame Menotti every aspect of the kitchen, which he found grotesque, useless (built to receive each day many discriminating guests, even though she lived alone and, by her own admission, didn't much like to cook), since that was his job, that was his life, and she couldn't have imagined that he had aspired to a university chair or that he'd once considered himself an expert on medieval literature, because nothing showed now of the fine erudition that he'd once possessed and that was slowly fading, slowly buried under the ashes of the worries burned without end.

Those that are in wedlock resemble the fish swimming freely in the vastness of the sea . . .

How could he extricate himself, he'd wondered in despair, cold and lucid, from this unending, pitiless dream that was his life?

. . . that comes and goes at will and comes and goes so much that eventually it encounters a creel . . .

"She's expecting you, go at once," said Manille.

Could he be referring to Fanta?

Rudy was sure of one thing, that if Fanta had stopped expecting him, her husband, she wasn't expecting Manille either. For some reason, Rudy didn't know why, she'd found Manille a big disappointment.

Manille turned on his heel.

"I've got to go to Madame Menotti's, is that it?" Rudy asked.

Without looking back at him Manille nodded, then returned to the showroom, where he'd left his two customers, a couple, sitting on barstools, their fat legs hanging awkwardly down to the ground, while he'd gone to speak to Rudy.

From far off the man smiled vaguely at Rudy.

He held his beret in his lap and Rudy could see, even at that distance, his bald pate shining over his pink forehead.

"They are in our midst!"

Might it be, he wondered, that this couple interested in a complete period kitchen in dark wood fitted with wrought-iron cupboard handles and peppered with fake wormholes formed part of the company of angels who, Mummy was certain, visited us regularly and who we could recognize if (thanks to Mummy's brochures) our souls were made alert to their presence?

As Rudy smiled back, the man immediately looked away, inscrutable.

. . . in which there are several fish that have been caught by the bait within, having found it sweet of smell and good of taste, and when our fish sees it he tries hard to get inside . . .

Rudy got up and went over to Cathie's desk, trying to act natural.

His anus was still burning terribly.

He picked up her phone. Cathie pursed her lips but said nothing.

As a junior salesperson he wasn't allowed a direct line.

He dialed his own number and let it ring a dozen or so times.

He suddenly felt his forehead and hands damp with sweat.

Fanta couldn't hear—or chose not to—or else, he thought, she couldn't answer because she was out or . . .

When he put down the phone his eyes met Cathie's. She was embarrassed, unsettled.

"It seems Madame Menotti wants to see me," he said cheerfully.

But he was in such pain that he felt his upper lip curling into the usual rictus. Unable to stand the burning itch any longer he scratched himself briefly, frenziedly, with one hand.

"I think that Madame Menotti is hopping mad, Rudy," Cathie said, rather regretfully, in a low voice.

"Oh? Why?"

The old vague impression that he'd fallen down on the job for Madame Menotti, not deliberately but through a negligent failure to pay close attention to his work, made his mouth suddenly feel dry.

So what had he done, or failed to do?

Madame Menotti, a lowly bank employee, didn't have much money. She'd taken out a loan of some twenty thousand euros to finance the purchase of this kitchen, and Rudy had had to juggle with different pieces of equipment taken from several models, some of them sale items, to meet the requirements, which were hardly modest, of this hard-nosed woman who, though well versed in money matters, suddenly affected inability to grasp why her itemized wish list added up to a lot more than she'd borrowed.

In many ways he'd shown himself to be receptive, committed, on the ball.

And yet, once the whole order had been placed, a sort of unpleasant aftertaste and a threatening premonition had stayed with him . . . *and circles about so that he finds the way through and goes inside, and trysts that he is in pleasaunce and delyte, as he trysts the others also to be, and once within he cannot go back . . .*

Oh God, what had he done now?

Since the start of his employment at Manille's four years ago (four years of his life!) he'd no recollection of ever having done anything exactly as it should have been done.

Either through boredom or resentment he'd piled up mistakes and peccadilloes. Some customers, when they came back for an additional purchase, recalled these lapses sufficiently well to tell Manille that this time they wanted nothing to do with Rudy Descas.

But in Madame Menotti's case he'd gone to a lot of trouble.

"How's your wife?" Cathie asked.

Startled, he blinked, and wriggled helplessly.

"Fine, fine."

"And the little boy?"

"Djibril? Fine, yes, I think."

Now she seemed to be gazing at him with the same taunting, rather distant smile as the man with the beret shortly before.

He was seized with panic.

What was she smiling about in her reddish halo?

And once within he cannot go back.

"You've really got no idea what Menotti wants from me?" he asked in an offhand way, knowing perfectly well that it was useless to pursue the matter but unable to make up his mind to leave without trying to get some clarification on Madame Menotti's concerns but also on the incomprehensible trials of his own life, of his whole existence.

He cannot go back.

Cathie stared at her screen, conspicuously ignoring him.

It then struck him that once he'd left the room he wouldn't get back in, that he wouldn't be allowed back in, and that people preferred, for a reason he couldn't discern, not to tell him so just yet—because they were afraid of him, perhaps?

"I did everything I could for Menotti, you know? Since I began working here I've never gone to so much trouble as I have over that blasted kitchen. I put in hours of uncounted overtime."

He was calm and he could feel his face radiating the warmth of his calm, light smile.

The sharp pain in his anus was also subsiding.

Since Cathie went on stubbornly pretending not to notice his presence, and because he suddenly thought that if he didn't come back to the office he would perhaps never see her again, he leaned down toward the tiny pink lobe of her almost translucent ear, and whispered, softly, calmly (as softly and calmly, he thought, as the young man he'd once been):

"I ought to bump off Manille, don't you think?"

She moved her head sharply away from his.

"Rudy, just back off!"

He raised his eyes and, through the picture window, looked once again at Manille's sunlit villa with its imposing, disproportionately large entrance bay, at this big low house very similar to those that rich businesspeople built for themselves in the part of town known as Les Almadies, and indeed very comparable, he said to himself, his heart missing a beat, yes indeed, very comparable, to the villa built by his father Abel Descas, who'd chosen to have his shutters painted not in the Provençal blue now popular everywhere but in a dark red that reminded him of his Basque origins, not suspecting, how could he—

but he cannot go back

—a red hardly less dark than the blood of his friend and partner would stain forever the very white, porous stone he'd chosen for the terrace.

Yes, Rudy thought, ambitious men like Manille or Abel Descas (whose strong legs were never obliged to graciously bend at the knee, were firmly planted on the ground) built houses that looked alike because they were the same sort of men, even though Rudy's father would have laughed at, or rather taken umbrage at, being compared to the owner of a kitchen dealership, he—Abel

Descas—who early on had left his province, crossed Spain and a bit of the Mediterranean, then Morocco and Mauritania, before pulling up in his valiant old Ford on the banks of the Senegal River, where—he straightaway said to himself, as he strove already to fashion his little family legend—he would found a vacation resort the likes of which the world had never seen.

Oh yes, Rudy thought, men of that sort, whose aims were practical but just as ardent as any aspiration of the spirit, never felt themselves struggling day after day against the icy blast of some endless, monotonous, subtly degrading dream.

Since he felt that Cathie was rigid with fear, her tiny immobile eyes striving desperately to avoid his own, he couldn't stop himself adding, before moving away from her desk, in a slightly trembling voice:

"If you had any idea all the tenderness I've got stored up inside me!"

She gave an involuntary throaty gurgle.

His father and Manille, although formidable in their different ways, weren't the sort of men to make women afraid, whereas he, good God, how had it come to that?

He picked up from his own desk Mummy's brochures, rolled them up, and stuffed them in a trouser pocket.

He crossed the large sunlit room, aware that his colleagues were probably watching him go with relief, or contempt, or something else he could only guess at.

. And yet, as he was approaching the glass door, his movements still affected by the sharp pain in his rectum, his thighs separated even though no excess of muscle pushed them away from each other (for he had slender, almost thin legs, and yet he was walking a bit like his father or Manille, men whose massive thighs forced their knees apart), he was amused at the thought that his colleagues had perhaps found in him their angel.

He moved forward, haloed in shimmering blondness, just as in the past when he left his little apartment in Le Plateau and walked calmly down the hot avenue, serenely conscious of the solid decency of his heart and the unalloyed plenitude of his honor.

He would like to have shouted to his colleagues in a nice, kindly, charming, unaffectedly cheerful way, "I am the Minister my mother talked to you about!"

Hadn't there been a time, he remembered uneasily, when Mummy used to bleach the pale flaxen hair of her little Rudy so that it looked even blonder, almost white?

He remembered the unpleasant odor of the peroxide, which ended up making him dazed and sleepy, sitting on a stool in the kitchen of the house where Manille had just informed him he'd spent so many Wednesdays, so Rudy must have been quite young when Mummy got it into her head to inflict on him that most conventional feature of the angelic aspect, because these sessions had been interrupted when they'd left to join Rudy's father in Africa.

Perhaps, he said to himself, Mummy had thought that the natural blondness of his hair would more than suffice over there to establish him as a seraph, or else she'd not dared to carry on with the practice in the presence of her husband, who, with incredulous, derisive bluntness, had dumped his own guardian angel and galloped off even farther into the shadows of his cynical calculations, of his more or less secret, more or less lawful, schemes and dodges.

"I'm your messenger from the order of Thrones!" he wanted to shout out, but he demurred, not wishing to look at his colleagues.

Suddenly, it pleased him to think that they would perhaps at that precise moment welcome such a revelation, as they saw him pass by in front of them with his rather stiff walk and his legs bizarrely spread, but for all that haloed with a fearsome, luminous majesty and sunny brilliance.

He hadn't been able to protect Fanta.

He'd claimed to be the guardian, in France, of her social fragility, but he'd let her down.

He pushed the door open and entered the showroom.

Manille's two customers were now at the stage of choosing the stools for the breakfast bar, where, Rudy was ready to bet, they were never going to eat, would never so much as lean their elbows upon to drink a cup of coffee, preferring the inconvenient little table they'd always used up till then. He knew they'd find a way of sneaking that table back into the brand-new kitchen that Manille would build for them, and when their children visited, and were astonished, almost to the point of anger, to see that they had reinstalled their greasy old table, with its grooves full of crumbs, at the end of the breakfast bar, blocking access to the fridge, they would, thought Rudy, justify themselves by saying that it was only temporary and that they would get rid of their dear table as soon as they found the right little piece of furniture for setting down their bags and cartons whenever they returned from shopping, which furnishing they still lacked.

Manille was getting them to feel the brown leatherette covers of a pair of dark wooden stools.

He stood beside them, infinitely patient, never pressing, never in a hurry to move on.

The man heard Rudy's footsteps from afar and looked up.

Rudy thought that he gazed at him more insistently than one might ordinarily, with an affable, friendly look, and he was moved.

Rudy had the impression that the man was making as if to raise his beret in greeting.

And whereas he would normally have been worried and embarrassed by a gesture like that and by such an insistent gaze, fearing some unpleasantness to come, he told himself cheerfully that the man may simply just have seen him somewhere before.

I am the spirit of the order of Dominions!

Yes, the guy had perhaps seen one of Mummy's tracts and, watching the haloed Rudy pass by, his heart had evidently been touched by a feeling of beatitude.

"Art thou the one that is to take care of me?" his look seemed to ask.

How to answer that?

Rudy smiled broadly, something he normally avoided because he was aware that rapture, like fear, caused his lips to twist and made him look nasty.

He mouthed, looking the guy straight in the eye, "I am the little Master of the Virtues!"

He hurried out of the showroom.

He was overcome by the heat in the parking lot. It brought him back down to earth.

Not, he mumbled, that anyone could reproach him for having knowingly abandoned Fanta to her lonely exile, and as for the fact that she didn't have the precise qualifications to teach in France, that wasn't his fault.

And yet what never left him was the certainty that he'd deceived her in bringing her here, since he'd turned his face away from hers and spurned the mission, implicitly accepted when they were still abroad, of watching over her.

The thing was, he was then recovering from utter mortification!

What a beating he received, what a beating!

It sometimes seemed that he could still feel it whenever he raised his arms, but especially when a smell of hot fuel oil arose from the baking asphalt of Manille's parking lot. Then with painful clarity he saw himself again lying prone on a similar asphalt surface softened by the heat, his back and shoulders crushed by sharp knees, his face swollen as he struggled to get up, to avoid all contact with the dusty, sticky tar.

Years later, that vision still made him blush with shame and astonishment.

But now he felt, for the first time, how automatic that response had become.

He breathed in deeply, soaking up the acrid smell.

He realized then that the opprobrium had left him.

Yes, it was certainly he whom teenagers from the Lycée Mermoz had beaten up before hurling him to the ground, crushing his chest against the asphalt, and ending up pushing his face, which he'd tried to keep clear of the ground, against the surface of the courtyard. It was still his cheek that would now always bear the fine scars, it was his shoulders that still ached slightly, and yet the abjection no longer clung to him, not that he could or would pass it on to someone else, but rather because he felt he'd accepted it and that now he had the chance of freeing himself of it, as from a recurrent, unending, cold, terrifying dream to which you submit, grinning and bearing it, in the knowledge that you're now going to be able to break free.

He, Rudy Descas, sometime literature teacher at the Lycée Mermoz and medieval specialist, no longer embodied the infamy he'd suffered.

He'd lost all honor and dignity and returned to France, dragging Fanta with him, knowing that the stigma would pursue him, because he'd internalized it and convinced himself that he was no more than that, even while hating it and fighting it.

And now that he was starting to accept it, he felt a great weight had been taken off his shoulders.

Now he could calmly and quietly review in his mind the images of that violent humiliation—and the humiliation no longer bore much relation to him as he was, at that moment, standing in the warm, dry air, and the dense, oppressive mass that had weighed down his heart and filled his chest he now saw leaving him, dissolving, as he remembered clearly the faces of the three boys who'd assaulted him and could even still smell on his nape the slightly sour breath (fear? excitement?) of the one who'd held him down—the three faces, so dusky and so beautiful in their unblemished youth, which only the day before in class with the others had looked up at him with a concentrated, innocent air as they listened to him talking about Rutebeuf.

He saw their faces again without being upset by it.

He wondered, "Well, what could they be doing now, those three?"

He began walking toward his car, putting each foot down firmly for the sheer pleasure of feeling the stickiness of the tar and hearing it detach itself with a tiny sound like a kiss.

He saw it all again without being upset by it.

How hot it was!

The hot poker in his anus again.

Yes, he saw it all again and . . .

What happiness, he said to himself.

He scratched himself, not without pleasure, aware that the itching would no longer lower him into the same abyss of anger and despair, that he no longer had any reason to consider these ordinary evils as a punishment or a demonstration of his inferiority.

He was now able to . . .

He laid his fingers on the red-hot handle of the car door.

He didn't take them off straightaway.

It burned him and it wasn't pleasant, but he seemed to perceive more clearly by contrast the new lightness of his spirit, the weight lifted from his chest, and the release of his heart.

Free at last! he said to himself.

How was that?

How could that be?

He gazed for a long time around him at the big black or gray cars of his colleagues and at the road in front of the parking lot lined with warehouses and villas. He raised his head to expose his face to the infernal sun.

Free at last!

Very well, he could go all the way despite the flush of embarrassment that he felt on the forehead he was proffering to the sky, he could very well go the whole way and test his newfound freedom by acknowledging, for the first time, that the three teenagers had not attacked him.

What remained within him of the old Rudy Descas objected.

But he held fast, even if the start of a panic attack, a feeling of helplessness, now made him shiver.

He opened the car door and flopped onto the seat.

It was stifling inside the vehicle.

He tried, however, to take in a big lungful of this overcooked air to calm himself down and banish the fear, the awful fear that was creeping up on him at the thought that, if he admitted that the boys had not attacked him, he also had to concede that it was he, Rudy Descas, literature teacher at the Lycée Mermoz in Dakar, who'd hurled himself on one of them, prompting the two others to come to their friend's aid.

True?

Yes, that's what must really have happened, eh, Rudy?

His eyes began to fill with acrid tears.

He'd worked so hard at persuading himself of the contrary that he was no longer sure what was true and what wasn't.

He was no longer sure.

He reached behind him, grabbed his old towel, and dabbed his eyes.

But could he glimpse the truth and not be afflicted by it?

Under the midday sun stretched the sizzling tar of the lycée's vast courtyard.

Rudy Descas was leaving the premises, happy, with a spring in his step, a young teacher loved by his pupils and by his colleagues, who included his wife, Fanta, and he had no need then—Rudy said to himself without bitterness—no need to imagine himself some minister of divine will just to feel himself haloed with benevolence and an air of subtle triumph and refined ambition.

The tar was clinging slightly to the soles of his loafers.

The contact had filled him with joy and he was still smiling to himself as he passed through the school gate. This smile had spread like an involuntary gesture of benediction upon the three teenagers who were waiting in the meager shade of a mango tree, their faces shining in the midday sun.

The three were all pupils of his.

Rudy Descas knew them well.

He felt a particular affection for them because they were black and came from modest backgrounds. One of them, he understood, was the son of a fisherman in Dara Salam, the village where Rudy and his parents had once lived.

Sitting in his car in Manille's parking lot, Rudy remembered what he always used to feel at that time, whenever his gaze fell on the fisherman's son: an exaggerated, resolute, anxious friendship that bore no relationship to the boy's particular qualities and that could suddenly turn to hatred without Rudy's realizing it, or even understanding that hatred, until it was no longer friendship that he actually felt for his pupil.

For the boy's face forced him to think of Dara Salam.

Horror-struck, he struggled against any vision of Dara Salam.

And this struggle mutated into a disproportionate affection for the teenager, an affection that was probably hatred.

But under the full midday sun of this unchanging, sweltering day in the dry season, as he was leaving the lycée happy and at peace with himself, his smile had enveloped the three boys equally, had flowed toward them, content, impersonal, with all the exquisiteness of an anointment.

Had the fisherman's son suddenly managed to guess that Rudy Descas's extreme kindness toward him was but a desperate way of containing the antagonism his Dara Salam face inspired in his teacher?

Was it that—the barely concealed hatred—which the teacher's smile obviously conveyed in the off-white glare of the midday sun?

The hot air quivered.

No puff of wind shook the gray leaves of the mango tree.

Rudy Descas felt so lucky, so flourishing, in those days.

Little Djibril had been born two years earlier. He was a smiling, voluble child. His forehead was not marked with a puzzled frown. Unlike later . . . when he would feel afraid of his father and uncomfortable in his presence.

Rudy had applied for a teaching post at a foreign university and his final interview with the head of the department of medieval literatures had gone splendidly. He was in no doubt, so certain about the outcome, that, out of sheer vanity, he'd already phoned Mummy to tell her he'd gotten the job.

Your son, the guardian of your mature years, a university teacher with a doctorate in literature.

Yes, life was good.

Even if it wasn't Fanta's nature to say so, he was sure she loved him, and through him the life they'd made together in the fine apartment they'd recently rented in Le Plateau.

He occasionally felt that Fanta loved Djibril even more than she loved him—that she loved the child with a similar, but much stronger love—whereas he'd believed that her love for him would merely be different in kind, and that he wouldn't lose out.

Now he thought he had lost out, that she'd rather drifted away from him.

But it scarcely mattered.

He then became so concerned about Fanta's well-being that

he accepted, even was pleased, that she was happy, even if it was rather at his expense.

So, yes, in this perfect life, it was only the memories of Dara Salam, which he had to struggle with every time he saw the teenager, that foreshadowed possible disaster ahead.

The young man had emerged from the shade of the mango tree, slowly, with effort, as if obliged to confront Rudy's fearsome smile.

In a calm, clear, decisive manner, he shouted:

"Son of a murderer!"

And, Rudy had said to himself later—and now in Manille's parking lot was once again saying to himself—that he'd been stabbed, literally, not just by what had been said but by the calm self-assurance in the voice of the boy, who hadn't had the tact, hadn't even taken the trouble, to insult him.

Without meaning to, the fisherman's son had uttered nothing but the plain and simple truth, because that was what it was: the truth. Perhaps it was only the teacher's smile, a false, suave smile, full of fear and hatred, that had allowed the truth to come out.

Rudy had dropped his briefcase.

Without knowing or understanding what he was going to do, he'd grabbed the boy by the throat.

Rudy was deeply shaken to feel under his thumbs the warm, moist, ringed tube of the boy's windpipe. He remembered that more vividly than anything else, and as he squeezed the boy's throat he recalled thinking only of the tender flesh of little Djibril, his son, whom he bathed every evening.

Without thinking, he stopped and turned his hands over and looked at them.

He seemed to feel again at the tips of his fingers, on the fleshy part of the first phalanges, that sensation of gentle resistance that had intoxicated him, and the floating, firm bump of the boy's Adam's apple that, drunk with exultant fury, he'd pressed so hard.

It was the first time in his life that he'd suffered such a fit of anger, the first time he'd hurled himself at anyone, and it was as if he was at last discovering his true nature, what he was made of and what gave him pleasure.

He'd heard himself groaning, gasping from the effort—unless it was the boy's grunts that he mistook for his own.

He'd pushed the teenager into the lycée courtyard, still clutching his throat, which he was squeezing with all his strength.

The young man had begun to sweat profusely.

Enough, enough of being nice, repeated a small, ferocious, triumphant voice in Rudy's head.

What had he said, the bastard?

"What's that you said, eh? Son of a murderer? Okay, then let's be true to our blood, eh?"

Were they of the same nature, the blood of his father's partner that had stained forever the fine porous stone of the terrace, and Abel Descas's own blood spattering the wall of his cell in Reubeuss prison, and the blood of this boy, the son of the Dara Salam fisherman, that would not fail to pour from his skull if Rudy managed to knock him over in the courtyard and then dash his head against the ground?

"Bastard," he'd growled mechanically, without being able to understand clearly why he was insulting the person who was giving him so much physical pleasure.

A violent pain shot through his back and shoulders.

He'd felt the neck soaked in sweat slipping through his fingers.

First his knees, then his chest, had hit the ground hard, taking his breath away.

He'd tried keeping his head as far off the ground as possible until some hand forced it down, grazing his cheek and forehead against the pebbles in the asphalt.

He'd heard the boys panting and hurling abuse at him.

Their voices were feverish but perplexed and without venom, as if the words they were hurling at him were just a part of the treatment he had brought on himself, which he'd obliged them to administer.

They were now wondering what to do with him, their literature teacher, whom they were kneeing hard in the back, not grasping, Rudy realized, quite how much they were hurting him.

Were they afraid, if they let him go, that he would attack them again?

He'd tried to mumble that it was over, that they had nothing to fear from him.

He succeeded only in dribbling on the asphalt.

His lips, crushed against the ground, had, in his attempt to move, gotten badly scraped.

Rudy switched on the ignition, put the car into reverse, and the old Nevada, chugging and smoking, moved out.

And whereas, for the past four years, he'd been studiously cultivating the theory of the profound cruelty of the three boys who, just for the hell of it, had sadistically attacked him, he knew now that it had all been a lie—oh, he'd always known it, but he'd refused to acknowledge it, and now he was refusing no longer, remembering the kindness, embarrassment, and astonishment he'd picked up from what the teenagers were saying as they held him down, unwittingly causing him a degree of pain he would never completely recover from, because they were searching for a way out of the situation that preserved their own dignity and security and also their teacher's, showing no desire for vengeance nor any wish to go hard on him, despite the fear and suffering he'd caused the boy from Dara Salam.

He'd understood—listening to them as they talked, with stupefaction but not rancor, nervously above him—that they fully realized, with their adolescent good sense, that their teacher had probably just lost it, even if it was the last thing they would have expected from that particular teacher.

Whereas he, Rudy, in fact hated the boy from Dara Salam.

Whereas he had, in fact, up to that moment in Manille's parking lot, hated all three of them, whom, in his heart, he'd held responsible for his forced return to the Gironde, for his troubles, for all his misfortunes.

There could be no doubt, he said to himself as he drove out of the lot and onto the road, that anger, illusion, and a general feeling of resentment had taken hold of him at that moment—when he'd chosen to cast himself as the boys' victim rather than seeing the facts plain: that he'd long harbored feelings of hatred, wrapped up in a smiling show of friendship, an animus issuing directly from Dara Salam, where Abel Descas had murdered his business partner.

Oh yes: no doubt, he said to himself, his present state of *dis*grace stemmed from that, from his cowardice, from his smug self-pity.

He went back the way he'd come an hour earlier, but at the rotary he went a little farther around the statue before turning into a wide road bordered by high banks, at the end of which stood Madame Menotti's house.

Just as he was wondering if it would be all right to ask Menotti if he could use her phone to try to get in touch with Fanta (what was she doing, good God, what was she thinking?), he saw right in front of him the pale breast and vast brown wings of a low-flying buzzard.

He took his foot off the accelerator.

The buzzard flew straight at the windshield.

It gripped the wipers with its claws. It rammed its abdomen against the glass.

Rudy shouted in surprise and braked sharply.

The buzzard did not budge.

With its wings spread out across the windshield, its head turned to one side, it glared at him with a horridly severe yellow eye.

Rudy honked.

The buzzard's whole breast shuddered. It seemed to be tightening its grip on the windshield wipers and, still giving Rudy a cold, accusing look, it screeched like an angry cat.

Slowly, he got out of the car.

He left the door open, not daring to get near the bird, which had moved its head slightly to continue watching him, now staring at him stubbornly, icily, with its other eye.

And, melting with anxious tenderness, Rudy thought, Good little god of Mummy's, nice little father, please let nothing have happened to Fanta.

He stretched out a hand, slightly shaking, toward the buzzard.

It let go of the wipers and screeched again, angrily, in a cry of irrevocable condemnation, and flew off, flapping its heavy wings.

As it rose above Rudy's head one of its claws grazed his forehead.

He could feel a heavy wingbeat against his hair.

He flung himself back into the car and slammed the door.

He was panting so hard that for a moment he thought the sound was being uttered by someone else—but no, these panicky, bewildered, hissing gasps were coming from his own mouth.

He grabbed the towel on the backseat and wiped his forehead.

Then he gazed for a long time, vacantly, at the bloodstained towel.

How was he going to convince Fanta that he now saw their situation in a whole new light?

How could he make her understand that, whatever he'd said to her that morning (if indeed those grotesque words he wasn't sure of remembering had truly passed his lips), he was a changed man, and that there was no more room, in the heart of this changed man, for anger and deceit?

Probing the wound on his forehead carefully with his finger, he said to himself fearfully, It was no longer necessary, Fanta, to send that avenging bird to me—really there wasn't . . .

Stunned, he set off again, driving with one hand, and with the other, unable to stop himself, fingering the crescent-shaped scratch on his forehead.

"It's not fair," he kept saying mechanically to himself, "it's really not fair."

A little farther on he stopped in front of Madame Menotti's house.

The road was lined with modest farmhouses that wealthy couples had bought and restored, eager to conceal the buildings' humble origins (short roof, low ceilings, narrow windows) with a good deal of lavish, meticulous interior decoration, or at least to make the shortcomings seem the result of deliberate choice, just like the copper piping, Moroccan floor tiles, and the vast bathtub set into the floor.

Rudy had realized that Madame Menotti's modest income scarcely made it possible for her outlay ever to match her neighbors' luxurious, obsessive extravagance, and that, for her, a new kitchen would remain the only manifestation of a sudden mad longing for comfort and splendor.

He'd also noted, with considerable anxiety and annoyance, that there was one realm in which Madame Menotti went a long way toward making up for her relative poverty. Within himself he referred to it as "wreaking almighty havoc."

He got out of the car.

He saw at once that Madame Menotti's wild, destructive, ham-fisted willfulness had dealt a mortal blow to an old wisteria root, thick as a tree trunk, that had been planted near the front door probably half a century earlier.

The first time Rudy had come to the house, thick bunches of sweet-smelling mauve flowers were hanging under the gutters, above the door and windows, clinging to a wire that the former owners had strung along the front of the building.

He'd stood on tiptoe to sniff the flowers, deeply moved, enchanted by so much beauty and fragrance offered free of charge, and he'd then congratulated Madame Menotti on the luxuriance of her wisteria, which reminded him, he said—oh yes, he, who never spoke of his past life, had let that slip—of the frangipani blossoms in Dara Salam.

He'd seen Madame Menotti purse her lips in a mixture of skepticism and vague annoyance—just like, he'd said to himself, a mother who had favorites being complimented on the child she didn't care for.

In a tone of dry condescension she'd complained about having to sweep up the leaves in autumn: so much dead foliage, so many shriveled petals.

She'd shown Rudy how, at the corner of the house, she'd already dealt with an enormous bignonia that had had the nerve to let its wild tangle of orange flowers climb all over the gray roughcast walls.

The slender branches, the glossy leaves, the strong roots, the dead corollas, all that lay on the ground waiting to be thrown on the bonfire, and Madame Menotti, as the heroine of a battle she'd won hands down, had pointed to it proudly and scornfully.

Crestfallen, Rudy had followed her in a tour around the garden. There was nothing but the pathetic remnants of a struggle that had been as absurd, as ferocious, as it had been reckless.

Madame Menotti wanted to clean everything up, make the place tidy, and lay down a lawn. In a destructive frenzy she'd taken it out on the hornbeam hedge (scalped), on the old walnut tree (sawn off at the root), and on the many rosebushes (dug up). After thinking better of it, she'd replanted the rosebushes elsewhere; now they were dying.

Madame Menotti still pressed on, satisfied that her acts of vandalism had established her proprietary rights. Seeing her fat bottom wobble as she moved between two piles of hundred-year-old box that she'd uprooted, Rudy had felt that, for her, it was as if nothing better demonstrated her omnipotence than the destruction of patient labors, of the memorials to the delicate, simple taste of all those numberless ghosts who had preceded her in that house and who had planted, sown, and arranged the vegetation in the garden.

And he was now discovering that Madame Menotti had cut down the wisteria.

He wasn't surprised. He was devastated.

The little house stood there, austere, stripped bare, sadly reduced to the mediocrity, which the leaves had concealed, of the materials used in building it.

Of the magnificent plant only a short stump remained.

Rudy walked slowly toward the garden gate.

He looked at the bare facade and sobbed.

Madame Menotti had opened her door when she heard the car approaching. She found Rudy standing at the gate, his cheeks wet with tears.

She was wearing a purple tracksuit.

She had short gray hair and glasses with thick black plastic frames that made her look perpetually cross. When she took them off, Rudy had already noticed, her face was that of a helpless, lost woman.

"You'd no right to do that!" he cried.

"Do what?" Madame Menotti looked exasperated.

Then he felt in his mouth again that taste of iron, that vague taste of blood that welled up in his throat whenever he thought of Madame Menotti and of what he still had to do despite all he'd already done and that for some obscure reason, perhaps out of weariness, he'd failed to do and then forgotten about.

He now recalled only the lapse, not what the lapse had involved.

"The wisteria!" he exclaimed. "It wasn't yours!"

"It wasn't mine?" Madame Menotti shouted.

"It belonged . . . to itself, to everybody."

His words were distorted and his voice faded away in embarrassment as he realized how futile his protest was.

It was too late, too late, in any case.

Should he not have attempted to save such an admirable wisteria?

How could he have imagined that Madame Menotti would spare it?

Once he'd witnessed her brutality toward a nature that in her eyes represented the enemy, the threat of invasion, how could he have turned his back on the wisteria, whose death sentence had been pronounced the moment she'd alluded sharply to the chore of sweeping up dead leaves?

He opened the gate and climbed up a few steps to her door.

The house now stood isolated in the middle of its grassy plot. The sun beat down on Madame Menotti.

The wisteria had given gentle shade to this same terrace, to these same concrete steps, recalled Rudy, grief stricken, and hadn't there also been, in the corner, a large bay tree that smelled of spices in the warm air?

Gone, the bay tree, like everything else.

"Monsieur Descas, you're an incompetent, you're a monster."

His eyes still damp with tears, but indifferent to what she might be thinking (it was as if shame could no longer reach him, however hard it tried), he met Madame Menotti's scandalized gaze.

He realized that she had gone well beyond the point of indignation, that she was now close to despair, to a sort of intoxication, wandering in a gray zone in which the slightest hitch must seem to her like a deliberate act of aggression.

He realized too that she was absolutely sincere, in her way.

A vague feeling of pity was now vying with a sense of grievance inside him. He suddenly felt downcast and very tired.

Once again his anus was itching painfully. Thinking with weary diffidence about the demise of the wisteria and without a thought for Madame Menotti's modesty or his own, he scratched himself fiercely, vigorously, through the thickness of his jeans.

Madame Menotti appeared not to notice.

She now seemed to hesitate between the need to bring him in (he was getting an inkling as to the nature of the problem, what she held against him) and an almost equally strong desire never to have anything to do with him again.

Finally she turned on her heels and gestured to him brusquely to follow her.

She was so upset, he could see her shoulders quivering.

It was the first time he'd been back to the house since he'd come to measure for the kitchen several months earlier.

Then, as he crossed the hall and the dining room behind her, a painful process of realization began. He felt an icy grip in the pit of his stomach as the dimensions of the problem became clearer to him. Then the brutal truth hit him.

He stopped in the kitchen doorway.

Horror-struck, he had difficulty restraining a hysterical fit of the giggles.

Without realizing it he started scratching himself frantically while Madame Menotti flopped onto a chair that was still wrapped in plastic.

She kept savagely pushing her glasses up her nose, to no purpose.

Her knee was quivering uncontrollably.

"Oh my God, oh my God," Rudy blurted out.

He felt himself blushing furiously with humiliation.

How, after so much hard work, had he managed to get his arithmetic so badly wrong?

He knew he wasn't very good at it, but when it came to designing the kind of kitchens he despised he'd secretly taken pride in his deficiencies, so much so that his arrogance had kept him from achieving any notable improvement in his skills.

He simply didn't wish to be good at the job.

It had seemed to him that his stubbornness was a bulwark against the complete disintegration of the erudition acquired in his former life: those arcane, those subtle bits of knowledge that he'd not had the strength, courage, or desire to cultivate and sustain and that were gradually losing their preciseness and substance.

But such an error was merely ridiculous, pitiful, and in no way a credit to the refined man he considered himself to have been; no, in no way, he thought, aghast.

He moved forward cautiously.

His eyes met Madame Menotti's and he remembered the wisteria. Still bearing the grudge, he looked away. Madame Menotti's gaze would now have appeared drained of the scandalized hatred he'd seen earlier, but he refused to meet it, thinking, I refuse to communicate with her, if that's what she expects.

Because he had the impression that she now felt a kind of dismay that was directed at no one in particular and was actually a plea for help and support, as if they were both looking at the consequences of an act of madness committed by someone else.

He then dared to venture toward the middle of the room, toward the square worktop with its marble and slate surface containing a vast cooktop under a bell-shaped hood, the centerpiece of this petrified, intimidating spectacle that had come to represent for Madame Menotti the essence of the concept "kitchen."

The counter was in place and the hood was attached to the ceiling.

But the cooktop was not under the hood but well to the side. Rudy understood at once that if one tried to move the counter in order to position the cooktop correctly, it would be impossible to maneuver around it easily.

Called upon to invest all his intelligence and mental stamina in making those calculations, he'd simply proved incapable of determining precisely the proper positioning of a four-burner cooktop relative to its hood.

"They're going to give you the sack, at Manille's," Madame Menotti said in a flat tone of voice.

"I fear so," murmured Rudy.

"I was going to invite a few friends in to see the kitchen tomorrow, now I'll have to cancel all that."

"Yes, probably a good idea," said Rudy.

Exhausted, he drew up a chair that was still in its packaging and flopped onto it.

How was he going to persuade himself that getting fired from Manille's wasn't a disaster?

What would become of the three of them?

He felt all the more inept because if he'd had the guts to probe the diffuse, nagging, subliminal awareness he'd had for a while that he was guilty of a particular form of carelessness in the case of Menotti, he could have pulled back in time to correct the mistake before building work began.

But he'd simply suppressed that awareness, not to be troubled by it, in much the same way, he thought, as he'd buried, far out of reach until today, the truth about the Dara Salam boy, the whole Dara Salam saga.

What would become of the three of them if he lost his job?

"Actually, I knew it," he murmured, "I knew I'd made a mistake!"

"Oh yes?" said Menotti.

"Yes, yes . . . I should have . . . dared to face up to the fact . . . to the possibility that I'd made a mistake, but I chose to close my eyes to it."

He looked at Madame Menotti, who took off her glasses and wiped them on her T-shirt, and he noticed that her face was calm, as if, everything having been said about the matter, there was no reason to go on feeling so cross about it.

He also noticed that the woman had fine features that were usually hidden behind her heavy glasses.

What would become of them?

His mortgage payments amounted to five hundred euros a month. What was going to happen to the house, to their family life?

"Would you like a cup of coffee?" Madame Menotti asked.

Somewhat surprised, he nodded.

He remembered the pleasant smell of coffee on Manille's breath.

"I've been dying for a coffee for quite some time," he said, his eyes following Madame Menotti as she hauled herself to her feet, grabbed a coffeepot, filled it with water, and then perched on the edge of the new countertop to pour a measure of coffee into the filter.

"All the same," he couldn't help saying, "that wisteria can't have been bothering you, it was so beautiful."

Absorbed by what she was doing, Madame Menotti didn't turn around or attempt an answer.

Her sneakers dangled above the floor.

He suddenly remembered other feet not touching the ground or scarcely appearing to touch it, the swift, indefatigable feet of Fanta flying above the pavements of Dakar, and he said to himself, That wisteria I cut down, and with bitter sweat pouring down his face he added, That's the wisteria I cut down, it wasn't bothering me and it was so beautiful. And he decided to leave unsaid the harsh things he'd been intending to say to Madame Menotti about the wisteria she'd cut off at the root.

A cold, bitter sweat was pouring down his face.

Nevertheless it seemed to him, in the light of what he was now prepared to admit to himself, that he was beginning to emerge from an old dream, from the old and unbearable dream in which, whatever he could say, whatever he could do . . .

"Here's your coffee," Madame Menotti said.

She poured some for herself and went back to sit on her chair. The plastic covering squeaked every time she moved.

They sipped their coffee in silence, and at last Rudy felt good, at peace with himself. The cold, bitter sweat on his forehead was beginning to dry, even though he realized that, objectively speaking, his situation had never been so depressing.

"I won't find work around here," he said calmly, as if he were talking about someone else.

And Madame Menotti replied in the same calm, detached tone of voice, licking her lips to show she'd finished her coffee and greatly enjoyed it, "No, not much chance of finding work around here."

Slightly embarrassed, he asked, "May I use your phone?"

She led him into her sitting room and pointed to the telephone on a pedestal table.

She kept pushing her glasses up her nose to little effect, but otherwise remained motionless by his side, not so much to keep an eye on him, he gathered, as to not be left alone in her bungled kitchen.

"You don't have a cell phone?"

"No," he replied, "it was too expensive."

Shame dealt a blow against the still-fragile carapace of his lucidity and self-esteem, but such attacks were routine, and he felt it was his duty not to give in to them, not to wallow in the paradoxical comfort of such a familiar sensation.

"It was really too expensive," he repeated, "and it was something I could do without."

"You did the right thing, then."

"Like your kitchen," he added, "too expensive and something you could have done without."

Gazing rather sadly before her, she said nothing.

For Madame Menotti it was still too soon, he felt, and it was more than she was capable of, to give up the hopes of happiness, frivolity, consistency, and peace enshrined in the supposed perfection of a kitchen from Manille's.

Besides, wasn't it what he'd implicitly promised her, when she'd phoned in distress one night and when he'd felt her resolution flagging, and he'd pointed out that she'd no chance of enjoying an enviably harmonious and well-ordered existence in an old kitchen with mismatched furnishings?

He dialed his own number again.

He let it ring for a long time, so long indeed that if Fanta had picked up the phone at that point he would have felt more anxiety than relief.

Next to the phone was the local directory. To while away the time he picked it up, thumbed through it with one hand, and deliberately went straight to the name of Gauquelan, the sculptor, and with a touch of unease noted that he lived not far away, in a new development occupied by wealthy former city dwellers who, like Madame Menotti's neighbors and to a lesser extent Madame Menotti herself, had bought rural properties that, at great expense, they were renovating.

Later, waiting on the doorstep to say good-bye to Madame Menotti, he thought he could smell the wisteria.

He stood there in the harsh glare of the sun. The heavy, intoxicating scent of the mauve clusters into which, drunk with gratitude, he'd plunged his nose a few weeks earlier now crept up on him once again, and he was deeply moved.

The scent probably came, he said to himself, from the pathetic heap of wisteria by the side of the house. It was spreading its fragrance one last time. Was it not, in its own way, saying, "You've done nothing, you've never tried doing anything for me, and now it's too late and I'm dying, slowly decomposing in my own perfume"?

He was overwhelmed with feelings of resentment.

To hide them, he lowered his head and stuck his hands in his back pockets.

From one of them he pulled out a brochure of Mummy's and brusquely handed it to Madame Menotti.

"They're among us," she read aloud. Puzzled, she asked, "Who are 'they'?"

"Oh, the angels," Rudy said with feigned nonchalance.

She snickered and crumpled up the brochure without opening it.

Feeling hurt on Mummy's behalf and sensing his anger rising again within him, he went quickly down the steps and, almost running, returned to his car.

He drove slowly, aimlessly, thinking there was no point in setting foot in Manille's place again, now that his goose was thoroughly cooked.

A feeling of pique still made it painful for him to think about his failure, because he would have loved to stomp out of Manille's and slam the door behind him rather than find himself sacked for a gross error of calculation on a project to which he'd given so much of himself, but then the dread inspired by the vision of his future was softened by a realization that there was nothing that could be done about it, that it was all in the order of things.

He ought not to crawl before Manille.

His head was spinning a little.

How had he managed to put up with such a life for four years? It was only an academic question, he realized, a purely formal, pretended bafflement, because he knew very well, actually, how people put up with long years of a paltry existence.

What he didn't know, rather, was how he could have fared *not* putting up with those bitter, pathetic years—what kind of man would he have been, what kind of man would he have become, what would have happened had he not settled for such mediocrity?

Would it have been a good thing or would he have fallen still lower than now?

And what would he have done with himself?

Really, it wasn't difficult getting used to a life of self-disgust, bitterness, and disorder.

He'd even gotten used to a state of permanent, barely contained fury, he'd even managed, after a fashion, to get used to his frosty, fraught relations with Fanta and the child.

At the thought that he was going to have to take a quite different view of his domestic situation he felt dizzy again, and although he'd long aspired to rekindle the love and tenderness they'd known before they'd left for France, he felt obscurely anxious. Would Fanta recognize what he'd newly become, wasn't she too weary, too mistrustful, and too skeptical to meet him at this point he'd arrived at?

You've come too late and I'm dying.

Where could she be at this precise moment?

Much as he longed to rejoin Fanta, he was afraid of going back home.

There was no need, Fanta, to send me that horrid avenging bird.

A voice kept cawing in his head: You've come too late, I'm dying, my feet have been cut off, I've fallen on the floor of your unfriendly house, you've come too late.

He was hungry now and Madame Menotti's coffee had made him terribly thirsty.

He was driving slowly with all the windows down along the quiet little road, between the thuja hedges and white fences beyond which occasionally shimmered the bluish water of a swimming pool.

Having left Madame Menotti's area behind, he noted that the neighborhood he was now in consisted of even larger houses, even more luxuriously and more recently restored, and it occurred to him that he was deceiving himself yet again in affecting to drive without a precise destination; he was annoyed to think that he, Rudy Descas, should have been itching to prowl around Gauquelan's place ever since noting the sculptor's address in Madame Menotti's sitting room, and felt he should no doubt admit having wanted to do it for quite a while, ever since he'd read about the municipality's having awarded Gauquelan more than a hundred thousand euros for the statue—whose face so closely resembled Rudy's—that had been installed on the rotary.

Tortured by heat and thirst, he wondered if he was not being cast back into the dangerous eddies of that tiresome, monotonous, degrading dream that left such a bitter aftertaste and from which by sheer force of will he was just beginning to extricate himself.

Should he not forget about Gauquelan, the man who'd inspired so much unjust, spiteful, uncalled-for rage?

Of course he should, and that's certainly what he was going to do—stop thinking that the man was in some mysterious, symbolic way responsible for Rudy's rotten luck, that he'd secretly taken advantage of Rudy's innocence to prosper while he, Rudy . . .

Yes, it was absurd, but merely thinking about it made him gloomy and irritable.

He could see again the photo in the local paper of this Gauquelan, with his missing tooth, fat face, and smug expression, and to Rudy it seemed unquestionable that the man had robbed him of something, just like all those clever, cynical people who benefit from the inability of the Rudy Descases of this world to get their grip of the brass ring.

That pathetic artist, Gauquelan, had succeeded because Rudy was languishing in poverty. In Rudy's eyes it was no coincidence: he couldn't shake the notion of cause and effect.

The other guy was growing fat at his expense.

The idea drove him mad.

What's more . . .

He managed a smile, he forced himself to smile, even though his dry lips were stuck together. Boy, was he thirsty!

What's more . . . it may have been silly, but that's the way it was, it had the perfect luminosity of unprovable truth: while Rudy's little soul was fluttering around unsuspectingly, the other had grabbed hold of it to create his despicable work, the statue of a man who looked like Rudy, even down to his pose of angry, terrified submission.

Yes, it drove him mad to think that, although they'd never met, Gauquelan had made use of him, that people like him exploited for their own benefit the trusting ignorance and weakness of those who failed to take steps to protect themselves.

He pulled up in front of a brand-new, black, wrought-iron gate with tips of gold. Feeling a little giddy, he said to himself that this was where Gauquelan lived, in that big house built of exposed stone blocks freshly scrubbed and pointed.

The tiled roof was new and the windows and shutters gleamed with white paint. On the wide terrace a set of pale wooden table and chairs stood in the shade of a yellow umbrella.

It was impossible, Rudy thought with pain, to be unhappy in a house like that.

How he'd love to live there with Fanta and the child!

The gate was purely notional since—and this was a detail that Rudy found particularly impressive—it defended nothing: on either side of the twin stone pillars there was a gap before the privet hedge began, through which it was easy to pass.

He got out of the car and closed the door gently.

He slipped through the gap and strode quickly to the terrace.

Total silence.

These houses had huge garages, so how could you tell whether anyone was in? Where Rudy or Mummy lived, a car parked outside proved beyond a doubt that the owner was at home.

Bending low, he went around to the back, where he found a door that he supposed opened onto the kitchen.

He pressed the door handle down, as if, he thought, he was letting himself into his own house.

The door opened and he went in, closing it nonchalantly behind him.

He stopped, nevertheless, alert to any sounds.

Then, reassured, he grabbed a bottle of water on the counter, checked that it was unopened, and drank it all, even though the water was barely chilled.

As he drank, he let his eyes wander over Gauquelan's large kitchen.

He noticed at once that it could not have come from Manille's, which offered nothing half as sumptuous, and that irritated him; it was as if Gauquelan had ordered from a more upmarket competitor as a way of further humiliating him.

Nevertheless, as a kitchen connoisseur, he judged it to be a really fine one, far more sophisticated, truth be told, than anything he could have designed.

The centerpiece was an oval counter in pink marble. It rested on a succession of white cupboards that curved elegantly, following the line of the stone.

Hanging over the whole was a glass cube, probably the hood. It seemed to be suspended solely by the miracle of its own refinement.

The floor, paved in traditional style with reddish sandstone flags, shone discreetly in the bright room. It looked as if it had been waxed and polished many times.

Yes, what a marvelous kitchen, he thought in a rage, built to cater every day for a large family gathered for slow-cooked food—he could almost hear a beef stew simmering on the magnificent stove, a professional eight-burner job in shining white enamel.

And yet the setup seemed never to have been used.

The marble surface was dusty, and apart from the bottle of water and a plate of bananas, there was nothing to indicate that anyone cooked or ate under the varnished beams of this big room.

Rudy crossed the kitchen and went into the hall, conscious of the lightness and suppleness of his refreshed, invincible self.

The air conditioning bolstered his self-assurance, because he'd stopped sweating so much.

He felt on his chest and back the cotton of his almost-dry shirt.

Oh, he said to himself in surprise, I'm not afraid of anything now.

He stopped in the doorway of the living room, which was situated opposite the kitchen on the other side of the hall.

He could hear, clearly, the sound of snoring.

Tilting his head forward, he could see an armchair. Sitting in it was a fat elderly man whom he recognized as Gauquelan from the newspaper photo.

With one cheek resting on the wing of the armchair, the man was snoring softly.

His hands rested palms up on his thighs, in an attitude of confidence and abandon.

His half-open lips produced an occasional bubble of saliva that burst when he next breathed out.

Isn't he grotesque, Rudy said to himself, slightly out of breath.

Snoozing peacefully like that while . . .

While what? he wondered, almost suffocated by a dizzying joyful malice.

While in his undefended house his nimble murderer prowls around him?

A murderer with a heart full of hatred?

He felt himself thinking clearly, rapidly.

In one of the drawers (fully retractable, thanks to tracks with shock absorbers) of that perfect kitchen there would no doubt be found a set of butcher's knives, the most fearsome of which could strike at Gauquelan's heart—piercing the thick skin, the muscle, the layer of hard dense fat like that surrounding a rabbit's small heart, thought Rudy, who occasionally bought from Madame Pulmaire at a cut rate one of the large rabbits that she kept in cages scarcely bigger than their occupants and that he was obliged to skin and gut himself even though he loathed it.

He was going to return to the kitchen, get that fantastic knife, and plunge it into Gauquelan's heart.

How calm, strong, and purposeful he felt! How he loved the feeling!

But then what?

Who would be able to link him to Gauquelan?

He alone was privy to the reasons he had for cursing the Gauquelans of this world.

He thought of his old Nevada parked in front of the house and stifled a giggle.

His ghastly car would give him away at once, but it was pretty unlikely that, in this neighborhood, and at this hour, anyone would have noticed it.

And even if they had . . .

He feared nothing now.

He looked hard at Gauquelan. From the living room door he watched this man sleeping—a man who'd shamelessly made so much money, and whose fat hands lay limply, trustingly, on his thighs.

Rudy's anus began itching again. He scratched himself mechanically.

His father, Abel Descas, had been in the habit of taking a siesta in the big, shady living room of the house in Dara Salam, where he used to sit in his wicker chair just as Gauquelan was now in his low armchair—heedless, confident, unaware of the crimes being dreamed up around him and of the crimes about to be hatched in his, for the moment, still heedless, confident mind.

Rudy wiped his hands—they had suddenly started sweating—on his trousers.

If his father's business partner Salif had taken advantage of Abel's siesta—of his afternoon nap and of his heedlessness, his confidence—to stab him, he (Salif) would no doubt still be alive, even today, and the death would have changed nothing as far as Abel's ultimate fate was concerned, since he (Abel) would kill himself a few weeks after Salif's murder.

Salif, Rudy recalled, had been a tall, slender man of slow, careful movements.

Had Salif stood on the threshold of the big, shady room gazing at Abel asleep, imagining that, absorbed in his strange afternoon dreams, Abel knew nothing of the crimes being plotted around him?

Had Salif so hated Rudy's father that, despite seeing the man's upturned palms resting on his thighs, he could have wished to kill him, or had he felt for Abel an affection in no way belied by his attempts to swindle his partner? Were these two tendencies—affection and treachery—present simultaneously in Salif's mind and intentions, but kept distinct, so that the one never interfered with the other?

Rudy had no privileged insight into what his father's partner Salif felt about Abel, and didn't know if Salif had really tried to cheat or whether Abel had mistakenly jumped to that conclusion, but now Rudy's thoughts were, despite himself, going back to the time when his father used to nap in the wicker chair. Rudy's thighs were getting damp and his trousers were clinging to them, and the itch was back with a vengeance. Feeling confused, angry, and upset, he was starting to wriggle once more, clenching and unclenching his buttocks.

Gauquelan hadn't stirred.

When he woke up and rubbed together those hands no longer innocent and carefree but impatient and eager to return to that contemptible métier of his that paid so well, when he laboriously hauled himself out of his dark green crushed-velvet armchair and raised his cold devious eyes to see Rudy Descas standing in the doorway, would he realize that his death—his brutal, misconstrued demise—had been dreamed up by this stranger, or would he think, rather, that he was looking at the unexpected face of a friend, mistaking that look of hatred for one of benevolence?

There must have been an afternoon, Rudy thought in a kind of panic, when his father had awoken from his siesta and from a possibly recurrent, cold, monotonous dream, had rubbed his eyes and face with hands no longer trusting but active and busy, had hauled from his wicker chair the supple heft of his trim, muscular frame, and had left the dark shady room in the quiet house, headed for Salif's office, a bungalow not far away. He was, perhaps, still letting float hazily through his mind the vestiges of a painful, vaguely degrading dream in which his partner was trying to rob him by artificially inflating estimates for the construction of the vacation resort Abel was planning. Perhaps as he walked toward Salif's bungalow he'd not dispelled the fallacy nurtured in some dreams that all the Africans around him had but one aim, to cheat him, even while feeling real affection for him, as Salif did, because those two impulses—friendship and deception—cohabited independently, without blending, in their minds and in their intentions.

Rudy knew he'd been somewhere on the property that afternoon when his father, perhaps carried away by the illusory certainty of a humiliating dream, had struck Salif in front of the bungalow.

He knew too that he'd been about eight or nine at the time, and that during the three years since he and Mummy had rejoined Abel in Dara Salam, a single fear occasionally tempered his bliss, a fear—though Mummy assured him it was groundless—of having perhaps one day to return to France, to the little house where, every Wednesday, a tall lad with straight, smooth legs like young beech trunks had monopolized Mummy's attention, laughter, and love and whose mere adorable presence had transformed Rudy, age five, into a nonentity.

On the other hand, what he couldn't work out was . . .

Without thinking he stepped into the living room and moved toward Gauquelan.

He could now hear the sound of his own heavy breathing, to which the other man's snoring seemed to reply with discreet solicitude, as if to encourage him to calm down and breathe more softly.

What he still couldn't work out was whether he'd been there when his father and Salif had it out, or whether Mummy had described it so graphically that he'd come to believe he'd seen it with his own eyes.

But how and why, then—not having been there herself—could Mummy have described so vividly what she'd only heard second-hand?

Rudy didn't have to close his eyes to re-create the effect of still being there or never having been there, whichever it was, the scene of his father shouting something at Salif, then, without giving him a chance to reply, hitting him hard in the face and knocking him down.

Abel Descas had been a strong man, and however gentle, trusting, and heedless they appeared when he was asleep, his big broad hands were used to handling tools, lifting heavy loads, and carrying sacks of cement, so that a single blow of his fist had been enough to knock Salif down.

But had Rudy really seen the tall, slim body of his father's partner bite the dust, or had he only imagined (or dreamed about) the almost comical way Salif had been flung backward by the force of the blow?

Suddenly he could no longer bear not knowing.

He looked at Gauquelan's hands and fat neck, telling himself that if he resolved to strangle the man it would not be easy, through so much flabby skin and flesh, for his thumbs to find their way to the rings of the windpipe.

Like him, his father, he thought, must sometimes have enjoyed his fits of hot, all-consuming, intoxicating fury, but he also allowed that it had been not rage but pitiless self-control driving Abel when he'd gotten into his 4×4 parked near the bungalow and slowly, calmly, as if setting off on an errand to the village, directed its huge wheels at Salif's body, at the unconscious form of his partner and friend, in whose mind affection and a possible taste for embezzlement had never been confused, and who therefore, if he had indeed cheated Abel, had meant no harm to the friend or even the notion of friendship, but merely, perhaps, to some simple abstraction of a colleague, a blank face.

Still gazing at Gauquelan, Rudy stepped backward, over the doorway to the living room, and stopped once more in the hall.

He covered his mouth with his hand, licked his palm, and nibbled it.

He wanted to snicker, to howl, to shout insults.

What could he do to find out?

What would need to happen for him to know at last?

"Oh God, oh God," he kept repeating. "Kind, sweet, little god of Mummy's, how can I find out, how can I get to understand?"

For what did Mummy herself, who wasn't there, know for certain about Rudy's presence or absence that afternoon in front of the bungalow when Abel, as calm as a man setting off to get bread in the village, had driven over Salif's head?

Was it possible that Mummy had told Rudy about the short, sharp sound, like that of a big insect being squashed, that Salif's skull had made under the wheel of the 4×4, and that Rudy had later dreamed about it until he believed he'd heard it himself?

Mummy was quite capable, he said to himself, of having described such a sound and of having told him about Salif's blood flowing in the dust, reaching the first flagstones of the terrace and staining the porous stone forever.

She was well capable of that, he said to himself.

But had she done it?

He scratched himself frantically but to no avail.

With eyes wide open he could clearly see the courtyard of the bungalow of corrugated iron and wood, the white pavement of the narrow terrace, and his father's big gray vehicle crushing Salif's head in the thick, heavy silence of a hot, white afternoon; panting with sorrow and disbelief, he could summon up the smallest details of that scene, whose colors and sounds never varied, that immutable tableau, which in his mind's eye he could even see from different angles, as if he'd been present in several places at once.

And in his heart of hearts he knew what his father's intentions had been.

Because, afterward, Abel had denied deliberately running Salif over; he'd pled jitteriness and irritation to explain the accident and his crazy driving, claiming that he'd gotten into the car with the sole idea of going for a spin to calm himself.

Rudy knew it was nothing of the sort.

He'd always known that his father had tried to blot the whole thing out, to convince himself that he'd never wanted to rid himself, so dishonorably, of his partner and friend who never in his heart had mixed . . .

He knew that in getting into the car and turning the key Abel was after revenge on Salif, a way of sustaining the pleasure of his exultant rage by pulverizing the man he'd knocked to the ground; Rudy knew it as well as—or even better than—if he'd felt it himself, because it wasn't his neck on the line, there was nothing to gain disputing the point.

So why was he so sure?

Was it because he'd been there and seen the way the car moved and realized that it was a furious, passionate, deliberate act of will that was directing the vehicle at Salif's head?

Rudy ran through the kitchen and out the back door, straight to the gate, and hurled himself through the gap in the hedge.

His shirt caught on the thorns. He pulled it roughly away.

Only when he was sitting in the Nevada again did he dare draw breath.

He gripped the steering wheel and lowered his head onto it.

Groaning softly, hiccupping and choking back his spit, he murmured, "What does it matter, what does it matter!"

Because that wasn't the issue, was it?

How could he be so blind as to believe that the fundamental question was whether, on that terrible afternoon, he'd been present or not?

Because that wasn't the issue.

It now seemed to him that fretting about this so much was just a distraction, albeit a painful one, a way of concealing the insidious progression of untruthfulness, criminality, perverse enjoyment, and insanity.

Trembling, he set off, and at the next junction turned right, to get away from Gauquelan's house as quickly as possible.

Why did he have to, even in the worst circumstances, be so like his father?

Who expected that of him?

He could still see, from where he'd stood in the doorway, Gauquelan's sleeping face and defenseless hands, while his own face had been deceptively calm, and he could recall his deceptively calm thoughts as he wondered in which drawer he'd find the most suitable weapon for killing Gauquelan with a single blow—he, Rudy, with his aspirations to pity and goodness, standing in the doorway of this stranger's living room and, beneath the calm and gentle exterior of a cultivated person, planning an act that, from the point of view of pity and goodness, was inexcusable.

His teeth were chattering.

Who would ever have expected him to be as violent and abject a man as his father, and what did he have to do with Abel Descas anyway?

He, Rudy, had been a specialist in medieval literature and a competent teacher.

The very thought of building a vacation resort for profit filled him with embarrassment and loathing.

So—as he clung to the steering wheel, well aware of driving carelessly and too fast along a country road far from Gauquelan's neighborhood—what inheritance did he feel he had to own up to?

And why should it have been necessary to keep Gauquelan from getting out of his armchair once his hands suddenly no longer seemed vulnerable and childlike . . . ?

Oh, thought Rudy as he swerved through the bends in the road, it wasn't Gauquelan who should never be allowed to awaken from his siesta, with his head full of deceitful visions that rubbing his eyes couldn't dispel, but rather Rudy's father, a man of murderous tendencies firmly, fanatically, rooted in his heart, where friendship and anger, affection for others and the need to destroy them, mingled incessantly.

And wasn't it that man's worthy heir who'd taken pleasure in throttling the Dara Salam boy and—just now—in spying on a stranger fast asleep?

Overcome with self-loathing, Rudy recalled having wept over

the murdered wisteria, and thought about his father's habit of
waxing sentimental about animals, at mealtimes occasionally talking of becoming a vegetarian, and making a show of covering his
ears whenever Mummy strangled a chicken out back.

On entering a village he slowed down and pulled up outside a
grocer's he knew slightly.

A bell tinkled as he opened the glass door.

The smell of cold meat, bread, and confectionary in the window made him realize how hungry he was.

Sounds of shouting and laughter on television filtered through a
curtain of plastic strips separating the shop from the grocer's living
room. The sounds grew louder as the woman slipped through the
curtain, parting the strips carefully to prevent the flies coming in.

Rudy cleared his throat.

The woman waited, her head cocked slightly toward the back
room so that she could go on listening to the program.

In a hoarse voice he asked for a baguette and a slice of ham.

Deftly, confidently, and (he thought, mechanically) with
unwashed hands, she lifted up the shiny ham, placed it on the
machine, cut a slice, popped it on the scales, then took a limp-
looking baguette from a large paper bag on the floor, felt it before
tossing it back and picking up another.

Despite the precision of her movements he noticed her absent
look, the way she kept listening for the sound coming from the
television, even though not a word was audible, as if she could stay
tuned just by following the varying intensity of the roar.

"Four euros sixty," she said, without looking at him.

This provincial France he knew so well suddenly made him

feel weary, oh yes—he reflected—terribly weary of inferior bread lying on the floor, of pale, damp ham, of hands like hers handling food and coins, bread and bills, in succession.

Those hands, indifferent to tainted bread, did they sometimes, he wondered, lie limp, fragile, palms up?

Then his feeling of disgust faded.

But there remained in his heart the nostalgic pang he felt whenever he remembered that during those long years spent in Dara Salam, and later in Le Plateau in the capital, he'd never felt the slightest repugnance when the hands of people serving him touched meat and coins at the same time.

Indeed he never felt any revulsion at anything, as if his joy, his well-being, his gratitude for the place had sterilized everyday transactions with a purifying fire.

Whereas here, in his own country . . .

As he left the shop he could hear behind him the swishing of the plastic curtain and the tinkling of the bell, then the heavy silence of midday and the thick, dry heat enveloped him.

The pavements on either side of the road were narrow, and the grayish houses all had their shutters closed.

He got back into the car.

It was so hot inside he felt slightly faint.

The very inside of his head felt hot and feeble. It wasn't an entirely disagreeable sensation, and in no way resembled the feeling of a furnace raging inside his skull when, stretched out on the ground in the lycée courtyard, his face pressed against the asphalt, he'd felt awkward, worried hands trying gingerly and laboriously to lift him up, first by the armpits and then by the waist as he remarked to himself confusedly, But I'm not all that heavy, until he realized that the delicate hands belonged to the terrified headmistress, Madame Plat.

Despite the shooting pain in his shoulders, he'd tried to help her, and he'd felt embarrassed for the two of them, as if Madame Plat had caught him in an intimate moment that nothing in their relationship could justify their sharing.

The three boys were standing erect, gathered together in silence and calm, as if waiting for justice to be done, so sure of their version of events as to feel no hurry to explain themselves.

Rudy's eyes had met those of the Dara Salam boy, who'd gazed back with a look of impassive, cold indifference.

He'd gently touched his Adam's apple as if to signify, no doubt, that he was still very badly hurt.

"Do you want me to call the nurse?" Madame Plat had asked. Rudy had said he didn't.

And although it was so hot inside his head that he couldn't say precisely what words were going to pass his lips, he'd embarked on a passionate, confused speech intended to completely exonerate the boys.

Puzzled and mistrustful, Madame Plat looked hard at Rudy's bloody temple and cheek.

She was a youngish laid-back woman with whom he'd always gotten along.

She was now looking at him suspiciously and somewhat fearfully. Rudy was starting to feel, as he talked, that his panicky defense of the three boys was working against him as much as them, and that Madame Plat was beginning to sense among all four some dubious, incomprehensible complicity or, worse still, some terror on his part of pupils whose vengeance he had reason to fear.

At that moment, he'd already concealed from himself what had really happened.

The truth he'd embrace in Manille's parking lot had already gone out of his head.

And thus had he convinced himself that in clearing the boys of all responsibility for provoking the confrontation, he was lying. It was they who attacked me, he thought to himself, because his fingers had already forgotten the warm neck of the Dara Salam boy, and what he was saying to Madame Plat—out of fear or shame at seeming to be a victim—was the opposite of the truth.

Later, in Madame Plat's office, he would stick to his guns: the boys had flung him to the ground because he'd deliberately, foolishly insulted them.

It's not true, it's not true, he was thinking, I've never hurt a fly, and his head was aching terribly and his shoulders were hurting dreadfully.

"But why did they do that? What did you say to them?" Madame Plat had asked, bewildered.

He said nothing.

She asked him again.

He still said nothing.

When he did say something, it was to affirm that the boys had been right to beat him up, because what he'd shouted at them was unforgivable.

The boys, when questioned in their turn, had said nothing. No one said anything about Monsieur Descas hurling himself at the Dara Salam boy.

Only Rudy's version of the story had been retained, i.e., that he'd said a vile thing to the boys and had brought a brutal reaction upon himself.

Madame Plat had advised Rudy to take sick leave.

His case was considered by a disciplinary panel and, as if out of nowhere, the insult "fucking nigger" was looked into as the one he'd allegedly hurled at the three boys.

Someone had remembered that, twenty-five years earlier, Rudy's father had humiliated and murdered his African business partner.

The disciplinary panel therefore decided to suspend Rudy.

He was panting, as if he'd been struck.

He could now, for the first time, remember that period, he could remember the smell of tar and the pressure of his fingers on the boy's windpipe, and the old pain was stirring.

As he awaited the verdict of the disciplinary panel, he'd spent a month in the apartment in Le Plateau.

He'd begun to hate that pretty three-room apartment in a newly built block of units that ran along an avenue shaded by poinciana trees.

He only went out to take his son for walks and to shop as close to home as possible, convinced that everyone was aware of his fall from grace and was laughing at him.

Wasn't it at that point too, he wondered, that he'd begun to dislike the child in a way he'd never owned up to and would indeed have hotly denied?

.   .   .

He set off and drove to the edge of the village.

He parked on a dirt track between two fields of corn, and without getting out began devouring the bread and ham, taking a bite first of the one and then the other.

Although the ham was watery and tasteless and the baguette limp, it was so good to be eating something at last that his eyes filled with tears.

But why, oh why, had he never been able to feel for Djibril the obvious love, so strong, joyous, proud, that other fathers seemed to feel toward their children?

He'd always made an effort to love his son, and that effort, previously disguised by his eagerness to please and the shortness of time actually spent with the boy, had been exposed during the long weeks he spent shut up in the apartment.

He'd have preferred then to hide away from everybody, but Djibril was there, always there, a witness to Rudy's downfall, to his degradation and the destruction of everything he'd done to make himself a man beloved and respected.

That the boy was only two made no difference.

This little angel had become his fearsome, watchful guardian, the silent, mocking judge of his fall from grace.

Rudy crumpled up the wrapping paper from the ham, tossed it in the back, and ate the rest of the bread.

Then he got out of the car and went toward the first row in the cornfield to urinate.

Hearing a wingbeat, the gentle flutter of feathers in the warm, still air above his head, he looked up.

As if on cue, the buzzard dived toward him.

He raised his arms to protect his head.

Just before touching him the buzzard swerved away, shrieking with rage.

Rudy jumped in the car, reversed out of the dirt track, and drove slowly along the road.

Although when he'd finished eating he'd been ready to go back home and see Fanta, he was now gripped with fear and irritation, so he deliberately went in the other direction.

The idea crossed his mind that the bird had perhaps been trying to tell him that he should indeed go back home as quickly as possible, but he rejected it, convinced deep down that the angry buzzard was, on the contrary, indicating that he should stay well away.

He felt his head throbbing.

"What for, Fanta, what for," he murmured.

Because wasn't he, in a sense, now worthier of being loved than he had been that morning?

And being on that lofty perch from which she could launch an attack bird that enjoyed her full support, could she not understand that?

Just as he would never again say those absurd, cruel things he'd uttered only in the white heat of anger, the same way as he would no longer let himself fall prey to a particular kind of humiliating, impotent, comforting rage, he would try no more to charm Fanta with seductive guile, because those things he said in the apartment in Le Plateau hadn't been intended to get at some honest truth or another but only to drag her back to France with him even at the risk (not considered at the time, almost beyond his concern) of her own downfall and the collapse of her rightful dreams.

He recalled the gentle, persuasive tones he'd managed to infuse into his voice, he who, after a month spent alone with Djibril, spoke only in a sort of hesitant croak. Then, even when Fanta came home in the evening, he felt too weary to utter more than a few words.

Quietly happy just to be back once more with her child, she took over with discreet alacrity from Rudy, even though they both knew that he hadn't had to do very much, and she busied herself so energetically with the toddler that Rudy could pretend there was no opportunity to get a word in.

He would feel relieved and would go out and lean on the balcony, watching the sun set over the placid avenue.

Big gray or black cars were bringing home businessmen and diplomats who would pass a few servant girls returning on foot carrying plastic bags, and those women who didn't pad wearily along flew above the pavement just as Fanta still did, seeming not to touch the ground except to use it as a springboard.

Then, sitting on opposite ends of the table, they'd eat the meal Rudy had prepared, and since by then Djibril had been put to bed, they could feign wanting to listen to the news on the radio and not have to speak to each other.

He would gaze furtively at her sometimes: at her small, shaven head, the harmonious roundness of her skull, the casual grace of her movements, her long slender hands, which, at rest, hung at right angles to a wrist that was so slender it looked as if it would snap easily, and her serious, thoughtful, conscientious air.

He was overwhelmed with love for her, but he felt too tired and depressed to show it.

Perhaps in some obscure way, too, he resented her for bringing home the daily action and images of a lycée he was no longer in touch with, her free movement in a scene from which he'd been excluded.

Perhaps, in some obscure way, he was insanely jealous.

Early on in his suspension, when he was supposed to be on sick leave only, he used to listen glumly to tidbits of news she thought would interest him, about colleagues and pupils and this and that; he'd gotten into the habit of leaving the room at that point, this evasion as effective an interruption as if he'd hit her in the mouth.

Wasn't it to avoid doing precisely that, that he'd walk out of the room?

But once he'd been informed of the panel's verdict—dismissal from his post and loss of his teacher's certificate—he'd recovered the gift of smooth talking and put it at the service of his unhappiness, dishonesty, underhandedness, and envy.

He'd assured her that it was only in France that they had a future, and that through her marriage to him she was lucky to be able to go and live there.

As for what she'd do there, no problem: he'd make it his business to get her a job in a middle school or a lycée.

He knew nothing was less likely, and yet his tone became all the more eloquent as he started to be assailed by doubts, and Fanta, being naturally honest, never suspected anything, perhaps particularly because he'd reverted to his former guise of the young man in love, the fiancé with the cheerful, tanned face and pale blond forelock that he tossed back with a puff of breath or jerk of the head, so that even if Fanta knew some people whose faces were adept at dissembling and lies, whom she therefore would never have trusted, behind that loving, tanned, open face, those eyes so limpid and pale, surely nothing could be concealed.

They'd spent long days visiting members of Fanta's extended family.

Rudy had remained on the threshold of the green-walled apartment where, a few years earlier, he'd first met the uncle and aunt who'd raised Fanta.

His excuse for not entering was that he felt unwell, but in truth he couldn't bear to look those two old people in the eye, not because he feared his lying mask would be torn off but rather because he was afraid of betraying himself and—standing in that greenish-blue room beside Fanta as she talked in proud, confident, determined tones about all the good things that awaited them over there—of being tempted to drop everything, to say to her, "Oh, they won't give you a teaching job in France," and of finally telling her about the crime Abel Descas had committed long ago and about the way he'd died, about why the boys had thrown him, her husband, to the ground, because Fanta, while not believing he'd insulted the pupils exactly as people said, must have thought he'd shown them some kind of disrespect or another.

He'd stayed put, not daring to go into the apartment.

He hadn't run away, he just hadn't gone inside.

He'd been content to defend his interests while avoiding any risk of letting the cat out of the bag.

Feeling very tired all of a sudden, he turned off the road into a plantation of poplars.

He parked on a grassy track where the last row of poplars gave way to a wood.

He was so hot in the car he thought he'd faint.

The ham and soft white bread sat heavy in his stomach.

He got out of the car and threw himself on the grass.

The earth was cool and smelled of damp clay.

Drunk with happiness, he rolled around a bit.

Then he stretched out and lay on his back with his arms crossed above his head, and turning his face toward the sun screwed up his eyes and through the slits looked at the white trunks and their tiny silvery leaves turning reddish.

"There was no need, Fanta . . ."

It was at first only a black spot among others high above him in the milky sky. Then he heard, and recognized, its aggressive, bitter shriek and, when he saw it diving toward him, realized it had recognized him, too.

He leaped to his feet, jumped in the car, and slammed the door just as the buzzard landed on the roof.

He could hear its claws scraping on the metal.

He switched on the ignition and rammed the stick shift into reverse.

He saw the buzzard fly off and land on one of the middle branches of a poplar. Tall and rigid, it looked at him askance, its mottled eye full of menace.

He did a three-point turn and drove away along the track as fast as he could.

The heat was stifling. He was in anguish.

Was he ever now, he wondered, was he ever now going to be able to get out of his car without the vindictive bird pursuing him relentlessly over his old misdeeds?

And what would have happened if he hadn't been made aware, precisely on this day, of his past misdemeanors?

Would the buzzard have appeared, would it have made itself known?

It's so unfair, he said to himself, on the brink of tears.

When he arrived at the little school, the children were coming out of their classrooms, which were all situated on the ground floor.

One after the other each door was flung wide and, as if they'd been pressing up against it to force it open, the children tumbled out onto the playground, staggering a little, looking rather frantic as they squinted in the golden light of the late afternoon.

Rudy got out of the car and looked up at the sky.

Reassured for the time being, he went up to the gate.

In the midst of the children who, at a distance, all seemed to look alike, to such an extent that they couldn't be told apart but formed a mass made up of the same individual multiplied bizarrely many times over, he recognized Djibril, even though, with his chestnut hair, gaily colored T-shirt, and sneakers, he differed little from the rest—that child was, of all the others, his child, and he recognized him at once.

He called out, "Hey, Djibril!"

The boy stopped in his tracks, and his wide-open, laughing mouth closed at once.

Feeling hurt and uneasy, Rudy saw his son's lively, animated features freeze with anxiety the moment he caught sight of the man standing behind the gate and all hope that it wasn't his father's voice evaporated.

Rudy waved to him.

At the same time he scrutinized the sky and above the noises in the playground tried to catch the sound of a possible curse.

Djibril stared at him.

He turned around deliberately and began to run.

Rudy called out to him again, but the boy paid no more mind than if he'd seen a stranger at the gate. He was now at the far end of the playground, immersed in a ball game that was unfamiliar to Rudy.

In truth, should he not know the games his son played?

Rudy thought that like any other father he could go into the playground, walk over to his son, seize him sternly by the arm, and take him to the car.

But apart from being afraid Djibril might start crying—something he wished at all costs to avoid—he was fearful of embarking on the wide-open space of the playground.

If the buzzard arrived, doleful, pitiless, where would he hide?

He went and sat in the Nevada.

He saw the school bus arrive and the children line up in the playground ready to get in.

As Djibril was leaving the playground Rudy jumped out of the car and trotted up to the bus.

"Come here, Djibril!" he said in a tone that was both cheery and insistent. "Dad's taking him home today," he said to the woman supervising the children on the bus. He ought to know her, he thought, at least by sight—but was it not the first time he'd fetched Djibril from school?

The boy left the group and followed Rudy. He kept his head down as if ashamed. He looked at nothing and no one, but he tried to act natural.

He held the straps on his schoolbag at the armpits and Rudy noticed that his hands were trembling slightly.

Rudy was about to put his arm around Djibril's shoulder in a gesture he never normally went in for. He had to think it through before doing so in order to make it look as natural as possible. Then, beside the acacias that lined the road, he saw a brown shape out of the corner of his eye.

Turning his head gingerly he looked at the calm, watchful buzzard perched at the top of one of the trees.

Frozen with terror he forgot to embrace Djibril. His arms hung stiffly and awkwardly down his sides.

It took a lot of effort to get to the car. He threw himself in with a groan. What do you want with me, what can you possibly want with me? he wondered.

The child got in the back and slammed the door with studied brusqueness.

"Why did you come and fetch me?" he asked. Rudy sensed that he was on the brink of tears and didn't answer straightaway.

Through the car window he gazed at the buzzard, uncertain as to whether it had seen him.

His heart was beating less fiercely now.

He drove off slowly so as not to attract the buzzard's attention. Perhaps it had learned to recognize the sound of the Nevada's engine.

When they were out of sight of the school, driving with his left hand he turned around to face his son.

The child was frowning, anxiously and uncomprehendingly.

It made him look so much like Fanta whenever she dropped her mask of indifference and revealed what she commonly felt—anxiety and incomprehension—about her husband and their life in France, that Rudy was momentarily annoyed with the boy and the old dark, aggressive emotions toward Djibril welled up inside him once again—as if the boy had only ever existed to judge the father—emotions that had burgeoned in him when, during his suspension from the lycée, he'd spent a mortifying month of indignity and bitter regret in the child's company.

It seemed to him now that, whatever he did, his son would blame him and be terribly afraid of him.

"I felt like coming to fetch you from school today, that's all," he said in his most amiable voice.

"And Mummy?" the boy almost shouted.

"What about Mummy?"

"Is she okay?"

"Yes, yes, she's fine."

Still a bit suspicious, Djibril nonetheless relaxed a little.

So as not to betray his own feelings, Rudy now looked straight ahead.

What did he know about how Fanta was at the moment?

"We're going to your grandmother's," he said, "you can spend the night there. It's been quite a while since you last saw her, hasn't it? Is that okay by you?"

Djibril grunted.

Choking suddenly with emotion, Rudy realized that the child was so relieved by his assurances about Fanta that all the rest—what was going to happen to him personally—was merely of secondary importance.

"Mummy's okay, you're sure?" the boy asked again.

Rudy nodded without looking around.

In the rearview mirror he could see the little pale brown face with its coal-black eyes, its flat nose and quivering nostrils like a heifer's, its thick lips, and he recognized all that and said to himself, That's my son, Djibril, and although that statement failed to resonate, although it sank inside him, he thought, like a stone, he was beginning to see, to take measure of both the innocence and the independence of the boy whose thoughts and intentions bore no relation to Rudy's, and who inhabited a whole intimate, secret world in which Rudy had no place.

The meaning of Djibril's existence didn't boil down to condemning his father—or did it?

Oh, that death sentence that the two-year-old with the stern look had seemed to pass upon his father: a man so debased, and so despised!

But the figure he saw in the rearview mirror was but a pensive —and for the moment pacified—schoolboy enjoying childhood reveries far removed from Rudy's preoccupations: it was his son, Djibril, and he was only seven.

"Tell me, are you hungry?" Just hearing himself ask this in a voice choked with emotion made Rudy embarrassed.

Like Fanta, Djibril took time weighing his responses.

Not, Rudy imagined, to work out what he really wanted, but to avoid laying himself open to anything that might be misinterpreted, as if everything he said could later be used against him.

How did we get to this point?

What sort of man am I, that they should need to tread so carefully with me?

Feeling demoralized, he didn't repeat his question, and Djibril remained silent.

His inscrutable face had a serious look.

Rudy felt a great awkwardness between them.

What should he say?

What did other fathers say to their seven-year-olds?

It had been so long, so long, since they'd been alone together.

Was it necessary to talk?

Did other fathers find it necessary?

"What was that game you were playing just now in school?"

"What was . . . ?" the child repeated after a few seconds.

"You know, when you were playing with a ball. It's not a game I know."

Djibril's eyes darted anxiously, hesitantly, right and left.

His mouth was half open.

He's wondering, "What's behind this sudden curiosity?" and since he can't work it out, he's looking for the best strategy, the best way to find out what underlies my question.

"It's just a game," the child said slowly, in a low voice.

"But what do you have to do? What are the rules?"

Rudy was trying to make his voice sound kindly and unthreatening.

He lifted himself up to smile into the rearview mirror.

But the child now seemed terror-struck.

He's so scared he can't think straight.

"I don't know the rules!" Djibril almost shouted. "It's just a game, that's all there is to it."

"Okay, okay, no problem. Anyway, you were enjoying yourself, weren't you?"

The child, still not looking any less anxious, mumbled something that Rudy didn't catch.

Rudy felt that his son was looking a bit like a half-wit. That annoyed and upset him.

Why was the child incapable of understanding that his father was only trying to get closer to him? Why didn't he make the effort to meet his father halfway? And the high intelligence that Rudy had, perhaps smugly, always credited him with, did it still exist, had it ever existed?

Or else, finding little stimulation at the village school where the teachers were narrowminded and hardly up to much—at least that was what, deep down, Rudy felt—and oppressed by the atmosphere of sadness, resentment, and dread that prevailed at home, the boy's intelligence had shriveled and withered, so that without it Djibril, his son, would be just like so many other children: not very interesting . . .

If Rudy felt no particular hostility toward mediocre children, he saw no reason to love them and didn't think it likely that he ever would.

He was sliding into a state of bitter affliction.

He was powerless to offer his son unconditional love, so that must mean he didn't love him. He needed good reasons to love. Was that what fatherly love amounted to? He'd never heard it described as depending on the qualities a child might or might not possess.

He looked at Djibril in the rearview mirror again; he looked at him intensely, passionately, alert to any sign of paternal feeling stirring within himself.

It was his son, Djibril; he'd recognize him even surrounded by other children.

Force of habit?

His heart was just a muddy pool into which, with a ghastly swish, everything was slipping.

Rudy's mother lived in a tiny, low-roofed, square house in a new housing development at the end of a village consisting of only one street.

When she'd returned to France with Rudy just after Abel's death she'd gone back to live in their old house deep in the countryside, and Rudy had gone to board at the nearest secondary school.

He'd gone to university in Bordeaux (he remembered the infinite desolation of the gray streets, the campus located far away in the dreary suburbs), and it was to the same old, isolated house that he occasionally went to visit Mummy.

Then, after taking his finals, he'd gone back to Africa and was appointed to a teaching post at the Lycée Mermoz.

Five years ago, after getting fired, when he'd returned to France under a cloud with Fanta and Djibril in tow, he'd found that his mother had left her house for that little villa with tiny square windows and a roof that, like a low forehead, made the whole place look mulish and stupid.

From the word go, he'd felt ill at ease in this neighborhood of houses that all looked alike, built on bare rectangular plots now artlessly graced with tufts of pampas grass and a few replanted Christmas trees!

He'd had the impression that in moving there Mummy was not only submitting to, but also ratifying, even anticipating in a smug, rather nasty way, the judgment of absolute failure that, at the end of her life, a supreme authority would be handing down.

Rudy had been burning to ask her: Was it really necessary to advertise her ruination in that manner? Hadn't her existence in the countryside been more dignified?

But as always with Mummy, he'd said nothing.

His own situation seemed nothing to brag about, either!

Besides, he'd soon realized that Mummy liked the neighborhood and that its large captive female audience made it much easier than before to peddle her stock of angelic brochures.

She'd made friends with women the very sight of whom filled Rudy with embarrassment and sadness.

Their bodies and faces bore all the signs of a brutal, terrible life (scars, bruises, skin turned purple through alcohol addiction). They were for the most part unemployed and willingly opened their door to Mummy, who tried to help them determine the name of their soul's guardian and then track it down—the angel none of them had ever seen and who had never come to their aid because it had never been correctly invoked.

Oh well, Rudy had finally said to himself, not without bitterness, Mummy was perfectly at home in her unlovely housing development.

He wandered around a bit on the grounds, lost as usual (that happened every time he visited), going up and down the same streets without realizing it.

Mummy's pocket handkerchief garden was one of the few not littered with plastic toys, bits of furniture, and auto parts.

The yellowish grass was overgrown because Mummy—completely taken up with her proselytizing—claimed no time to mow the lawn.

Djibril got out of the car very reluctantly, leaving his schoolbag on the backseat. Rudy, getting out in his turn, grabbed it.

He could see from the terrified look on the boy's face that he'd just realized his father was going to leave without him.

But he has to see his grandmother from time to time, Rudy thought, very upset.

How distant, now, seemed the morning of this very same day when, informing Fanta he'd collect Djibril and take him to spend the night at his grandmother's, it had dawned on him that he hadn't so much wanted to give Mummy a nice surprise as to prevent Fanta from leaving him!

Because why would he suddenly get it into his head to try to please Mummy that way?

Even if he couldn't agree with Fanta's claim that his grandmother didn't love Djibril—because that would be to make the mistake of seeing Mummy as an ordinary person who simply loved someone or didn't love them—it seemed obvious to Rudy that ever since the child was born, ever since Mummy first leaned over his crib, examined his features, and found that he in no way corresponded, had no hope of ever corresponding, to her idea of a divine messenger, and so had never really taken the trouble to bond with the child: it seemed obvious to Rudy that it was this attitude—benign indifference—that Fanta had taken for hostility.

Rudy put his hand on Djibril's shoulder.

He could feel the little, pointy bones.

Djibril let his head fall against his father's stomach. Rudy ran his fingers through the boy's silky curls, feeling the beautifully smooth, perfect, miraculous skull.

His eyes suddenly filled with bitter tears.

Then he heard a cry above them, a single angry, threatening shriek.

He took his hand away and pushed Djibril toward the garden gate, so brusquely that the boy stumbled.

Rudy steadied him, gripping him tightly, and they crossed the overgrown lawn to the front door. Rudy thought it looked as if he were dragging the child along against his will.

But, terrified and distraught, not daring to look up at the sky, he had no intention of letting go.

But, moaning, Djibril shook himself loose. Rudy didn't try to stop him.

The child looked at him in fear and bafflement.

Rudy forced himself to smile and banged on the door.

If the buzzard was going to swoop down on Rudy before Mummy opened the door, what would become of his attempts at restoring his honor?

Oh, all would then be lost!

The door opened almost at once.

Rudy dragged Djibril inside and closed the door.

"Well, well," said Mummy in a cheery voice, "what a surprise!"

"I've brought Djibril to see you," Rudy murmured, still in a state of shock.

There was no need to do that, Fanta, there was no need to do that now . . .

Mummy stooped down toward Djibril's face, looked at him closely, and kissed the boy's forehead.

Ill at ease, Djibril wriggled.

She stood up next to kiss Rudy, and he felt from the quivering of her mouth that she was happy and excited.

That made him slightly anxious.

He guessed that her feverish cheeriness was due not to their presence but to something that had happened before their arrival and that their visit would in no way disturb, being negligible, superfluous alongside this mysterious source of exultation.

He felt jealous about that, both for himself and for Djibril.

He placed his two hands heavily on his son's shoulders.

"I thought you'd like to keep him for the night."

"Ah!"

Nodding gently, Mummy folded her arms, and her searching gaze played on the child's features again as if trying to estimate his worth.

"You could have warned me, but all right, it'll be okay."

Rudy remarked with some displeasure that she seemed particularly youthful and amiable today. Her short hair had been freshly dyed, a nice ash-blond color.

Her powdered, very pale skin was stretched over her cheekbones.

She was wearing jeans and a pink polo shirt, and when she turned around to go into the kitchen, Rudy saw that the jeans were quite tight and hugged her narrow hips, her small buttocks, and her slender knees.

In the tiny kitchen all in dark wood, a boy was sitting at the narrow table having his tea.

He was dipping into a glass of milk a shortbread cookie that Rudy recognized as being like those Mummy made for special occasions.

He was about Djibril's age.

He was a beautiful child with pale eyes and fair curly hair.

Rudy nearly retched.

He had in his mouth the taste of ham and soft white bread.

"There, you sit down here," Mummy said to Djibril, pointing to the other chair in front of the small table. "Are you hungry?"

She asked that with an air of hoping that his reply would be in the negative. Djibril shook his head. He also declined her invitation to sit down.

"It's a little neighbor, I've got a new friend," said Mummy.

The blond child didn't look at anyone.

Assured, confident, he was eating happily, diligently, his lips wet with milk.

Rudy felt certain, at that moment, that there was no other explanation for Mummy's eager bliss, for the hard sheen of happiness on her face, than the presence in her kitchen of this boy feasting on the shortbread she'd baked for him.

No, there was no other cause for the quivering of her lips and trembling of her skin but the boy himself.

It was equally clear to him that he wouldn't leave Djibril with Mummy, not that evening nor any other, and having decided this, he felt immensely relieved.

Holding his son close he whispered in his ear, "We're both going home, you're not staying here, okay?"

Then, since Djibril was probably hungry and, at least for a short time, might as well sit at Mummy's table, Rudy pulled up a chair for him and poured him a glass of milk.

"Come," Mummy said to Rudy, "I've got something to show you."

He followed her into the living room filled with heavy, useless furniture, navigable only by narrow corridors with complicated angles.

"What do you think?" asked Mummy in a tone of feigned detachment.

He could hear her voice trembling with desire, impatience, and delight.

"I use him as a model, he is an excellent sitter. I won't let go of him."

She let out a brief, shrill laugh.

"In any case, no one takes care of him at home. Good heavens, he's so beautiful, don't you think?"

From the table covered in pens, paper, and brochures tied together with string, she picked up a sheet of paper, which she showed to Rudy.

It was the sketch for a more developed drawing.

Clad in a white robe, Mummy's little neighbor was shown flying above a group of adults frozen in what was presumably intended to look like an attitude of fear or ignorance. The execution was clumsy.

In a strained, sharp, but delighted tone Mummy explained, "He's there, above them, and they've not yet recognized him, it has not yet been granted to them to see the light, but in the next drawing they will be enlightened and their eyes will be opened and the angel will be able to take his place among them."

Rudy was overwhelmed by a feeling of weary disgust.

She's stark, staring mad, and in the most ridiculous way. I can't and shouldn't cover up for her any longer. Poor little Djibril! We'll never set foot in here again.

Rudy thought his mother had read his mind because at that moment she smiled tenderly at him, stroked his cheek, and patted the back of his head with her cold, damp hand. Rudy found that rather disagreeable.

Since she was short, he could see her fairly heavy breasts revealed by the plunging neckline of her polo shirt. They appeared swollen with milk or with desire.

He looked aside and backed away to get her to remove her hand.

She only talks to me about boring things that get on my nerves, but the things I still need to know she won't ever take it upon herself to tell me, because she lost interest in all that long ago.

"Did anyone ever find out," he began slowly, awkwardly, "who provided my father with a gun?"

She stiffened momentarily with surprise, but that was perceptible only during the time it took her to put the sketch down and turn toward him. Her dry lips parted slightly in an annoyed, pinched smile.

"That's all over and done with," she said.

"Did anyone find out?"

She sighed ostentatiously, coquettishly, annoyed at his insistence.

She flopped down in an armchair, seeming almost to disappear in the flabby folds of the oversize rosy vinyl upholstery.

"No, obviously, no one ever found out, I'm not even sure if an investigation was ever carried out, you know the country, you know how things were. When all's said and done, what does it matter? You can get hold of anything in prison as long as you can pay for it."

Mummy's voice once again took on that bitter, rancorous, flat, stubborn tone that Rudy had heard ever since she'd returned to France some thirty years earlier, and that her passion for angels and the almost professional way she disseminated her propaganda about them had made her gradually forsake.

He heard it again, intact, unaltered, as if the memory of that time had to be accompanied by the voice and feelings associated with it.

"Your father had the wherewithal to pay, it wasn't a problem. He hadn't been in Reubeuss six weeks before he'd found a way of getting hold of a revolver; as you're well aware he knew how things were done, he knew the right people, he knew the country. He'd decided he preferred to die rather than rot in Reubeuss and endure a trial in which he knew he was bound to be convicted."

"He told you that? That he preferred to die?"

"Well, not in so many words, but there are ways of implying such things. At the time, even so, I'd never have imagined he'd go that far: have a gun delivered to his cell. No, I'd never have imagined that."

And, as always, that sullen, bitter, vaguely whining tone in Mummy's voice that used to so upset Rudy in the past, creating a feeling of guilt that he hadn't managed to make her happy merely by his kindly, considerate presence at her side, by the mere fact that he existed, the only child of this lowly woman.

"There were no individual cells, not even for six or seven people, he was in a room with sixty other men and it was so hot—or so he told me when I went to visit him—that he was practically fainting most of the time. I did what I could, I tried to get to know his guardian angel, but faced with his ill will, his negative attitude, his disbelief, what could I hope to achieve?"

Rudy wanted to ask—nearly did ask—"Was I there when my father ran his 4×4 over Salif? Did I actually see that?"

But a deep reluctance, a vivid, burning hatred, stopped him from uttering these words.

How he loathed his father for obliging him to formulate such terrible questions.

It seemed to him that whatever had really occurred between Salif and his father that afternoon, his father was at least guilty of having made it possible for such words to stick to him, even if only in the form of a question.

Nevertheless, filled with disgust, he didn't ask that question.

It was Mummy who started speaking about his father again, perhaps because she'd sensed how much spite and disapproval had been conveyed by her silence.

"He'd convinced himself that he was done for," she continued in her caustic, plaintive, monotonous voice, "that the police investigation, or whatever it was, considered him guilty as hell and so wouldn't be impartial, whereas it could already be proved that this Salif had indeed swindled him, I could see that right away when I went through your father's papers. It was, after all, justified, I don't mean the blows and the rest, but the anger, the fight, because this Salif, when all's said and done he should have been your father's best friend out there, it was your father who'd given him board and lodging and taken him on as his business partner, and there Salif goes and starts doing the one thing Abel couldn't forgive or even understand: cheating him outrageously, without a hint of a problem between them, not a change in Salif's smile or friendly voice whenever they met. All that could have been said at the trial. I went through every estimate Salif had drawn up, for bricklaying, joinery, and plumbing, and I went to see the contractors and lo and behold they were all one way or another in cahoots with Salif or with Salif's wife and God knows who else, it jumped right out at you that they were inflated, those estimates, and that Salif had worked it all out, how he was going to be able to line his pocket along the way. Me, I could never understand how Abel could trust that one so blindly, you have to watch your back constantly over there, people are out to jew you the whole time. Friendship, that doesn't exist over there. They may believe in God, but the angels, they despise, think they're funny. When you went back there to try to make a living, I knew it wouldn't work out, I was certain of it, and as you can see, it didn't work out."

"If it didn't work out," said Rudy, "it was because of my father, not the country."

She snickered with a little triumphant acrimony.

"That's what you think. You're too white and too blond, naturally they would have taken you for a ride, they would have done everything to destroy you. Even love, that doesn't exist over there. Your wife, she married you out of self-interest. They don't know what love is, all they think about is money and status."

He left the room and returned to the kitchen. He felt his anger assuaged, almost eliminated, by his intoxicating, invigorating decision never to visit Mummy again, and he thought, She can come if she feels like it, thinking too, Manille & Co., that's all over and done with, what joy, to feel young, light as a bird, in the way he hadn't since the time he'd first met Fanta and walked down the boulevard de la République in the warm, pale, dazzling morning light, in the simple, clear awareness of his own honesty and goodness.

Slumped on his chair, Djibril hadn't touched his milk or short-bread.

The other boy was still eating with concentration and delight. Djibril looked at him with glum alarm.

"You see, he wasn't hungry," Mummy said as she walked in.

Outside, as they moved toward the car, Rudy put his arm around Djibril and had the sense of having glimpsed on the ground, just in front of the Nevada, an indistinct lump of something that had no reason to be there.

But the thought was so fleeting and superficial and, besides, he was so proud and happy to be taking Djibril home to Fanta that he forgot what his eyes had perhaps seen almost as soon as he'd wondered whether his eyes had seen anything.

He let Djibril in and dropped the schoolbag at his feet, and for the first time in ages—it troubled Rudy to think—the child shot him a big wide smile.

He got in too and started the engine.

"Home," he said with gusto.

The car moved forward.

It passed over a big, soft, dense mass that threw it slightly off balance.

"What was that?" asked Djibril.

A few yards on Rudy pulled over.

"Oh my God, oh my God, oh my God," he murmured.

The child had turned and was looking out of the rear window.

"We've run a bird over," he said in his clear voice.

"It's nothing," Rudy muttered, "it doesn't matter now."

COUNTERPOINT

WAKING FROM her daily siesta, emerging from hazy, satisfied dreams, Madame Pulmaire gazed for a moment at her hands resting contentedly on her thighs then looked toward the living-room window opposite her armchair and saw on the other side of the hedge her neighbor's long neck and small delicate head that seemed to emerge from the bay tree like a miraculous branch, an unlikely sucker looking at Madame Pulmaire's garden with big wide eyes and with lips parted in a big, calm smile that greatly surprised her because she couldn't ever remember seeing Fanta look happy. Hesitantly, shyly, she raised a rather stiff, withered hand flecked with liver spots, and waved it slowly from right to left. And the young woman on the other side of the hedge, the strange neighbor called Fanta who'd only ever looked at Madame Pulmaire with a blank expression, raised her hand too. She waved to Madame Pulmaire, she waved to her slowly, deliberately, purposefully.

PART

III

*W*HEN HER HUSBAND'S parents and sisters told her what was expected of her, what she was going to have to do, Khady knew already.

She hadn't known what form their wish to get rid of her would take, only that the day would come when she'd be ordered to leave, that much she'd known or gathered or felt (that is to say, before tacit understanding and unexpressed feelings had gradually established knowledge and certainty) from the earliest months of her settling in with her husband's family following his death.

She remembered her three years of marriage not as a time of serenity, because the longing, the terrible desire for a child, had made each month a frantic climb toward a possible blessing, then, when her period came, a collapse followed by gloomy despondency before hope returned and, with it, the gradual, dazzling, breathless ascent day after day, right up to the cruel moment when a barely perceptible pain in her lower abdomen let her know that it hadn't worked this time—no, those years had certainly been neither calm nor happy, because Khady never did get pregnant.

Still, she thought of herself as a string stretched to the limit, strong, taut, vibrating in the impassioned confinement of these expectations.

It seemed to her that she'd not been able to concentrate on anything, throughout those three years, other than on the rhythmic alternation of hope and disillusionment, so that disillusionment—provoked by a twinge in her groin—might quickly be followed by the stubborn, almost ridiculous surge of hope regained.

"It'll perhaps be next month," she would say to her husband.

And, careful not to show his own disappointment, he would reply in a kindly way, "Yes, for sure."

Because that husband of hers had been such a nice man.

In their life together he'd given her full latitude to become that desperately taut string that resonated with every emotion, and he'd surrounded her with kindness, always speaking to her with prudence and tact, exactly as if, busy with creating a new life, she needed to be surrounded by an atmosphere of silent deference in order to be able to perfect her art and give form to her obsession.

Never once had he complained about the overwhelming presence in their life of the baby that never got conceived.

He'd played his part rather selflessly, she said to herself later.

Wouldn't he have been within his rights to complain about the inconsiderate way she pulled him toward her or pushed him away at night, depending on whether she thought her husband's semen would be of any use at that moment, about the way, during her non-ovulating period, she made no bones about not wanting to make love, as if the expenditure of useless energy could damage the only project she then cared about, as if her husband's seed constituted a unique, precious resource of which she was the keeper and which should never be squandered in the pursuit of mere pleasure?

He'd never complained.

At the time she hadn't seen how noble his behavior was because she wouldn't have understood that he could have complained about—or even simply rejected the legitimacy, necessity, and nobility of—the asceticism (ascetic only in a sense, since their tally of sexual encounters was impressive) that this mania to have a child subjected them.

No, for sure, she wouldn't have understood that at the time.

It was only after the death of her husband, of the peaceable, kindly man she'd been married to for three years, that she was able to appreciate his forbearance. That only happened once her obsession had left her and she'd become herself again, rediscovering the person she'd been before her marriage, the woman who'd been able to appreciate the qualities of devotion and gallantry that her man possessed in abundance.

She then felt a great unhappiness, remorse, hatred almost, about the mad desire to get pregnant that had blinded her to everything else, in particular her husband's illness.

Because must he not have been ill for some time to die so suddenly, early one pale morning during the rainy season? He'd scarcely gotten out of bed that day to open as usual the little café they ran in a lane in the medina.

He'd got up and then, with a sort of choking sigh, almost a muted sob, a sound as discreet as the man himself, he collapsed at the foot of the bed.

Still in bed herself and barely awake, at first Khady hadn't imagined that her husband was dead, no, not for a second.

For a long time she would blame herself about the thought that had flashed through her mind—oh, a year or more later, she was, actually, still angry with herself—about this thought: Wouldn't it be just their rotten luck if he fell ill just at that moment, a good two weeks after her period, with her breasts feeling slightly harder and more sensitive than usual, leading her to suppose she was fertile, but if this man was so unwell as to be incapable of making love to her that evening, what a mess, what a waste of time, what a horrid letdown!

She'd gotten up in her turn and gone over to him, and when she'd realized he was no longer breathing but just lying there inert, hunched up, his knees almost touching his chin, with one arm trapped under his head and with one innocent, vulnerable hand lying flat, palm upward, on the floor, looking, she'd said to herself, like the child he must have been, small and brave, never contrary but open and forthright, solitary and secretive under a sociable exterior, she'd seized his open palm and pressed it to her lips, tortured at the sight of so much decency in one human being. But even then stupefied grief was battling it out in her heart with an unabated, undeflated exultation at the thought that she was ovulating, and at the same moment as she was running to get help, diving into the house next door, unaware of the tears pouring down her cheeks, that part of her still obsessed with pregnancy was beginning to wonder feverishly what man could, just this once, step in for her husband to avoid missing the chance to get pregnant this month and break the exhausting cycle of hope and despair that,

even as she ran shouting that her husband was dead, she saw looming, were she forced to pass up this opportunity.

And as her reason returned, and it began to dawn on her that
this fertile period would be wasted, and likewise the months
to follow, a huge disappointment—a feeling that she'd put
up with all that (hope and despair) for three whole years to no
purpose—contaminated her grief at this man's death with an
almost rancorous bitterness.

Couldn't he have waited for two or three days?

Such thoughts did Khady still, now, reproach herself for having
entertained.

After her husband's death the owner of the café threw her out
to make way for another couple, and Khady had had no choice but
to go and live with her husband's family.

Her own parents had handed her over to be brought up by her
grandmother, long since dead, and after not seeing them during
her childhood for long stretches, Khady had finally lost touch with
them altogether.

And although she'd grown up to be a tall, well-built, slender young woman with a smooth oval face and delicate features,
although she'd lived for three years with this man who'd always
had a kind word for her, and although she'd managed, in the
café, to command respect with an attitude that was unconsciously
haughty, reserved, a little frosty, and thereby preempt any taunts
about her infertility—despite it all, her lonely, anxious childhood, and later her vain efforts to get pregnant, which, while sus-
pending her in an intense, almost fanatical emotional state, had
all dealt their barely perceptible but fatal blows to her precarious

self-esteem: all that had conditioned her to find humiliation not in the least abnormal.

So that, when she found herself living with in-laws who couldn't forgive her for having no means of support and no dowry, who despised her openly and angrily for having failed to conceive, she willingly became a poor, self-effacing wretch who entertained only vague impersonal thoughts and inconsistent, pallid dreams, in the shadow of which she wandered about vacantly, mechanically, dragging her indifferent feet and, she believed, hardly suffering at all.

She lived in a three-room rundown house with her husband's parents, two of her sisters-in-law, and the young children of one of them.

Behind the house there was a backyard of beaten earth shared with the neighbors.

Khady avoided going into the yard because she feared being peppered with sarcastic comments about her worthlessness and the absurdity of her existence as a penniless, childless widow, and when she had to go there to peel the vegetables or prepare the fish she huddled so closely inside her batik, with only her quick hands and high cheekbones showing, that people soon stopped paying her any attention and forgot all about her, as if this silent, uninteresting heap no longer merited a rude or jeering remark.

Without pausing in her work she would slide into a kind of mental stupor that stopped her taking in what was going on around her.

She then felt almost happy.

She seemed to be in a blank, light sleep that was devoid of both joy and anguish.

Early every morning she would leave the house with her

sisters-in-law. All three carried on their heads the plastic bowls of various sizes that they would sell in the market.

There they found their usual spot. Khady would squat a little to one side of the two others, who pretended not to notice her presence, and, responding with three or four raised fingers when asked the price of the bowls, she stayed there for hours on end, motionless in the noisy bustle of the market, which made her slightly dizzy and lulled her back into a state of torpor shot through with pleasing, unthreatening, pallid dreams like long veils flapping in the wind, on which there appeared from time to time the blurred face of her husband smiling his everlasting kindly smile, or, less often, the features of the grandmother who'd brought her up and sheltered her and who had been able to see, even while treating her harshly, that she was a special little girl with her own attributes and not any old child.

So much so that she'd always been conscious of her uniqueness and aware, in a manner that could neither be proved nor disproved, that she, Khady Demba, was strictly irreplaceable, even though her parents had abandoned her and her grandmother had only taken her in because there hadn't been a choice, and even though no being on earth needed her or wanted her around.

She was happy to be Khady, there'd never been a chink of doubt between herself and the implacable reality of the person called Khady Demba.

She'd even happened on occasion to feel proud of being Khady because—she'd often thought with some amazement—children whose lives seemed happy, who every day got generous helpings of chicken or fish and wore clothes to school that weren't stained or torn, such children were no more human than Khady Demba, who only managed to get a minuscule helping of the good things in life.

That now was still something she never doubted: that she was indivisible and precious and could only ever be herself.

She just felt tired of existence and weary of all the humiliation she had to undergo, even if it didn't cause her any real pain.

All the time they were sitting together at their stall her husband's sisters never once spoke to her.

On the way back from the market they were still quivering with pleasure, as if all the feverish, impassioned hubbub of the crowd still filled them with excitement and they had to shake it off before getting home, and still they never stopped needling, shoving, and pinching Khady, irritated and titillated by the impregnable firmness of her body, the cold scowl on her face, knowing or surmising that she would blot everything out as soon as they began tormenting her, knowing or surmising that the most cutting remarks were transformed in her mind into reddish veils, which started to get entangled a bit, if fleetingly, with the others, her pallid beneficent dreams—knowing it, surmising it, and feeling silently irritated by it.

Khady sometimes stepped quickly aside or began walking at a dauntingly slow pace, and the two sisters soon started losing interest in her.

On one occasion, one of them shouted, "What's the matter, you a mute?" when she turned around and noticed the lengthening distance between themselves and Khady.

Khady couldn't prevent her mind from taking that in. The expression surprised her by revealing what, without realizing it, she already knew: that she hadn't opened her mouth in quite a long while.

The chattering in her dreams, made up vaguely of the voice of her husband, her own, and that of a few nameless people from the past, had given her the impression that she had been speaking from time to time.

She was seized with a sudden panic: if she forgot how words were formed and uttered, could she count on having a future, even a tiresome one?

She sank back into numb indifference.

But she made no effort to say anything, fearing that she mightn't succeed and that a strange, disturbing sound would reach her ears.

When her in-laws—backed up by their two daughters, who, for once, were content to listen in silence—told Khady she had to go, they didn't expect her to reply, because they weren't asking her a question but giving her an order, and, although her apathy was now being tempered by anxiety, Khady said nothing, asked nothing, believing perhaps that by her silence she avoided the risk of their intentions concerning her person acquiring greater precision, of her departure becoming a reality, as if, she would later tell herself, her husband's parents had the slightest need to hear their words answered by any words of hers in order to be assured of the reality and validity of what they were proposing.

No, they had no need to hear anything she might have to say, none whatever. Khady knew that for them she simply did not exist.

Because their only son had married her against their wishes, because she had not produced a child, and because she enjoyed no one's protection, they had tacitly, naturally, without animus or ulterior motive, separated her from the human community, and so their hard, narrow, old people's eyes made no distinction between the shape called Khady and the innumerable forms of animals and things that also inhabit the world.

Khady knew they were wrong, but she had no way of telling them so other than by being there and looking obviously like them. But she knew that would not be enough, and she'd ceased concerning herself with proving to them that she was human.

So she listened in silence, focusing on the patterned skirts worn by her two sisters-in-law sitting on each side of their parents on the old sofa, their hands lying palms up on their thighs, with a guileless fragility that wasn't in the women's nature but that all of a sudden presaged their death—which unveiled and prefigured the innocent vulnerability of their faces when they would be dead—and those defenseless hands were so similar to those of her husband, their brother, after his life had suddenly left him that Khady felt a lump in her throat.

Her mother-in-law's voice—dry, monotonous, threatening—was still spelling out what must have been, Khady thought distantly, a number of disagreeable recommendations, but she was no longer making any effort to understand.

She barely heard about someone called Fanta, a cousin who'd married a white man and was now living in France.

She opened her mind once again to those insipid pipe dreams that had for her stood in place of thoughts ever since she'd first come to live with these people, forgetting, indeed being quite incapable of remembering, her terror a few moments earlier at the notion of having to leave, not that she wished to stay (she wished for nothing), but as she believed those dreams would not survive such a radical change in her situation, and she would have to ponder, undertake, and decide a number of things (including where to go), no prospect, given her present languor, could have been more terrifying.

Gray snakes on a yellow ground biting their tails, and cheery women's faces, brown on a red ground above the inscription "Year of the African Woman," adorned the cloth from which the sisters had made themselves skirts; the snakes and faces, repeated several times, were monstrously crushed by the folds of the fabric, and they danced in a cruel ring inside her head, displacing the kind, cloudy face of her husband.

It seemed to Khady that the two sisters, whose gaze she normally avoided, were gazing at her derisively.

One of them straightened her skirt without taking her eyes off Khady, and now her hands, as they smoothed the fabric insistently, seemed to Khady as dangerous, provocative, and indecipherable as they'd earlier appeared helpless and artless when upturned and at rest.

Khady was hugely relieved when with a wave of her hand her mother-in-law indicated that she was done and that Khady could leave the room.

She'd no idea what had just been said to her about the circumstances of her departure—when she'd leave, where she'd go, with what aim, or how—and since for the next few days no one spoke to her again or paid her any mind, and she went to market as usual, the worrying possibility of her world being turned upside down got mixed up in her head with the memory of the printed snakes and faces, taking on their phantasmagorical and absurd character before sliding into the oblivion to which all pointless dreams are consigned.

Then one evening her mother-in-law prodded her in the back.

"Get your things," she said.

And since she was afraid Khady might take what didn't belong to her, she spread out on the floor of their shared bedroom one of Khady's batiks, placing on it the only other one she herself possessed, together with an old faded blue T-shirt and a piece of bread wrapped in newspaper.

She folded the batik carefully and tied the four corners together.

Then slowly, with an air of solemnity full of pique and regret, she drew a wad of cash from her bra, and (knowing that Khady had no bra of her own?) slid her hand roughly under Khady's belt and into the top of her panties, tucking the money between the elastic and the skin, which she scratched with her yellow nails.

She added a piece of paper folded in four, which contained, she said, the cousin's address.

"When you get over there, to Fanta's, you'll send us money. Fanta must be wealthy now, she's a teacher."

Khady lay down on the mattress she shared with her sister-in-law's children.

She was so terrified she felt sick.

She closed her eyes and tried to call to mind those chalky, shimmering dreams that protected her from intolerable contact with a reality that her anxious, grief-stricken heart full of remorse and doubt had made her a part of, tried desperately to detach herself from the feeble, timorous person she was, but that night her dreams weren't up to battling life's intrusions. Khady was left face-to-face with her terrors, and no effort at willed indifference could free her from them.

Her mother-in-law came to fetch her at dawn, silently indicating to her to get up.

Khady stepped over her sisters-in-law lying on the second mattress, and although she had no wish to hear their harsh, mocking voices or see their pitiless eyes shining in the gray light of dawn, it seemed to her a bad omen that the two women were pretending to be asleep at the moment of her departure into the unknown.

Was it because they were sure of never seeing Khady again that they chose to avoid the trouble of looking at her, of waving a hand, of lifting a kindly, angelic palm toward her to say good-bye?

That was it, no doubt: Khady was walking toward her death, and so, swayed by the very understandable fear of getting involved somehow in her fate, they chose to have nothing further to do with her.

Khady stifled a moan.

In the street a man was waiting for her.

He was dressed in Western clothes: jeans and a checked shirt. Although the sun had barely risen he wore gleaming sunglasses, so that when tiny, anxious Khady, her bundle pressed against her chest, was pushed toward him by her jumpy, irritated, impatient mother-in-law, she couldn't tell whether he was looking at her, but she could see herself reflected in the twin mirrors of his glasses.

She noticed his habit of biting his lower lip, so that the lower part of his face was constantly moving, like the jaw of a rodent.

Her mother-in-law quickly put a few banknotes in his hand and he stuffed them in his pocket without looking at them.

"You mustn't come back here," she murmured in Khady's ear. "You must send us some money as soon as you get over there. But if you don't make it, you mustn't come back here."

Khady made as if to clutch the old woman's arm, but she slipped quickly inside the house and shut the door behind her.

"It's this way, follow me," the man said in a low, flat tone.

He started down the road without bothering to make sure Khady was behind him, as if, she said to herself, following in his footsteps, tottering clumsily in her pink plastic flip-flops while he seemed to leap along on the light, thick soles of his sneakers, he didn't doubt for a second her interest in accompanying him, or as if, having been paid in full, he couldn't care less what she did.

Such lack of concern about her Khady found somewhat reassuring.

As soon as she stopped thinking about that, taking care not to get left behind or lose one of her flip-flops, she found her mind being invaded by the usual fog, this time shot through not with the dead faces of her husband or grandmother but with the images she saw as she followed in the man's footsteps along streets that she couldn't recall ever having been down before, although, she suddenly thought, she could have walked through them in her usual stupor and mental prostration without remembering it—whereas it seemed to her that, this morning, the most humble scenes along the way were gently insisting on their permanence in a kind of rear projection on the screen of her dreams.

Was it possible that, now finding herself cast into the unknown, wrenched from her dangerous torpor, she was being protected in spite of herself?

What surprised her more was the twinge of grief she felt on seeing a pregnant woman sitting under a mango tree feeding a small child boiled rice.

She'd not felt for a long while—not since she'd gone to live with her husband's family and everything had frozen inside her—that great distress at not having had a baby, that immense, bitter grief unconnected with any reflex of shame in the face of those around her.

And now she was gazing at the woman instead of merely glancing at her, unable to take her eyes off that swollen belly and the smeared lips of the little boy, and thinking sadly, Won't I, Khady, ever have a child? She was however less sad than surprised at being sad, at identifying the emotion that, in an obscure, almost gentle way, stirred a part of her that had grown accustomed to feeling merely sluggish or terrified.

She hurried on because the man in front of her was walking quickly.

A young woman who could have been her, Khady, in her previous life came out onto the pavement and removed the wooden panel that covered the only window of her drinks stall, and on seeing that long, slender body, narrow at the hips and shoulders, with barely a perceptible waist, but as compact and vigorous in its slimness as the body of a snake, Khady recognized a shape very much like her own, and she reawakened to the action of her own muscles in enabling her to move so quickly, of their forgotten vigor and unfailing presence, of the whole of her young body, which she no longer paid the slightest attention to but which she now remembered and rediscovered in the bearing of this unknown young woman, who was arranging on the counter the fizzy-drink bottles she was about to sell and who, with her calm, focused reserve, could have been Khady, in an earlier life.

The man was now leading her down the avenue de l'Indépendance.

Schoolboys in blue shorts and white tops were moving slowly along the pavement, holding pieces of bread that they bit into from time to time, scattering crumbs as they went, with the crows hot on their heels.

Khady hurried, caught up with her guide, and began trotting in order to stay alongside him, her flip-flops making such a racket on the asphalt that the suspicious crows flew away.

"We're nearly there," the man said in a neutral tone of voice, less to reassure or encourage Khady than to forestall a possible question.

She wondered then if he was embarrassed to be seen walking alongside this woman with her faded batik, short unadorned hair, and feet white with dust, whereas he, with his fitted shirt, sunglasses, and green sneakers, obviously took particular pride in his appearance and cared what people thought of him.

He crossed the avenue, turned into the boulevard de la République, and walked down toward the sea.

Khady could see crows and gulls flying in the soft pale blue sky. She was aware of watching them in their flight and was surprised, almost fearful, of this awareness, saying to herself—not clearly but limply and confusedly, her thoughts still impeded by the fog of her dreams—saying to herself, It's been a while since I've come this way, to the seashore where her grandmother sent her as a child to buy fish from the boats that had just landed their catch.

She then felt so completely sure of the indisputable fact that the thin, valiant little girl haggling fiercely over the price of mullet and the woman accompanying a stranger toward a similar shore were one and the same person with a unique, coherent destiny that she was moved and felt satisfied and fulfilled. Her eyes were stinging, and she forgot the uncertainty of her situation, or, rather, its precariousness no longer appeared so serious in the dazzling radiance of such a truth.

She felt the ghost of a smile playing on her lips.

Hello, Khady, she said to herself.

She remembered how much, as a little girl, she'd enjoyed her own company, and that she never felt lonely when she was by herself but when she was surrounded by other children or by members of the numerous families that had employed her as a servant.

She remembered too that her husband, a kindly, placid, taciturn, and slightly withdrawn character, had given her the reassuring impression that she'd no need to give up her solitude and that he didn't expect her to, any more than he imagined she'd attempt to draw him out of himself.

And for the first time perhaps since his death, as she went, half running, along the boulevard, gripping her flip-flops with her toes to keep them from falling off, as she felt on her forehead the still mild heat of the blue sky, as she heard the shrieking of the crows in their fury at being always hungry, and as she saw them at the edge of her field of vision, the innumerable dark specks in their jerky whirls, for the first time in a very long while she missed her husband, precisely because of the kind of man he had been.

She felt a knot in her chest.

Because that was such a new sensation for her.

This pain was very far from the dizzying disillusion and resentment she'd felt when—because of that unexpected death—she faced the certainty that she wouldn't have a child anytime soon, and the bitter realization that she'd gone to all that trouble for nothing; very far, too, from the no less bitter regret at having forfeited a life that had been perfectly suitable. This feeling of hurt over her loss took her by surprise and upset her, and with her free hand—the other gripping her bundle—she struck her breasts with little taps as if to make herself believe that she suffered from a form of physical imperfection.

Oh, that was it, all right: she wanted her husband to be there—or simply to be somewhere in that vast country of which she knew only this town (even only a small part of this town), a country whose borders, extent, and shape she had merely the vaguest notion of—in the end she wanted her husband to be there so she could remember his smooth, dark, calm features and feel secure in the knowledge of that face remaining unchanged, warm and animated, waving like hers, somewhere on earth, a heavy flower on its stalk. Khady now turned her own face mechanically toward that of the stranger ("That's where the car will pick people up, it'll be here soon"), the unknown, disdainful face twitching disconcertingly, the living presence that Khady couldn't fail to acknowledge beside her own, whose heat she could feel close to her cheek and whose faint odor of sweat she could smell, whereas what her husband's face might look like now she had no idea and couldn't even imagine.

That beloved face, she would have endured never seeing it again if she could have been sure that, even far removed from her, it was intact, warm and damp with sweat.

But the thought that it would exist forever only in the memory of a handful of people suddenly filled her with sadness and pity for her husband, and although she ached and kept hitting her chest, she couldn't help feeling lucky.

The man had stopped at the bottom of the boulevard near a small group of people laden with packages.

Khady had put her bundle down and sat upon it.

She let her body relax and wiggled her toes on the thin plastic soles of her flip-flops.

She'd pulled her batik almost up to her knee to let the sun play on her dry, cracked, and dusty legs.

She wasn't bothered that she didn't matter to anyone or that no one gave her a single thought.

She was herself, she was calm, she was alive, she was still young, and she was in excellent health; every fiber of her being was savoring the kindly warmth of the early-morning sun, and her twitching nostrils gratefully sniffed the salty air blowing in off the sea, which, though not visible, she could hear just at the bottom of the boulevard like a surge of blue-green radiance in the morning light, like the glint of bronze against the soft blue of the sky.

She half closed her eyes, leaving only a slit through which to watch the man assigned to drive her pacing nervously up and down.

To drive her where?

She'd never dare ask him; in any case she didn't want to know, not yet anyway, because, she wondered, what would her poor brain do with the information, knowing as little as it did of the world, knowing only a small number of names, names of things in everyday use but not the names of what cannot be seen, used, or comprehended.

Whenever memories of the school to which her grandmother had briefly sent her insinuated themselves into her dreams, it was all noise, confusion, jibes, and scuffles and a few vague images of a bony, mistrustful girl quick to scratch the face of anyone who attacked her, who, squatting on the tiled floor because there weren't enough chairs, could hear (but couldn't discern) the rapid, dry, impatient, cross words of a teacher who luckily paid her not the slightest attention, whose perpetually scandalized look (or perpetual looking for something to be scandalized by) passed over the girl without seeing her, and if the girl was content to be left in peace she wasn't in the least afraid of that woman or of the other children, and if she put up with humiliation she wasn't, for all that, cowed by anyone.

Khady smiled inwardly. That small, cantankerous girl was her.

She touched her right ear mechanically and smiled again at the feeling of the two separate parts of her lobe: a child had jumped on her in class and torn off her earring.

Oh no, she'd never learned or understood anything at school.

She would simply let the litany of indistinguishable words—uttered in a toneless voice by the woman with the unlovely face and annoyed expression—wash over her. She'd no idea what sort of things the words referred to; she was aware that they involved a language, French, which she could understand and even speak a little but couldn't follow in the woman's rapid, irascible delivery. Meanwhile, a part of her remained constantly on the alert for that group of children who might at any moment launch a surprise attack and kick or slap her when the teacher turned around to face the blackboard.

That was why, today, all she knew of life was what she'd lived through.

She therefore preferred that the man imposed on her as her guide or companion or protector didn't inflict on her ignorant mind—were she to ask him where they were going—the pointless torment of a vocable it couldn't possibly recognize, since she was well aware that her fate was linked to the obscure, even bizarre and quite unmemorizable name.

It wasn't that her fate bothered her all that much, no, but why spoil this brand-new, beneficent feeling of pleasure at the warm atmosphere and slight odor of fermentation, of healthy rot, rising from the pavement on which her feet were resting contentedly and her body was relaxing in that state of complete immobility that it knew so well how to attain—why risk spoiling all that for no good reason?

The people around her were doing much the same as they waited, sitting on large tartan plastic bags or cardboard boxes tied with string, and although Khady looked straight in front of her through half-closed eyelids, she could tell from the absence of vibration, from a certain stagnant quality of the air around her, that the man—shepherd or jailer or protector or secret caster of evil spells—was the only one fidgeting, pacing feverishly up and down the sandy, uneven pavement, bouncing and hopping about involuntarily in his green sneakers exactly like (Khady thought) the black and white crows nearby—black crows with broad white collars—whose brother he perhaps was, subtly changed into a man in order to carry Khady off.

Her equanimity was disrupted by a shudder of dread.

Later, after it turned so hot that Khady had wrapped herself in the batik packed the night before and the small group of individuals had become a tumultuous crowd, the man suddenly grabbed her by the arm, pulled her to her feet, and pushed her into the back of a car already occupied by several others, then jumped in himself, protesting loudly, scornfully, and indignantly; it seemed to Khady that he was furious at finding so many people in the car, that he'd been assured it wouldn't be so, and that perhaps he'd even paid for it not to be.

Unsettled, she stopped listening, feeling the hot anger of this man against her thigh and his anxious, quivering exasperation.

Was he hiding behind his reflective lenses the small, hard, round eyes, the fixed stare of the crows, was he concealing under his checked shirt curiously buttoned up at the neck that collar of whitish feathers they all wore?

She shot him a sideways glance as the car started moving slowly and with difficulty out of the square that was now filled with minibuses and other big, heavy vehicles like theirs into which there clambered, or tried to, large numbers of people whose words and occasional shouts and cries mingled with the aggressive shrieks of the black-and-white crows flying low over the roadway—she looked at the man's mouth, which never stopped twitching, and at the feverish quivering of his neck, and she thought then that the crows opened and closed their black beaks ceaselessly in much the same way, that their black-and-white breasts—black trimmed with white—jerked rhythmically in a similar fashion, as if life were so fragile that it had to signal, or warn of, how delicate and vulnerable it was.

She wouldn't have put a question to him for all the world.

Because what she feared now wasn't that he would say something that corresponded with nothing in the little she knew, but
that, on the contrary, he would remind her of his fellow crows and
conjure up the dark, far-off place to which he was perhaps taking
her: she, Khady, who hadn't earned enough in the family to pay for
her food and who was being put out in this way, but, oh, were those
banknotes tucked in her waistband intended to pay for her passage
to that undoubtedly baleful, terrible place?

Enveloped again by the fleeting confusion into which she had
previously been plunged, but without the gentle slowness that had
protected her, she was on the verge of panic.

What was she supposed to think, what was she failing to understand?

How was she to interpret the clues to her misfortune?

She vaguely remembered a story her grandmother used to tell
about a snake, a violent and invisible creature that had several
times tried to carry the grandmother off before a neighbor had
managed to kill it even though it couldn't be seen, but she was
unable to recall any mention of crows, and that frightened her.

Should she have remembered something?

Had she already, at some time past, been warned?

She tried to move away a little from her companion by pressing up against the two old women on her left, but the one closest
elbowed her purposefully in the ribs without looking at her.

Khady then tried to make herself as small as possible by hugging her bundle tight.

She stared at the folds of skin on the back of the driver's shaven
head and tried not to think about anything, just allowing herself
to note that she was now hungry and thirsty, reflecting longingly

on the piece of bread her mother-in-law had packed, feeling its hard edges against her chest, her head swaying left and right as she was thrown about roughly by the car bouncing up and down as it went along a wide, badly rutted road that Khady could see unfolding rapidly between the head of the driver and that of the front-seat passenger, through the cracked windshield: a soothing view, despite the jolts.

The road was lined by cinder-block houses with corrugated-iron roofs in front of which small white hens were pecking and lively children were playing, houses and children such as Khady had dreamed of having with her husband (he of the kindly face): a house of well-laid cement blocks and with a shiny roof, a tiny, clean yard, and bright-eyed children with healthy skin, *her* children, who would romp about at the roadside without a care in the world although it seemed to Khady that the car was going to gobble them up as surely as it was swallowing the fast, wide, rutted road.

Something inside her wanted to shout a warning to them about the danger and to beg the driver not to devour her children—they'd all inherited her husband's kindly face—but the moment she was about to utter it she held back, feeling horribly ashamed and frustrated to realize that her children were only crows with unkempt plumage pecking in front of the houses and sometimes grumpily flying off when the cars passed by, black and white and quarrelsome, sailing toward the low branches of a kapok tree, and what would people say if she got it into her head to try and protect her crow-children, she who by chance still had the face and name of Khady Demba and would keep her human features only as long as she remained in that car staring at the fat shaven nape of the driver and thus out of his clutches, this ferocious light-footed bird, what would people say about Khady Demba?

She jumped violently as the man gripped her shoulder.

Having already gotten out of the car he pulled her toward him to make her get out too, while the other women pushed her unceremoniously (one of them complaining that their door was jammed).

Khady stumbled out, still half asleep, leaving the stuffy heat of the car for the suffocating humidity of a place that, if it didn't remind her of anywhere in particular, wasn't unlike the neighborhood she'd been living in, with sandy streets and pink or pale blue or roughcast walls, so that she began to lose her fear of having been brought to the crows' lair.

The man gestured impatiently for her to follow him.

Khady took a quick look around her.

Stalls lined the little square where the car had parked among others just like it, long, badly dented vehicles, and a crowd of men and women was moving between the cars haggling over fares.

Khady noticed in a corner the two letters WC painted on a wall.

She pointed them out to the man, who'd turned around to make sure she was still there, then ran to relieve herself.

When she came out of the latrines, he'd disappeared.

She stopped exactly where he'd stood a few moments before.

She undid her bundle carefully, tore off a piece of bread, and began eating it slowly.

She let each mouthful dissolve on her tongue because she wanted to savor it fully. It was stale, so rather bland and tasteless, but she enjoyed eating it. At the same time, her eyes darted from one end of the square to the other trying to find the man who held her fate in his hands.

Because now that the crows were no longer to be seen anywhere (only pigeons and gray sparrows were flitting here and there), she was much less afraid of a possible family connection between those birds and the man she was with than of being abandoned there: she, Khady Demba, who had no idea where she was and didn't care to ask.

The sky was dull and overcast.

From the dimmed brilliance of the light and the low position of the pink halo behind the pale gray of the sky Khady guessed with some surprise that night was drawing in, meaning they'd been driving for several hours.

Suddenly the man was standing in front of her again.

He thrust a bottle of orange soda toward her.

"Come on, come on," he breathed in an urgent, edgy tone of voice, and Khady began trotting behind him again, her flip-flops scraping along the dusty ground, taking big gulps straight from the bottle and, in a state of focused, lucid terror, pausing to inhale the distant smells of putrefaction blowing in from the sea and the crumbling facades, facades such as she'd never seen before, of enormous houses with sagging balconies and dilapidated columns that seemed, in the fading light of violet dusk, to take on the look of very old bones propping up the ravaged body of some large animal. Then the faint smell of rotting fish became more insistent as the man turned toward one of those half-collapsed monsters, and pushed a door open to let Khady into a courtyard, where she saw nothing at first but a pile of sacks and bundles scarcely darker than the violet dusk of the fading day.

The man whispered to her to sit down but Khady remained standing close to the door they'd just come through, not out of any wish to disobey him but rather because in the awesome effort she was making, within her limited powers and sparse points of reference, to force her unbridled, impulsive, timorous mind to note then try to interpret what her eyes were taking in—in that terrible feat of will and intellect, her body had frozen, her legs had stiffened, and her knees had been transformed into two tight balls as hard and inflexible as two knots on a tree branch.

Between herself and the other people there was but one connection: they all found themselves huddled together in the same place at the same time.

But what was the nature of—and the reason for—that connection, and was the situation a good one for them and for her, and how would she recognize a bad situation, and was she a free person or not?

That she was capable of formulating such questions surprised and troubled her.

Her laboriously inquisitive mind was suffering under the burden of so much reflection, but she was not displeased at the progress of that hard work within her, indeed she found it fascinating.

The man didn't insist on her sitting down.

She could smell the chalybeate odor of his sweat and feel, too, the almost electrical vibrations of his anxious excitement.

For the first time he took off his sunglasses.

In the semidarkness his pitch-black eyes seemed very round and shiny.

Khady was gripped again by her old fear that the man had something to do with crows.

She glanced at the blurred mass of packages and of people sitting or lying among them. She would have been scarcely surprised to see wings flapping there, recognizable in the dark by their white fringes, or hear those white-fringed wings beating against invisible sides. She felt then that in this very fear of hers an escape was being plotted, an attempted flight toward the pallid, dreamy, solitary lands she'd just left—only that very morning, in fact—and she forced herself to suppress her anxiety and to concentrate on nothing but the immediate reality of imminent threat she discerned in the man's gleaming eyes, on the voracious hiss of his voice asking for, indeed demanding, money.

"Pay me now, you have to pay me!"

Khady suddenly realized that he might be attributing her motionlessness, her lack of reaction, to a reluctance to give him what he wanted, so she softened her stance and facial expression and opened her mouth in a kind of conciliatory smile that he probably couldn't see in the dark.

As if from a great distance she could hear herself cawing—and wasn't it a bit as if she were imitating the man's voice?

"Pay you? Why must I pay you?"

"I brought you here, it was agreed!"

Abruptly turning her back on him she slid her hand along her belly, felt around, and pulled out five warm, damp banknotes, so soft and worn they looked like bits of rag.

She spun around and shoved the notes into the man's hand.

He counted them without looking at them.

Satisfied, he muttered something to himself and stuffed the notes in the pocket of his jeans. Seeing him so easily placated, Khady immediately regretted having given him so much.

She had the vague feeling that she would have been ready now to ask him, not the name of the town he'd brought her to nor the name of the place they found themselves in, but the reason for their journey—that she would now have been in a position to listen to him and try to learn something, but she was loath to speak to him again, to hear her own voice and then his, the rasping sound of his throat being cleared, which reminded her of the cry of those ferocious black birds with the white wingtips.

But he'd already turned on his heels and left the courtyard.

And though she'd not known all day whether he was her jailer or her guardian angel, fearsome or benevolent, though she'd been afraid to look him in the eye, his disappearance blocked the calm, studious, rapt flow of her newly directed, controlled thought, and Khady slipped back into the faintly anguished mists of her monotonous daydreams.

She slid to the ground and curled up on her bundle.

She lay prostrate, neither awake nor sleepy, and was almost unaware of what was going on around her. In the depths of an inertia interrupted by occasional jolts of anxiety she was conscious only of feeling hot, hungry, and thirsty. Then a sudden commotion made her lift her head and start to get up.

All the people in the courtyard had stood up, responding, Khady hastily supposed, to the arrival of a small group of men.

There was much whispering among the previously silent crowd.

The darkness was heavy and deep.

As she crouched Khady could feel the sweat running down her arms, between her breasts, and at the back of her knees.

She heard short, deliberately stifled shouts coming from the three or four men who'd just entered, and although she hadn't grasped what they were saying, either because she was too far away or because they were speaking a language she wasn't familiar with, Khady understood, from the busy, preoccupied, muffled rustling that ran through the crowd, that what the people in the courtyard had been waiting for was now at last to happen.

Her head was buzzing.

She picked up her bundle and, a little unsteadily, followed the slow procession to the door.

Hardly had they reached the sandy street, dimly lit by a thin crescent moon, than silence fell once again on the group walking slowly in a spontaneously organized single file behind the men whose arrival had put an end to the long wait in the courtyard, and even the small children, strapped to their mothers' backs, were quiet.

Dogs were howling in the distance.

Apart from the rustling of people's clothes and the noise of their flip-flops scraping the sand, that was the only sound to be heard in the darkness.

The last houses disappeared.

She then felt her thin plastic soles sinking into deep sand, still warm on the surface but cold underneath. The march of one and all around her was slowed, impeded by the mass of fine sand that filled their slippers and flip-flops and suddenly froze their toes and ankles, whereas their foreheads were still pouring with sweat.

She was aware, too, almost in advance, almost before it happened, of an end to the prudent hushed consensus that had prevailed in the street, and she guessed, from an imperceptible quiver, from a more pronounced sound of breathing running through the moving, undulating crowd, that the danger, whatever it was, of being heard and noticed had passed, or else perhaps the tension had reached such a point now as they were approaching the sea that the need for restraint could be set aside and forgotten.

Shouts broke out. All Khady could distinguish was a change of tone, to one of considerable anguish.

One child started to cry, then another.

The men in front leading the group halted and shouted orders in a feverish, menacing tone.

They'd switched on flashlights, which they shone in people's faces as if they were looking for someone in particular.

Then, in the sudden flashes of harsh white light, Khady was able to see, in fleeting fragments, the dazzled, half-closed eyes and faces of those who up till then had seemed to form an undifferentiated mass.

They were all more or less young, like her.

One man with a calm, rather sad air made her think momentarily of her husband.

The beam of light flashed across her own face and she thought, Yes, me, Khady Demba, still happy to utter her name silently and to sense its apt harmony with the precise, satisfying image she had of her own features and of the Khady heart that dwelled within her to which no one but she had access.

But she was afraid now.

She could hear the waves crashing close by, and out at sea she could see other lights, less harsh, yellower, bobbing up and down.

Yes, she was very afraid.

With a fierce effort that made her dizzy she tried frantically to connect what she was seeing and hearing—flickering lights, the roar of the surf, men and women assembled on the beach—to something she'd heard in her husband's family, at the market, in the yard of the house she'd been living in, and even before that, in the little café she ran where she thought of nothing all day but of the child she so longed to conceive.

It seemed she ought to have been able to remember snatches of conversation or the odd word heard on the radio, things caught on the wing and stored vaguely in her mind along with other information of no interest at the time but not without the potential one day to acquire it—it seemed to her that, without having paid attention to the subject at one stage in her life, or thinking it important, she'd nevertheless known what such a combination of elements (night, flickering lamps, cold sand, anxious faces) signified, and it seemed to her that she still knew, but for her stubborn sluggish mind blocking access to a region of sparse, jumbled knowledge to which possibly, certainly, the scene before her was in some way connected.

Oh, she was very afraid.

She felt as if she'd been prodded in the back and was being pushed forward by the abrupt surge of the group toward the sound of crashing waves.

The men with flashlights were getting increasingly nervous and were shouting more and more insistently as people got nearer the sea.

Khady felt her flip-flops getting submerged in the water.

She now clearly saw lights moving in front of her and realized that they must be coming from lamps hung on the bow of a boat. Then, as if she'd had to work out what it was all about before being able to see it, she made out the shape of a large craft not unlike those whose landing she waited for when, as a little girl, she'd been sent by her grandmother to buy fish on the beach.

The people in front of her went into the water, holding their bundles above their heads, then climbed into the boat, helped up by those already on board, whom Khady could make out in the yellowish, fragile, swaying lights, their faces calm and preoccupied, before she too moved forward awkwardly in the cold sea, throwing her bundle in before letting herself be pulled up into the boat.

The bottom was filled with water.

Gripping her bundle, she crouched on one of the sides.

An indeterminate, putrid smell rose from the wood.

There she remained, stunned and dazed. Such a large number of people were still climbing into the boat that she was afraid of being squashed or suffocated.

She staggered to her feet.

Seized with terror, she was panting.

She pulled up her wet batik, put a leg over the edge of the boat, grabbed her bundle, and lifted the other leg.

She felt a terrible pain in her right calf.

She jumped into the water.

She waded back to the beach and began running along the sand. It got increasingly darker as she left the boat behind.

Although her calf hurt a great deal and her heart was beating so fast that she felt sick, she was filled with delirious, fervent, savage joy at realizing, clearly and indubitably, that she'd just done something that *she* had resolved to do, once she'd decided—very quickly—how vitally important it was for her to leave the boat.

She realized too that such a thing had never happened before:

making a decision, quite independently, about something that mattered to *her*. Her marriage, for instance: because it represented a way to cut loose from her grandmother, she'd been only too eager to accept when this quiet, gentle man—a neighbor at the time—had asked her for her hand. It certainly wasn't—she thought as she ran, gasping for breath—because she thought that her life was her own and that it involved choices that she, Khady Demba, was free to make, oh, certainly not. It was *she* who'd been chosen: by a man who'd turned out fortunately to be a good husband. But she hadn't known it then: at the time she'd just felt grateful, relieved, to have been chosen.

Exhausted, she collapsed in the sand.

She was barefoot: her flip-flops had remained in the water or perhaps at the bottom of the boat.

She touched her injured calf and felt blood running from her torn flesh.

She told herself she must have caught her leg on a nail as she leaped out of the boat.

It was so dark she couldn't see the blood on her hand even when holding it close to her eyes.

She rubbed sand on her fingers for a long while.

What she could see—far away, much farther than she thought she could have run—were small yellowish lights, motionless in the distance, and the powerful white beam of a torch, probing the darkness continually, jerkily, enigmatically.

At dawn she realized, before she'd even opened her eyes, that what had aroused her was not anxiety, nor the sharp pain in her calf, nor the still feeble brightness of the day, but the imperceptible sensation of tingling on her skin, of someone's motionless, insistent stare. In order to give herself time to regain her composure she pretended to be still asleep, while quite alert.

She suddenly opened her eyes and sat up on the sand.

A few yards away a young man was kneeling. He didn't lower his eyes when she looked at him. He just cocked his head slightly and held his hands up with their palms toward her to indicate that she had nothing to fear. She scrutinized him furtively and cautiously. Flipping through her mental images of the previous evening with a speed and lucidity she no longer thought herself capable of, she recognized one of the faces she'd glimpsed, pale in the beam of the torch, just before climbing into the boat.

He seemed younger than her, about twenty perhaps.

With a high, shrill voice, almost like a child's, he asked, "You okay?"

"Yes, thanks, and you?"

"I'm okay. My name's Lamine."

She hesitated a moment, then, not quite managing to suppress a proud, almost arrogant note creeping into her voice, she told him her name: "Khady Demba."

He got up and sat down beside her.

The deserted beach of grayish sand was covered in garbage (plastic bottles, rubbish bags split open, and the like), which Lamine eyed with cold detachment, looking to see if any of it could possibly still be of use, passing from one item to the next, promptly forgetting each one the moment he'd dismissed it, consigning it to oblivion as though it had never existed.

His eyes fell on Khady's leg. His face was twisted in horror, but he tried to hide it clumsily behind a hesitant smile.

"You're really hurt, aren't you?"

A bit peeved, she looked down in turn.

It was a gaping wound, encrusted with dried blood covered in sand.

The dull nagging pain seemed to get worse the more she looked at it. Khady let out a groan.

"I know where we can get some water," Lamine said.

He helped her to her feet.

She sensed the nervous strength of his rawboned, tight body, like a coiled spring, as if it were being kept firm, hardened by the constant vigilance and the privations he'd endured, no less than by his ability to blot them out, just as he seemed to negate, to banish from his mind, any object on the beach that was of no interest.

Khady knew her own body was slim and robust, but it did not compare to this boy's, tempered in the icy water of unavoidable deprivation, so that for the first time in her life she felt luckier than another human being.

She checked to make sure that the wad of banknotes was still there, held in her elastic waistband.

Then, refusing his offer of help, she walked beside Lamine toward the row of houses and shops with corrugated-iron roofs that lined the beach above the high-water mark.

At every step, the pain intensified.

And because, on top of that, she was very hungry, she yearned to be able to acquire an insensible, inorganic body, with no needs or desires, nothing but a tool in the service of a plan that she still knew nothing of but that she understood she'd be made to learn about.

Well, she did know one thing. And this she knew, not as she usually knew things—that is, without knowing that she knew—but in a clear and conscious way.

I can't go back to the family, she said to herself, not even wondering (because it was useless) whether that was a good thing or just an extra source of unhappiness. Thinking clearly and calmly, she was well aware that she had, in a way, made a choice.

And when Lamine had told her of his own intentions, when—in a rather strident voice interrupted by little nervous giggles when he couldn't think of a word or seemed afraid of not being taken seriously—he'd assured her that he'd get to Europe one day or die in the attempt, that there was no other solution to his problems, it appeared to Khady that all he was doing there was making her own plan explicit.

So, in deciding to join him, her conviction that she was now in control of the precarious, unsteady equipage that was her existence hadn't been shaken in any way.

Quite the opposite.

He'd led her to a pump in the center of town so that she could wash off the sand sticking to her wound. Then he explained that he'd tried several times to leave, that he'd always been prevented by unforeseen circumstances, sometimes large impediments, sometimes small (last night it had been the ramshackle condition of the boat), but that he now had sufficient knowledge of what he might find to brave the obstacles and evade or overcome all eventualities, of which there couldn't be that many and surely he'd seen them all.

Khady instantly recognized that he was up to speed with things she couldn't even imagine, and that by staying with him she'd benefit from absorbing his knowledge, instead of having to grope her own laborious way to it.

How remarkable she found it that she hadn't said to herself, What else can I do, in any case, but follow this boy? but rather had thought that she could take control of the situation and profit from it.

Racked with pain, she washed her torn calf.

The two pieces of flesh were clearly separated.

She tore a strip off the batik that contained her belongings and wrapped it tightly around her calf, binding together the two flaps of the wound.

Throughout the heavy, still days that followed, the place remained grayish, but the light was bright, as if the shimmering metallic surface of the sea were diffusing a leaden glare.

It seemed to Khady that she'd been granted a reprieve so she could steep herself in information such as she'd never acquired in twenty-five years; and discreetly, too, without appearing to learn anything, an instinctive caution having stopped her revealing to Lamine how ignorant she was.

He'd brought her back to the courtyard their group had departed from.

Many new people were gathered there, and the boy went around collecting orders for food and water, which he then ran to get in town.

He never asked Khady to pay for what he'd bring back for them to eat (omelet sandwiches, bananas, grilled fish), and Khady never offered, because she'd decided never to talk about anything that hadn't already been aired, confining herself to short replies to questions that were equally laconic, not mentioning money since Lamine didn't, questioning him on the other hand with suppressed eagerness about the journey he was planning and the means of achieving it. On that topic she tried to conceal her hunger for information behind an air of gloomy, bored restraint; she felt a veil of morose impenetrability covering her face, just as it had done in her husband's family, hiding her wan, tepid thoughts behind it.

Oh, how fast her mind was working now! Sometimes it got in a muddle, as if intoxicated by its own abilities.

It was not too sure now whether the ardent young man standing before it was Khady's husband or a stranger called Lamine, or why exactly it had to remember everything that came out of that mouth with the hot, almost feverish breath, and it felt tempted—at rare, very brief moments—to flush itself clean and return to its previous state, where nothing was demanded of it except to avoid getting involved in anything to do with real life.

Khady memorized, then, at nightfall, lying in the courtyard, filed away the new pieces of information in order of importance.

What had to be kept continually in mind was this: the journey could take months, even years, as it had for a neighbor of Lamine's who'd only reached Europe (what "Europe" was exactly, where it was situated, she put off until later to find out) five whole years after leaving home.

This too: it was imperative to buy a passport. Lamine had reliable connections for getting one.

And then: the boy now refused to go by sea from this coast.

The journey would be longer, much longer, but it would go through the desert and arrive at a certain place where you had to climb to get into Europe.

And then, and then: Lamine had said many times—his suddenly mulish, inscrutable, smooth face shining with sweat—that he didn't mind dying if that was the price of pursuing his aim, but to go on living as he had done up till now, that he refused to do.

Although Khady spontaneously blotted out everything to do with the boy's earlier life, although she tried not to listen to anything she thought inessential, whatever was likely to upset or embarrass her, even, inexplicably, to fill her with a muted sadness, as if her own earliest memories were being revived rather than his, she couldn't help retaining the fact that a stepmother—his father's new wife after his mother's death—had for years beaten Lamine so hard he'd almost gone mad.

He pulled up his T-shirt to show her the pinkish, slightly puffy marks on his back.

He'd gone to the lycée and failed the baccalaureate twice.

But he wanted badly to go on studying, he dreamed of becoming an engineer. (What did that mean? Khady wondered despite herself, trying hard not to get interested.)

When after a few days she made to remove the cloth protecting her calf, it was stuck so hard to the wound that she had to wrench it off, causing such pain that she couldn't help crying out.

She wrapped a strip of clean cloth tightly around it.

She limped from one corner of the courtyard to another, trying to habituate herself to the hindrance, to train her body to cope with the slower pace and constant pain, until they became a part of her that she could forget or ignore by relegating it to the status of other merely circumstantial matters, like the painful stories of Lamine's past, that served no useful purpose but merely risked deflecting and slowing down the still budding, precarious development of her thinking by insinuating into it elements of turmoil and uncontrollable suffering.

She similarly let her eyes flit across the faces of the people who arrived ever more numerous each day in the courtyard—and her look, she knew, was neutral, cold, and a permanent discouragement to anyone attempting conversation, not because she was afraid of being asked something (she had no fear of that) but because her mind panicked at the mere possibility of hearing about painful, complicated lives and being told at great length about things she found difficult to understand since she lacked the principles for interpreting matters in life that others seemed to possess as a matter of course.

One day the boy took her through narrow, sandy streets to a barber shop where a woman in the back took photos of her.

A few days later he came back with a worn, creased, blue booklet that he gave Khady, telling her she was now called Bintou Thiam.

His eyes had a look of pride, triumph, and self-assurance that put Khady slightly on guard.

She had a passing feeling that she was becoming feeble again and subject to the decisions, knowledge, and inscrutable intentions of others. Through sheer weariness she was briefly tempted to accept this subordination, to stop thinking about anything and to let her mind once again drift in the milky flow of its dreams.

Feeling a little disgusted, she pulled herself together.

She thanked the boy with a nod.

She felt terrible shooting pains in her calf that made it hard for her to think straight.

But though still determined not to discuss money unless he did, she couldn't ignore the issue, nor the fact that Lamine had bought a passport for her and was behaving as if it were obvious that she had no money, or that one way or another she'd pay later—that worried her to the point that she sometimes wished he'd disappear, vanish from her life.

But she was becoming attached to his eager features, his adolescent voice.

She surprised herself by looking at him with pleasure, almost with tender amusement, when, hopping about the courtyard like the delicate birds with long spindly legs that she remembered seeing as a child on the beach (although she thought she couldn't now remember what they were called, she could see that everything had a name even if she didn't know it, and realized with embarrassment she'd once believed that only those things whose names she knew possessed one), he moved from one group to another, busying himself with a spirited, childlike innocence that inspired confidence.

He was possessed of a particular intuition.

She was beginning to grow impatient, but never for a moment thought to complain about it, when he announced they'd be leaving the next day. It was as if—she thought—he'd guessed that without realizing it she was starting to get bored, and had decided it was a bad thing: but why?

What could that matter to him?

Oh, she certainly felt affection for the boy.

That night, in the darkness of the courtyard where they were lying, she felt him moving close to her, hesitantly, as if unsure of her reaction.

She didn't rebuff him; rather, she encouraged him by turning toward him.

She pulled her batik up and, carefully rolling the banknotes in them, slipped her panties off and laid her head on them.

It was years since she'd made love: not once since her husband's death.

She carefully stroked the boy's heavily scarred back and was surprised at the same time by the extreme lightness of his body and by the almost excessive gentleness and delicacy (because she could barely feel he was there) with which he moved within her. Almost as a reflex, recalled by the sensation of a body on top of hers, even one so different from her husband's compact, heavy frame, there came back to her the prayers to be got with child which she'd never ceased murmuring at the time and which had prevented her having an orgasm by distracting her from the necessary concentration on her own pleasure.

She vehemently chased all such prayers away.

She was filled with a kind of well-being, a sort of physical comfort—nothing more pointed than that, nothing at all like what her sisters-in-law giggled and sighed about between themselves—but it made Khady feel happy and grateful to the boy.

As he pulled away from her he inadvertently bumped against her calf.

An explosion of pain tore through Khady.

She was panting and almost fainted.

She could hear Lamine murmuring anxiously in her ear and—suffering so much that she felt surprised, almost detached, a stranger to a self that was in such violent pain—she said to herself, Who ever cared about me the way he does, this lad, and so young too! I'm lucky, I'm really lucky . . .

Before dawn they clambered onto an open-bed truck where so many people were already huddling that it seemed impossible for Khady to find any room for herself.

She perched on a pile of sacks in the back, high up above the wheels.

Lamine advised her to grip the string on the packaging firmly so as not to fall off.

He was sitting astride a box right next to her and Khady could smell on their arms, pressed close together, the slightly sharp odor of his sweat mingling with hers.

"If you fall, the driver won't stop and you'll die in the desert," Lamine whispered.

He'd given her a leather flask filled with tepid water.

Khady had seen him give the driver a wad of bills, explaining that he was paying for her too, then he'd helped her onto the truck, since her leg seemed to have become so heavy she couldn't manage it alone.

Lamine's barely contained excitement—which he attempted to conceal by fussy, precise gestures (such as frequently checking that the top of the water bottle was screwed on tight) and by continual warnings, repeated in a soft, slow voice ("Hang on tight, if you fall off the driver won't stop and you'll die in the desert")—she could sense from the slight twitch of his face: she found herself infected by his slightly intoxicated eagerness, so that she felt neither afraid nor humiliated at being helped in the simplest ways by the boy, nor by the constant support he gave her, such as cupping his hands together to give her a leg up onto the truck; none of that called into question the idea she now had of her own independence, of being free from constraints imposed by the will of others. In much the same manner she endeavored not to see, in the money that Lamine had given the driver on her behalf, anything that amounted to a personal commitment on her part.

For Khady Demba, all that was of no consequence.

If it pleased Lamine to play a crucial role in her liberation, she was sincerely grateful to him for that—yes, she felt a great deal of affection for the boy, but it didn't make her accountable in any way.

Her head was spinning a little.

There was no relief now from the intense pain in her leg. It mingled with a feeling of joy that also appeared to be urging her fiercely onward.

As it moved off, the truck juddered so violently she was nearly thrown from her perch.

Lamine grabbed her in the nick of time.

"Hold on tight, hold on tight!" he shouted in her ear, and close up in the rosy light of dawn she could see his thin, hollow cheeks and the pale chapped lips he moistened often with his tongue, and his eyes: a bit wild, a bit frantic, she thought, like those dark and terrified eyes of a large yellowish dog that had been cornered in the market by women armed with sticks determined to make it pay for the theft of a chicken—Lamine's were just like the dog's eyes, filled with innocent terror, that had met hers in the market and pierced her numb, cold heart and had for a brief moment aroused strong feelings of sympathy and shame.

Was it for her that Lamine had been so afraid?

She was to recall, with dull remorse but without bitterness, how very attentive Lamine had been toward her.

She would remember all that, never thinking, however, that he'd sought to deceive her. In thinking back to his concern for her, the sadness she would feel, though at some remove, would be more for him than herself: it would be the boy's fate that would affect her to the point of shedding a few cold tears, whereas she would judge her own destiny dispassionately, almost with detachment, as if she, Khady Demba, who had never wagered on life as much hope as Lamine did, had no reason to complain about losing everything.

She had not lost much, she would think, insisting with that imponderable pride, that discreet, unshakable assurance, I'm me, Khady Demba, even as she would get up, with sore thighs, the lips of her hot, inflamed vagina still swollen, up from that sad excuse for a mattress—a piece of grayish, stinking foam, actually—that throughout those long months was to be her place of work.

She'd not lost much, she thought.

Because, however great her exhaustion or intense her affliction, she would never regret that period of her life when her mind wandered in the foggy, numbing protective confinement of her frozen dreams, the time she lived with her husband's family.

Nor would she have missed for anything the years of her marriage when the longing to get pregnant occupied every thinking moment.

Truth to tell, she would regret nothing, even while plunged in the reality of a horrific present that she could see only too clearly, to which she would apply thinking full of both pragmatism and pride (she would never have pointless feelings of shame, she would never forget the value of the human being she was: Khady Demba, honest and true)—a reality that above all she considered transitory, convinced that this period of suffering would have an end, and that while she would certainly not be rewarded (she couldn't believe she was owed anything for having suffered) she would simply move on to something else. She didn't yet know what that would be, but she was curious to find out.

As for the chain of events that had brought them—her and Lamine—to this point, she had a precise picture of that and was trying, calmly and coldly, to understand it.

After a day and a night on the road, the truck had stopped at a border.

All the passengers had gotten out, formed a line, and shown their passports to soldiers who shouted one word that Khady did understand even though it was not her language.

Money.

Those who put their hands up to indicate that they had none, or who offered too little, were then so badly beaten that some fell to the ground, where, even lying there, they were sometimes thrashed further by a soldier who seemed mad with rage at this hard job he had of hitting people, the trouble they put him to.

Khady began to tremble all over.

Lamine, next to her, had gripped her hand.

She could see his jaw quivering as if behind those lips shut tight his teeth were chattering.

He'd held out his passport to the soldier and a roll of banknotes, pointing to Khady and then himself.

The man had taken the notes with the tips of his fingers, contemptuously, and thrown them on the ground.

He'd given a soldier an order. The soldier hit Lamine in the stomach.

The boy doubled over and fell to his knees without a word, without a groan.

The soldier had taken out a knife, lifted one of Lamine's feet and slashed the sole of his shoe. He'd felt the slit, then he'd done the same with the other foot.

And when, with his bony knees knocking, Lamine had straightaway staggered to his feet, as if it was more dangerous to lie prostrate than face his enemy, Khady could see two thin lines of blood running into the dust from under his shoes.

The commander had then turned to her. Khady had shown him the passport that Lamine had procured for her.

Clearheadedly, even though she couldn't stop shivering, she'd slipped her hand under her batik and drawn out the thin wad of banknotes, which, soaked in sweat all this time in the elastic of her panties, looked like a piece of greenish rag. She had placed the money delicately and respectfully in the man's hands while clinging tight to Lamine to make it clear that they were an item.

.   .   .

It was now several weeks—she wasn't sure how many—that they'd been holed up in this desert town, not where the soldier had slashed the soles of Lamine's feet but in another one, farther on from their original point of departure, where, once through that first checkpoint, they'd been brought by the truck.

Those travelers who still had money, either because they'd managed cleverly to hold some back or because for some obscure reason they hadn't been beaten or searched, had been able to pay the driver to take them on the next leg of their journey.

But Khady, Lamine, and a few others had had to stop here, in this town infested with sand, with low sand-colored houses and with streets and gardens covered in sand.

Exhausted and famished, they'd lain down to sleep in front of a sort of bus station where the truck had dumped them.

Other trucks, laden with their human cargo, were waiting, ready to leave.

When Khady and Lamine had awoken at dawn, numb with cold, they were covered in sand from head to foot. Khady's leg was hurting so much that it seemed to her, in flashes, that her suffering couldn't be real, that either she was struggling inside the cruelest nightmare of her entire life or she was already dead and was being made to understand that her death was just that: an unbearable—yet abiding—constant physical pain.

The cloth she'd used to bind her calf several days earlier was embedded in the wound.

It was damp under the grains of sand, impregnated by the seepage of a foul, reddish liquid.

She hadn't the strength to take it off, even though she knew she ought to—all she managed to do was gently move her leg, which was stiff and shot through with pins and needles. In the end she got up, shook the sand out of her hair and clothing.

She hopped around a bit.

On the ground sand-covered shapes were stirring.

She came back to Lamine, who was now sitting up. He'd taken his shoes off and was inspecting the soles of his feet, which the soldier's knife had cut while searching the boy's shoes.

A crust of dried blood made a dark line on the hard, broken skin.

She knew that the boy, though in pain, wouldn't show it or ever speak about his wounds; she knew too that her questioning look would be met only by a deliberately gloomy expression masking his humiliation (oh, how humiliated he was, how sorry she was for him, and how upset too at not being able to take on the humiliation for him, she who could bear it, who was so little affected by it), because what convincing explanation could he give, if not of their failure, at least of such a setback occurring so early in their journey, he who had assured her that he knew the ropes, knew about all the obstacles and dangers likely to be met with on the road?

She was aware of it, she understood and accepted it: the mortification he was feeling, which left him with that blank look and made him seem remote, so different from the intense, friendly boy he had been.

Understanding it, she didn't hold it against him.

What she didn't then know, what would only gradually become clear but what at the time she was unequipped to envision, was that the boy was doubly humiliated, both by what had happened the day before and, as a matter of deduction, by something that hadn't yet happened, something that Khady, who, though not naive, was too inexperienced to have yet intuited but that he, Lamine, knew would happen: that was why—Khady would later understand—he'd felt so ashamed in her presence, ashamed both at knowing she didn't know and ashamed at the thing itself: that was why, out of fear and unwillingness to have anything to do with Khady's innocence, he was so withdrawn from her.

Had he, later on, said anything specific to her?

She couldn't remember exactly.

But it seemed to her that he hadn't.

They'd simply wandered around, each limping in a different fashion (he trying to step only on the outer edges of his feet, she hopping along with irregular steps, trying to favor her sore leg), through streets heavy with dry, dusty heat under a yellowish, shimmering, sand-colored sky.

Lamine's close-cropped hair, face, and chapped lips were still covered with sand.

Dazed and desperate to find some shade, they'd sought out a cheap place to eat, with earthen walls and no windows, where, in the semidarkness, they'd eaten tough, stringy pieces of grilled goat's meat and drunk Coke, both knowing that they'd no money left to pay even for this meager fare, and Lamine retreated into a bitter, heartrending detachment behind which—he perhaps thought—he could take refuge alone with his indignity without it contaminating Khady, he who knew what was going to happen while she—he perhaps believed—still did not. But she'd had an inkling when, chewing the last piece of meat and washing it down with a last gulp of Coke, her eyes had met the hostile, half-closed eyes of the woman who had served them and who, breathing noisily, slumped on a chair in the darkest corner, had been scrutinizing the two of them, her and the boy. Khady had wondered then how they were now going to pay what they owed. In a way the woman's unfriendly, judgmental, inquisitive gaze had given her the answer.

Throughout this period she would cling ferociously to the conviction that only the reality of physical pain had to be taken into account.

Because her body was in a permanent state of suffering.

The woman made her work in a tiny room that gave onto a courtyard at the back of the chophouse.

There was a foam mattress on the hard floor.

Khady spent most of her time lying on it, dressed in a beige slip. The woman would bring a customer in, usually a wretched-looking young man who, like Khady and Lamine, had fetched up in this town, where he scraped together a living as a houseboy, and who often on entering the hot stuffy room would cast frightened looks around him as if caught in a trap of what was hardly—Khady thought—his own desires but the machinations of the woman who tried to inveigle every diner into visiting the room at the back.

The woman would then lock the door and go away.

The man would then lower his trousers with almost anxious haste, as if it were a matter of getting a tiresome and vaguely threatening obligation over with as quickly as possible. He'd lie down on Khady, who—to avoid jolting it as best she could—would move aside her injured leg, on which the woman put a fresh bandage each day. He would then enter her, often groaning in surprise, because a recent attack of pruritus that made Khady's vagina dry and inflamed also caused his penis some discomfort. She summoned all her mental strength to counter the multiple shooting pains in her back, her lower abdomen, and her calf, thinking, There's a time when it stops, feeling on her chest half hidden by the lace edging of her slip and on her neck the man's copious sweat mingling with hers, thinking again, There's a time when it stops, until the man finished his labors and, in a murmur of pain and disappointment, promptly withdrew.

He would then bang on the door and they would both hear the slow, heavy tread of the woman coming to open it.

Some customers would complain, saying that it had hurt, that the girl was infected.

And Khady thought with surprise, Ah, "the girl," that's me, almost amused to be the one referred to that way, she, Khady Demba, in all her singularity.

She would remain lying there a while after the other two had gone.

Breathing slowly, with her eyes wide open, she would calmly inspect the cracks in the pinkish walls, the corrugated-iron ceiling, and the white plastic chair under which she'd put her bundle.

Lying perfectly still, she could hear the blood throbbing calmly, softly, in her ears, and if she moved slightly, the sucking sound of her wet back on the mattress—which was also soaked in sweat—and the tiny lapping noise made by her burning vulva, and then, feeling the pain oozing gently away, overcome by the youthful, tempestuous vigor of her solid, willful physique, she would think, calmly, almost serenely, There's a time when it stops, so calmly, so serenely, that when the woman came back not alone, as she usually did, to wash her, nurse her, and give her something to drink, but in the company of another customer whom—with a vague gesture of regret or excuse in Khady's direction—she would bring in: even then Khady would experience only a brief moment of dejection, weakness, and disorientation, before once more thinking calmly, There's a time when it stops.

After imposing one customer after another upon her, the woman would take care of Khady with motherly solicitude.

She'd bring a towel and a bucket filled with cool water and gently wash Khady's nether regions.

In the evening they would sit down together in the courtyard and Khady would eat a solid meal of goat's meat and boiled corn washed down with Coke, keeping back a portion for Lamine.

The woman would take off Khady's bandage, smear fat on the wound, which was swollen and foul smelling, and bind it up again with a clean piece of cloth.

And as they sat there, full up, enjoying the quiet of the cool evening, Khady would turn to look at the woman. In the dusk she could see only the outline of a round, kindly face, and it sometimes seemed to her that she'd gone back to the time of her childhood, which, although harsh, muddled, and often grim, had had its happier moments, such as when Khady sat in front of the house at her grandmother's feet to have her hair done.

Just before nightfall, Lamine would arrive.

He slipped into the courtyard—Khady thought with a touch of pity and disgust—like a dog afraid of getting a hiding, but even more of finding his bowl empty. Lamine was at once quick and stooping, keen and furtive. Khady and the woman pretended not to notice, Khady out of delicacy and the woman out of scorn, and Lamine would pick up the full plate and carry it to Khady's room, where the woman allowed him—or at least didn't forbid him—to spend the night, on the unspoken proviso that he'd be gone by dawn.

Before going to bed, the woman would give Khady a small part of the money she'd earned.

Khady would also turn in, going back to the pinkish room lit by a grimy bulb hanging from the tin roof.

Seeing Lamine, once so energetic, crouched in a corner scraping his plate with his spoon, made Khady feel her aches and pains all come flooding back.

Because what—beyond the faintly tired evidence of her own honor now forever secured, and the rather weary awareness of her irrevocable dignity—could she set against the incurable shame the boy felt?

Perhaps he'd have preferred to see her humiliated and in despair.

But he carried the whole burden of despair and humiliation. Khady felt that, without realizing it, he held it against her. That was why she'd have preferred him not to be there in the evening, filling up the cramped space with his bitterness and his silent, obscure, unjust reproaches.

She also knew that he bore a grudge over her refusal to let him now make love to her.

Her reason—the one she gave herself and the one she told him—was that her swollen, ulcerated vagina needed a rest.

But this she guessed too: Lamine was ashamed of her, and for her, as much as he was ashamed of himself.

That annoyed her.

What right had he to include her in his feelings of abjection just because he lacked her strength of spirit?

She didn't see why she should put up with pain in her genitalia just to satisfy his needs.

Silently, wearily, she would slide down onto the mattress.

What he did all day long in the dry, suffocating heat of the town, she didn't care to be told.

She would feel a sullen pout beginning to play on her lips, aimed at discouraging any timid wish he might have for a chat.

Meanwhile her fingers would start moving mechanically toward the wall to stroke its nooks and crannies and, just before she fell asleep, a wild surge of joy would make her exhausted body quiver all over as she recalled suddenly, pretending to have forgotten, that she was Khady Demba: Khady Demba.

She awoke one morning to find Lamine gone.

Curiously, she understood what had happened before noticing his absence; she understood as soon as she woke up and leaped toward her bundle, which was wide open. She'd left it, tightly knotted, under the chair. She pulled out its meager contents—two T-shirts, a batik, a clean empty beer bottle—and groaned as she took in what she'd guessed before remarking anything else: that all her money was gone.

It was only at that instant she realized she was alone in the room.

In her distress she started making little whimpering sounds.

She opened her mouth wide. She felt she was suffocating.

Having awoken in the certainty that something bad had been done to her, had she, during the night, heard something, or had she had one of those dreams that foretell in precise detail what's about to happen?

She rushed out, limping so badly that she nearly fell over at every step, crossed the courtyard, and went into the chophouse, where the woman was drinking her first coffee of the day.

"He's gone! He's stolen everything from me!" she shouted.

She slumped down onto a chair.

With rather distant pity, the woman eyed her coldly and knowingly.

She finished her coffee, slightly spoiled by Khady's entry, and clicked her tongue. Then she got up heavily and, taking the girl in her arms and cradling her awkwardly, promised she'd never throw her out.

"No risk of that," Khady whispered, "with what I bring you."

In utter dejection she thought that she'd have to start all over again, that everything had to be endured once more, and even worse, because her body was so horribly bruised, whereas the night before she'd worked out that just two or three months' more work would suffice to enable her and Lamine to continue their journey.

As for the boy, well, she'd already forgotten him.

It wouldn't be long before all recollection of his name and what he looked like would fade from her mind. In retrospect she would see his betrayal as just one more cruel blow of fate.

Whenever she looked back to that period, she would round down to about a year the time she'd spent at the chophouse and in the pinkish room, but she knew that it had probably lasted a great deal longer and that she, too, had gotten bogged down in the sand of the desert town, like most of the men who visited her, who'd come from several different countries and who'd been wandering around the place for years, their eyes flitting apathetically over everything but seeming to take nothing in. They'd lost count of how long they'd been there, and people back home must have thought them dead because, in their shame over their situation, they'd failed to keep in touch with their families.

With their inert and impenetrable manners, they'd often linger by Khady's side, having seemingly forgotten what they'd come for or thought it so exhausting and pointless that in the end they preferred just to lie there, neither asleep nor really alive.

Month after month Khady got thinner and thinner.

She had fewer and fewer customers and spent a good part of her day in the semidarkness of the chophouse.

Still, her mind was clear and alert, and she was sometimes overwhelmed with joy when, alone at night, she murmured her own name and once again savored how perfectly suited it was to her self.

But she was losing weight and getting weaker all the time, and the wound in her leg was slow to heal.

One day, though, she reckoned she'd saved up enough to try to leave.

For the first time in months she went out into the street, and limping in the scorching heat she made her way to the parking lot where the trucks left from.

She came back stubbornly each day, trying to work out which of the numerous men hanging about the place she should link up with so as to be able to get onto one of the trucks.

And she was no longer surprised by the harsh, combative tone in her own hard, sexless voice as she asked questions in the few words of English she'd picked up at the chophouse, any more than she was surprised by the reflection, in a truck's rearview mirror, of a gaunt, gray face with matted, reddish hair, a face with pinched lips and dry skin that happened, now, to be her own and of which, she thought, one couldn't be sure it was a woman's face, any more than it could be said that her skeletal body was a woman's, and yet she was still Khady Demba, unique and indispensable to the orderly functioning of things in the world, even though she now looked more and more like the lost, sluggish, scrawny creatures roaming the town, in fact so much like them that she thought, What difference is there between them and me, basically?, after which she laughed inwardly, delighted to have told herself a good joke, saying, It's because I'm me, Khady Demba!

No, nothing surprised her anymore; nothing, any longer, made her afraid, not even the great weariness she felt all day long that caused her thin limbs suddenly to feel so heavy that she labored to lift a spoon to her mouth and to put one foot in front of the other.

To all that, too, she'd grown accustomed.

Now she looked upon exhaustion as the natural condition of her body.

Weeks later, in a forest the name of which she'd forgotten, among trees that were unfamiliar to her, her state of great weakness would prevent her from leaving the makeshift tent of plastic and foliage in which she was lying.

She'd no idea how long she'd been there, nor how it was possible for the sunlight filtering through the blue plastic to reveal her arms, legs, and feet that were so thin and so far gone. She felt herself weighing so heavily on the earth that it seemed gravity was causing her to sink into it as soon as she closed her eyes.

And she, Khady Demba, who was ashamed of nothing, was

dying of shame at seeing herself like that: huge, unwieldy, and immovable.

A damp, strong-smelling hand was lifting her head, trying to put something into her mouth.

She tried to prevent it, because the smell of that something and of the hand holding it sickened her, but she had so little strength left that her lips parted in spite of herself and she let a sort of insipid, sticky paste slide down her gullet.

She felt cold all the time. The cold was so deep and awful that it couldn't be assuaged either by the blanket covering her or the warm hands that occasionally massaged her.

And while she hoped to find in the earth being hollowed out under the weight of her enormous body the warmth that she thought would get her back on her feet, as soon as she closed her eyes she encountered an even greater cold, against which the bluish sun filtering through the plastic was of no effect, any more than was the humid, stuffy, and (to judge by her profuse sweating) probably warm air inside the tent under the trees.

Oh, she was certainly cold and every inch of her body was hurting, but she reflected with such intensity on how she might forget the cold and the pain that when she saw again in her mind's eye the faces of her grandmother and of her husband—the two people who'd been good to her and had reinforced her in the view that her life, her person, had no less meaning and value than theirs—and when she wondered if the child she'd so longed to bear could have prevented her falling into such a wretched situation, she realized that these were only thoughts and not regrets, because she didn't lament her present state, didn't want to change it, and even found herself in a way delighted, not at her suffering but simply at her condition as a human being confronting as bravely as possible all sorts of perils.

She got better.

She could sit up and eat and drink normally.

A man and a woman who appeared to be living together under the tent gave her a little bread and some boiled wheat that they prepared outside on a log fire in an old saucepan without a handle.

Khady remembered that she'd traveled in the truck with them.

They were both taciturn, and besides had no language in common with Khady, beyond a few words of English; still, she grasped eventually that they had been trying for years to get to Europe and that the man had managed to live there for a while before being expelled.

They both had children somewhere whom they hadn't seen in a long time.

The tent was part of a vast encampment of shacks or tarpaulins lofted on poles, and men in rags were moving among the trees, carrying branches or tin cans.

Khady'd noticed she had nothing anymore: no bundle, passport, or money.

Both the man and the woman spent their days making ladders. After watching for a while how they did it, Khady went in search of branches and worked in her turn at building a ladder, dredging up from memory a story she'd been told (by the nameless faceless boy of her thwarted ascension) about a wire fence separating Africa from Europe, and questioning in her new hoarse, rough voice the man and the woman, who replied with a few words that she didn't always know but that, linked to others she had learned, or translated summarily by a sketch drawn on the ground, ended up corresponding fairly closely to what she'd gathered from the boy. The couple tossed in her direction bits of string, which they used to tie each rung of the ladder to the uprights. They did so reluctantly and with some annoyance, as if, Khady thought calmly, having robbed her of all she possessed, as she assumed they had, they could hardly refuse to help her however much they didn't like it.

She left the forest with the woman, and they followed a tarmac road to the gates of a town.

She was limping badly and her damaged calf could be seen below the hem of her old batik.

They begged in the streets.

Khady held her hand out as the woman did.

In an incomprehensible language people hurled what must have been insults at them. Some spat at their feet. Others gave them bread.

Khady was so hungry she bit violently into the bread.

Her hands trembled.

Her gums were bleeding. They left traces of blood on the bread.

But her heart was beating gently, calmly, and she felt the same way: gentle and calm, beyond reach, shielded by her unshakable humanity.

A short time later barking, shouting, and the sound of people running echoed through the camp.

Soldiers were pulling down the shacks, tearing off tarpaulin covers, and scattering the stones where cooking fires had been lit.

One of them grabbed Khady and ripped her batik off.

She saw him hesitate and realized he was repulsed by her thin body and the blackish marks on her skin.

He punched her in the face and threw her on the ground, his mouth twisted in anger and disgust.

Later, much later, weeks and months later perhaps, with every night in the forest feeling colder than the last and the sun seeming every day to look paler and hang lower in the sky, the men who'd been elected—or who'd appointed themselves—as leaders of the camp announced that the assault on the fence would take place the day after next.

They set off at night, dozens and dozens of men and women among whom Khady felt particularly flimsy, almost impalpable, a mere puff of wind.

Like the others she was carrying a ladder, which, though light, seemed to weigh more than she did, just as things sometimes—absurdly—do in dreams, and yet, as her enormous heart beat within the little bony cage of her fragile, burning chest, she limped along no slower than her companions.

They walked for a long while in silence through the forest, then over stony fields where Khady stumbled and fell several times, but she picked herself up and returned to her place in the group, she who felt herself but an infinitesimal displacement of air, a glacial nuance of the atmosphere—so cold was she, so cold through and through.

They arrived at last in a deserted area bathed in a white light that resembled the brightness of the moon made incandescent, and Khady saw the fence they'd all been talking about.

As they moved forward dogs began barking and shots rang out. Khady heard a voice made strident and uneven by anxiety: "They're firing in the air," then the same person, perhaps, shouted the agreed-upon signal, a single word, and everyone began running toward the fence.

She ran too. Her mouth was wide open but she couldn't breathe. Her eyes were staring and her throat was blocked. Already the fence was there and she leaned her ladder against it. Then, rung by rung, she climbed up until she reached the top and gripped the fence.

She could hear all around her shots being fired and cries of fear and pain. She couldn't tell if she was shouting too, or if it was the sound of the blood throbbing in her skull, enveloping her in an endless threnody. She tried to go higher, remembering that a boy had told her you must never, never stop climbing until you've reached the top, but the barbed wire was tearing the skin off her hands and feet and she could now hear herself screaming and feel blood running along her shoulders and down her arms. She kept telling herself never to stop climbing, never, repeating the words over and over again while no longer understanding them, then giving up, letting go, falling slowly backward, and thinking then that the person of Khady Demba—less than a breath, scarcely a puff of air—was surely never to touch the ground, but would float eternal, priceless, too evanescent ever to be smashed in the cold, blinding glare of the floodlights.

COUNTERPOINT

EVERY TIME Lamine was paid for his work, in the kitchen at the back of the restaurant *Au bec fin,* where he was an evening dishwasher; at the warehouse where he unpacked goods for supermarkets; on a construction site or in the metro: wherever he went to sell his labor, every time euros passed from a foreigner's hand into his own, he thought of the girl, he silently begged her to forgive him and not to haunt him with curses and poisoned dreams. In the room he shared with others he slept with his money under the pillow and dreamed of the girl. She was either protecting him or—on the contrary—wishing he was in the pit of hell. And when, on bright days, he raised his eyes and let the sun warm his face, it wasn't unusual for the sky to cloud over suddenly for no obvious reason, and then he would talk to the girl and tell her softly what had become of him, he would give thanks to her, a bird would vanish in the distance.

Marie NDiaye was born in Pithiviers, France, in 1967 and spent her childhood with her French mother. Her father was Senegalese. Educated at primary and secondary level in France, NDiaye studied linguistics at the Sorbonne, and obtained a grant from the French Academy that enabled her to stay in the Villa Médicis in Rome. She started writing when she was about twelve or thirteen years old and was only eighteen when her first work was published. NDiaye was awarded the prestigious Femina literary prize for her novel *Rosie Carpe* in 2001 and the Goncourt Prize, France's highest literary honor, in 2009 for *Trois femmes puissantes*. She lives in Berlin.

A NOTE ON THE TYPE

Pierre Simon Fournier *le jeune,* who designed the type used in this book, was both an originator and a collector of types. His services to the art of printing were his design of letters, his creation of ornaments and initials, and his standardization of type sizes. His types are old style in character and sharply cut. In 1764 and 1766 he published his *Manuel typographique,* a treatise on the history of French types and printing, on typefounding in all its details, and on what many consider his most important contribution to typography—the measurement of type by the point system.

Composed by North Market Street Graphics, Lancaster, Pennsylvania
Printed and bound by RR Donnelley, Harrisonburg, Virginia
Designed by Maggie Hinders